FLU

WAYNE SIMMONS

Proudly Published by Snowbooks in 2010

Snowbooks Ltd.
120 Pentonville Road
London
N1 9JN
Tel: 0207 837 6482
Fax: 0207 837 6348
email: info@snowbooks.com

www.snowbooks.com

British Library Cataloguing in Publication Data
A catalogue record for this book is available from the British Library.

ISBN 978-1-906727-19-2

Printed and bound by J F Print Ltd., Sparkford, Somerst

For the birds, the pigs, the mad cows...

PROLOGUE

Finaghy, Northern Ireland

17th June

There was a woman screaming in his face.

She was one of many crowding around him. But he couldn't hear her. With the headgear he was wearing, Sergeant George Kelly couldn't hear what any of them were saying. Just muffled words. Muted. Censored. Like sounds you would hear under water.

But he could *see* her talking, *see* her screaming.

And he knew she was swearing.

It was something about the way her lips were moving. Shaping the words as if they were heavy. Teeth showing. Almost growling rather than speaking. Or maybe laughing. Because, with every fuck-shaped word she mouthed, there was at least the *hint* of a smile.

It didn't matter, of course. None of their words mattered to George when all he could hear was the rhythmic sound of his own breathing. A mechanical mish-mash of pumps and compression as sanitised air flowed, noisily, through rubber tubing into his facemask and lungs. Steady and dependable.

Pure and uninfected.

He felt a hand on his shoulder. Looking to the corner of his visor, he saw his constable, Norman Coulter, also in breathing apparatus, also fighting through the confused and excited crowd. Norman smiled, as if enjoying himself, rolling with the mob as if on some fairground ride. George knew it was just bravado, though. Maybe the big man was drinking on the job again. Or maybe he had something even more taboo flooding through his system. George didn't care. Not now. He couldn't blame the poor bastard for taking the edge off, regardless of how he did it. In fact, he wished he'd had the wit to take a drink himself.

Together, the two men waded their way through the sea of silently angry people, their cries and protests as muffled as the swearing woman's rants. The crowd was constantly shifting, like marbles in a tin. It was like being on a ship. Waves of people rabid with emotion, slapping against each other. George almost felt sick with the constant impact of body upon body.

They moved through the car park into the nearby tower block of flats. It was the fifth time they'd been to this particular block, in Finaghy, but the thirteenth time they'd been to a call *like this*. George had been counting. He wished he hadn't been counting, because the number 'thirteen' had always bugged him. It wasn't that he was particularly superstitious, but there was something about numbers and codes that unnerved him. He hated maths, unable to understand them. But you feared what you didn't understand. That's what they said, anyway.

The crowd was becoming increasingly lively, increasingly aggressive. But George remained focused, shoving his way through the confused and frenzied people with resolve. The angry woman remained, somehow, in his face, despite the heavy numbers. She was still screaming, still shaping f-words. How she managed to keep up with him, he wasn't sure. He knew that if she had been giving Norman that kind of abuse, he'd not be quite as passive. But George wasn't going to risk the use of force where he didn't have to. He'd seen this all before. They were on the cusp of something nasty. A riot, a breakdown. A loss of order, or control. They needed to tread very carefully. The crowd was scared and confused. One wrong move could set them off like a bucket of fireworks.

Still the woman screamed at him, as he fought his way up the stairwell. He wondered if she was a relative of the 'patient'. Or maybe just a family friend. Looking at her, he reckoned she was more likely just another nasty bitch sent to try his patience. Some troublemaker using the whole drama to offload her general beef with the police. He'd seen her type before. He wondered what would make a person so bitter, so one-dimensional in their thinking. He couldn't understand that mentality at all. Didn't she understand the pressures he, and other officers, suffered on a daily basis? How they were first on the scene of everything nasty? Breaching the frontline of every flare-up? Protecting, negotiating, tolerating?

(enforcing?)

But George was adamant he was going to hold his cool a little longer, regardless of his anger. Especially on his thirteenth –

(*thirteenth what*?)

No one back at the station had given *these types* of calls a name yet. He'd been on twelve (now thirteen), yet remained unaware of a codeword, number, colour or any other way to distinguish such calls from more 'routine' police work. It suddenly dawned on George how odd that was.

When it first hit, George had felt the same as everyone else. Confused, scared, unsettled. He'd seen the signs on television. The news reporting a rise in workplace absence. The shutting down of small businesses. Houses falling to ridiculously low prices, people trying to flee to Europe, America, anywhere that would take them. But then the airports closed, all exits in and out of Ireland blocked. Eventually, hospitals and medical centres became overrun with patients. Private healthcare intervened, but the demand was overwhelming. The posters, first advising of helplines to ring if sick, then advising of martial law. *Anyone found outdoors after curfew would be detained,* they said. And it was then that George's role changed, his perspective shifted. He became one of those *administering* detention. Today, he was *administering* much worse.

They took the next flight of stairs by storm. He noticed Norman, in front, pushing through the dwindling crowds, quite aggressively, as they neared the second floor. Bodies were less thick, now, but still in his face like lights at a show. George filed behind Norman's ram-like hide, allowing the bigger man to do all the donkey work. He wondered if it would have been better to take the lift, avoiding the heavy throng of people for the relative calm of spinning cogs and levers. But the numbers continued to thin as they got closer to flat 23. Word must have got out, he thought. Another person infected. 'Get out, get the police out and stay out' as the well worn advert on television instructed.

Yet, it certainly hadn't got through to one person - the swearing woman still persisted. George could actually hear what she was screaming at him, now, even through the oxygen mask. It was mostly obscenities, as he suspected. She didn't trust the police, warning George that she was watching every 'fucking' thing he was 'fucking' doing and would record it on her 'fucking' phone if he did anything out of 'fucking' line. He gritted his teeth and continued to ignore her. He hated her type, and he *really* hated her.

When they reached flat 23, the crowds had diluted. There were only a few people milling about outside. Most of them stood back as George and Norman approached. A couple of paramedics, wearing even more elaborate breathing apparatus than George and Norman, came out to meet them. They didn't introduce themselves, nor did they exchange any pleasantries. They simply nodded to George to confirm, subtly, their diagnosis.

It was flu.

The people huddled around the doorway, mostly relatives of flat 23's tenants. They seemed reluctant to step back. The paramedics did their best to gently persuade them, but in the end it was Norman's handgun, brandished assertively in the air, that ultimately convinced them what a good idea it would be to make room. There were a few shrieks from a rather inconsolable older woman; George left her to the paramedics to comfort and, most likely, sedate. This was the way of such things. Desperate measures for desperate times.

George followed Norman into the flat, closing the door in the face of the swearing woman who had been tailing him like some mad banshee with Tourettes. He got a little satisfaction out of that, but it seemed wildly inappropriate to admit it. Even to himself.

George steadied himself, leaning against the wall for a short, precious moment. His breathing was slowing. He could hear the air more clearly as it pumped through the tank into his mask. Norman was beside him, patting him on the shoulder to ask if he were okay. He *wasn't* okay. He *couldn't* be okay. Because this was where it got messy. This was the bit he had hated most about all twelve previous calls. They called it 'risk management.' He didn't know if that was the correct title or not. But what did it matter in a situation like this, anyway? These words, these terms dreamed up by bureaucrats in 'think tanks.' 'Protocol' and 'viable' and 'procedural.' None of them bore any relevance to the real world. None of them meant anything, here in this flat, to these people. They offered no comfort to anyone within this awful crescendo to a brutal, anonymous and necessary evil.

They moved through the hallway of the small flat, finding a tearful young woman. The television was turned up loud in another room. George could hear a lively debate about symptoms and signs of the flu. It was pretty much all people were talking about, on the radio, the TV, the street. The television sounded old, tired, jaded. Its speakers were muffled, buzzing as if a fuse had blown somewhere. An overtired doctor was reciting government rhetoric, hardly sounding like he believed it himself. The studio audience were almost as vicious as the crowd outside.

The woman didn't introduce herself, simply retreating through into another room on seeing the two cops. She didn't look scared of them or surprised to see them. But she wasn't going to shake their hands, either. George didn't expect pleasantries. Cops were like angels of death, now. Expected, even summoned, but never welcomed.

George shook his head, looking to his colleague. The bigger cop shrugged, dismissively. He followed the young woman, George filing in behind him. He wondered if it was she who was infected, or a partner or husband. Nothing seemed *obviously* wrong with her. But appearances were deceiving. A simple sneeze seemed all that was needed to determine someone's health. A tickly cough, runny nose. All previously harmless symptoms of a minor cold or flu. Barely noticeable, before. Now, they were like the first nails in the coffin. Enough to send shivers down a man's spine. Like the bells ringing out during the Great Plague.

George's heart sank as they were led into another room, that of a little girl. Pink Barbie wallpaper lined the walls. A faded Disney Princess duvet covered the bed in the centre of the room. A couple of posters, cut out of magazines and comics, were cellotaped, roughly, above her headboard. A little girl with a fever lay under the covers, a bucket in the corner holding her vomit, a bedpan seeming to contain fresh excrement. A thick line of blood was seeping out of her nose, constantly being attended to by her young mother with a heavily soiled handkerchief. She couldn't have been more than six years old.

The young woman turned to them, petitioning them in what seemed to be some kind of Eastern European dialect. While George couldn't understand what she was saying, he was pretty sure he got her meaning.

He looked, again, at the little girl. His sister had a child the very same age. They clearly shared the same interests, his little niece having similarly themed decor in her room, albeit with a little more cash spent on it. Where was this little girl from, though? Romania? Probably one of the many Eastern Europeans George would have seen on an almost daily basis. Selling papers at traffic lights. Begging in the street. Busking, maybe. Sometimes the perpetrators of petty crimes. They were far from welcome in Belfast. Even less so in rural areas. George always wondered how they put up with the constant abuse they received, the slander and the slogans on the wall. Probably couldn't understand much of it, he thought. The darker side of Belfast lost in translation.

He bent down by her bedside. The girl was barely conscious, but he talked to her, nonetheless.

"Hi, sweetie," he said, not sure what else to say. It was what he called his niece. He suddenly felt guilty about using his special name for her with someone else.

Not that it mattered, of course. His words were probably meaningless, anyway. Muffled by the equipment he was wearing. Dulcet tones murmured to a drained body, delirious with fever. It really wasn't likely that she even *heard* him. But George thought he should say *something*. Even just for the mother's sake.

He placed his gloved hand over the little girl's brow. It was radiating heat to such an extent that he could even feel it through the fabric, as if it were a hot plate. He brushed the sweaty hair away from her eyes, took a fresh tissue from a nearby box and removed some of the ever-increasing blood and bile seeping from her nose. She suddenly began to cough, spitting a dark smear across his visor. He quietly removed it, before dipping another tissue in water and patting her burning forehead with it. Then he continued to clean her, using more dampened tissues.

"Shhhh..." he said, each time she sputtered. "It's going to be okay."

But it wasn't going to be okay. It was clear that her condition was pretty far advanced. Yet, underneath the mess, when he wiped her face clean, he found a beautiful little girl. Strikingly beautiful. George looked to the mother, hoping this would be the face she would record in her memory. The one to remember her daughter by.

George then looked to his partner, standing, awkwardly, by the bed. Big Norman looked even bigger when compared to such a small, weak child. Like a bear watching over her. A giant from some fairy tale. The big man looked more than just uncomfortable as he stared at the scene before him. He seemed moved. It was as if even *his* heavy and jaded heart was melting at the bedside of this child, this innocent little creature who did not deserve what was happening to her.

George shook his head, sighing heavily under all the tubes and glass. He pulled himself to his feet, feeling the weight of his oxygen tank.

"Christ," muttered Norman. George pulled the big man aside so they could discuss the situation more privately. His visor was steaming up, and it was difficult to make out any expression on Norman's face. "This is a hard one, mate. What do we do?" asked Norman. But he knew well enough what they were meant to do. He'd accompanied George all twelve times before this.

"We have to stick to protocol," said George, hating the word as he used it. Yet, somehow it seemed appropriate to use a 'think tank' word to describe something indescribable. Something clearly wrong, yet masked as right under nonsensical language and jargon.

Protocol. Procedural.

Norman just stared back at him, as if George, too, were infected. Infected by nonsense, by bureaucracy. Infected by the very words he was using. It troubled George to see Norman look at him like that. It shamed him. He was suddenly aware of the sweat building under his mask. His breathing, fast and heavy. His hands, sticky and itchy under his plastic-lined gloves. Whether it was the screaming woman having riled him, or the little girl on the bed, or the fucking words leaving his mouth, he really didn't feel well.

(maybe it was flu?)

"Fuck protocol," Norman said, suddenly. He was never a fan of the 'think tank' mentality. "I'm not going to quarantine a six-year-old girl. Not like this. No way."

"We could lock the mother in, too." George offered. It was a terrible thing to say. He knew that. But he also knew it was as close as he was going to get to being the *right* thing to say. The most honest, the most human thing.

"Are you serious?" Norman said, almost laughing. But his superior *was* serious. Very serious.

"It's the only thing we *can* do," George said, pressing one hand against the wall beside him. "For the little girl, anyway. Let's face it, the mother's probably infected." It was true. This flu was airborne. Those within the vicinity of the infected usually contracted the virus quickly afterwards. George felt sick even thinking about it. He was still heating up under all the protective clothing, feeling close to ripping it all off. He suddenly felt trapped in his head gear, trapped in the tower block, this breeding ground for germs and disease and fear and venom. "It's either that or leave the little girl in here alone."

Norman sighed, heavily. He began to pace the hallway like some kind of animal. A big animal. Even bigger looking than normal, with the riot gear and breathing apparatus. He was not a man who was known for benevolence. Huge, cumbersome, with an attitude to policing that suited his burly appearance. Maybe that was why he never progressed from constable, regardless of the time he had spent in the force.

"Do we tell them?" he asked, finally, pointing in the general direction of the little girl's bedroom. He couldn't even turn to look at them.

"Best not to," George replied. "We're best just leaving right –"

"Jesus Christ!" Norman exclaimed, dumbfounded. "This is *really* fucked up."

George knew that Norman found a lot of things to be 'fucked up.' Things like the recent reform of the force. Or the positive discrimination during recruitment, since the reform. But Norman reserved '*really* fucked up' for especially messed up things. Things that made your mind bend, such was the insanity. Things that were too funny, too ridiculous, too appalling.

Too unfair.

"It *is* really fucked up," George replied, his voice raised a little. "But that's the world we live in, now..."

The crowds outside were getting worked up again, and it was making George nervous. He fought to remain heard over the crying woman with the sick child, the swelling tide of people, that fucking swearing woman with the phone and his own dirty, guilty conscience.

They left the flat, quietly. The woman probably didn't even notice them slip out. But the crowd was waiting for them. They went wild at first sight. It was as if George and Norman were celebrities, attending some movie premiere. Only the reception was far from positive. The reception was everything that was negative curled up in a fist. The screaming banshee woman had her phone out, as expected, piously recording everything that was going on. When she saw George exit, she immediately aimed it at him, her eyes almost radiant with sick delight.

George couldn't have hated her more.

Several others in the crowd were doing similarly. A sea of phones fought to record all that went on – some for altruistic reasons, no doubt, others not so much. George looked at them each in the eye, quietly judging them.

Someone spat at him, the gob smearing across George's visor obscuring his vision. He wiped it off with a gloved hand.

This is REALLY fucked up, he thought.

The paramedics weren't faring much better. Two of them were embroiled in a very heated exchange. Other police had reached the scene, maintaining a perimeter around the flat's entrance by linking arms.

Several yellow-suited men stood outside, tools, welding equipment and metal sheets at their side. They, too, wore breathing apparatus. George nodded to them, silently. They moved in without uttering a word. He could hear them firing up their gear as they got to work sealing the windows. This drove the crowd even wilder, surging them forward in an almighty push.

The police, struggling to keep their arms linked, strained against the sudden pressure as the welding continued. One of the paramedics lost his balance, falling to the ground. An officer tried to help him up, before also succumbing to the riotous throng.

The workmen exited the flat. The young woman from inside, realising what was happening, tried to follow them, but they closed the door on her. George could hear her pounding on the wood.. She was screaming. George turned away, catching Norman's eye.

(REALLY fucked –)

The crowd moved in, some breaking through the police perimeter. As George watched, Norman stood forward, brandishing his firearm again. It was an attempt to restore peace, but a young lad, barely in his teens, grabbed Norman's arm, wrestling the gun from his grasp. The gun went off in the heat of the moment, the young lad falling to the ground, wounded, before being trampled by the crowd.

"Jesus..." George whispered.

His visor was steaming up again, lending the whole scene even more of a surreal feel. Through misty glass, he watched Banshee Woman recording the falling lad, enthusiastically, before shifting her phone camera's angle to record a baffled looking Norman. The other cameras didn't follow suit, though, and that struck George as odd. They were recording something at the *back* of the crowd, something, seemingly, coming up the stairwell.

The crowd's pitch suddenly doubled. The paramedic on the ground had lost his breathing apparatus in the sudden jolt. He reached down to retrieve it but never made it back up again. The crowd surged forward once more. People were being squashed at the front, swearing and calling for help as others were pushed, helplessly, against them. Shrieks could still be heard from the other side of the door, where a young woman and her six year old were being sentenced to death. Someone, and George wasn't sure if it was by accident or design, had produced a gun of their own and managed to shoot themselves with it.

George watched Norman fall to the ground, the big man's frame rolling up as he tried to defend himself. The crowd pushed further, some people tripping over him and scrambling to the ground as if playing some kind of chaotic rugby match. But Norman rose up like a big, ugly phoenix, gripping his breathing apparatus tightly with one hand, swinging his other to connect fist with face. His patience was obviously gone, making him as feral as the crowd.

One of the welders, working on the door, turned, nervously, swinging his flame, by mistake, into the face of a middle aged man. The man grabbed at his suddenly melting skin, screeching. Blisters broke across his face like popcorn. The smell was terrible, the scream deafening. Even George could hear it, its shrill explosion high pitched over the mechanical sounds of his quickened breathing.

George grabbed Norman by the oxygen tank on his back, pulling him quickly down the corridor. The crowd was getting even thicker, more and more numbers pouring up the stairwell. This wasn't just your average riot or disturbance. This was something worse than that. It had a rawness to it, a desperation George had never felt before.

Noticing the door to a nearby flat open, George motioned to Norman. They both darted in, quickly, to escape the crowd. They slammed the door shut, tight, feeling the swelling numbers immediately crush against it. Norman locked it, slipping the key chain across as if it would make them more secure. Both men stood back from the door, breathing heavily.

"Fuck me," said Norman.

It was quiet once more. George could hear a different television broadcasting the same debate. This television was better, the sound clearer. The doctor's voice, older and more measured, tried, in vain, to interrupt the ranting of a younger man. The younger man had lost his whole family to the virus. He wanted to know what was being done, what measures were being taken. *I'll show you what measures*, George thought.

An older woman with a tight, red face stood in the hallway, wrapped in her dressing gown. She was yelling at them to 'get the hell out of here'. She called George a 'pig' . He'd been called it many times before. Its familiarity almost comforted him. George raised his hand at her, shushing her. The old woman stepped back nervously.

"Are going to shoot me!?" she exclaimed, pointing at him with a shaking hand.

"What?!" he said, baffled. But he wanted to. He wanted to shoot all of them, suddenly. The old woman. The crowds outside. The swearing woman. The ranting man on the television. It was an instinctual reaction, born out of raw fear. Maybe he even wanted to shoot himself. "Of course not," he said, moving away from her, as if frightened he *might* shoot her. "We just need you to be calm."

"There's nothing here for you," she said, suddenly, both hands vibrating, her head staring at the wall. "He's dead, you know. So you can both just leave."

"Dead? Who's dead?" Norman asked, looking around him. But she didn't answer, still lost in the moment. She was shaking all over now, quivering like thunder. George could sense an anger and grief within her, tearing her from the inside out. It was beaming off her like fire. Lighting everything it touched, consuming her. A part of her, maybe, felt relieved to have someone to blame for everything, someone to transfer all of her frustration onto. The tears in her eyes erupted, as if volcanic.

"Leave!" she yelled, at them. "Leave now!"

"Listen, we're just going to move into the living room to make a call on the radio," George argued.

"No," she yelled, "that's where Frank's resting."

"Who's Frank?" asked George, baffled and exasperated. Couldn't he get just one word of sense out of *anyone* today? The crowd outside were clawing at the door like wolves. It was making George nervous. His oxygen tank was pumping air faster, noisier. They wanted blood. They wanted *his* blood. There seemed to be no escape, no respite. And George really needed to escape.

He moved into the living room, despite the old woman's protests. The television was turned up loud, drowning out the sounds of the crowd. Floral wallpaper clung to the walls. Old, dusty furniture littered the room. A couple of china dogs stood by the TV, as if guarding it. A mahogany coffee table stood proudly beside them, polished like a shiny button. But then there was the sofa, blood stained and sweaty, like a pile of old rags. An older man lay across it. It was probably Frank. He was very clearly dead, all the tell-tale signs present and accounted for. The bloody gore gathering around the nose and mouth. Dead eyes, staring deep into space. A still chest. One arm hanging over the chair's edge, limply.

"W-when did Frank die?" Norman asked the old woman, uncomfortably. The big guy was still clearly shaken up by the little girl and all that happened outside. Such a hard man, yet this all had softened him.

"About an hour ago," she said, still crying. Her tiny, sinewy hands clasped an old, bloody tissue as if it were made of gold. It was probably Frank's blood gathered there, George thought. He could only guess how many years the two of them had been together. He noticed a picture on the wall, presumably of the couple getting married, decades ago. This was her world. This dusty old flat with her pictures and her ornaments and her memories. The tissue. The things she considered important, precious. Outside, the rest of the world was crumbling, but hers had already been levelled.

The crowds hammered at the door, viciously. He could hear them, now, over the television. It sounded like the drumbeat of a dead army coming. George turned to look back through the small hallway at the failing door. He could hear another round of gunshots, fired by God-knows-who. The sound of shattering wood. He watched with horror as the door caved in against repeated force, its chain snapping like thread.

But then something very odd happened. A sharp movement caught the corner of George's visor. He turned back towards the sofa, as quickly as his bulky equipment allowed him to. He was just in time to see old Frank rise up from his deathbed, blankets falling at his feet like dead snakes.

"Jesus!" he heard Norman cry from the corner of the room. Even Frank's wife was unnerved, scrambling away from her suddenly resurrected husband as if he were a ghost. And, by all accounts, he pretty much was.

"Wait," Norman said, stepping backwards, himself. "Frank? Frank, are you–"

"He was dead!" spat Mrs Frank, now hanging onto George as if for dear life. "I was a nurse! I should fucking know! My Frank was dead!"

Like some stilted creature from a horror B-movie, Frank simply stood there, as if enjoying all the audience's attention, lapping up the dramatic intro music. Then he stepped forward, shuffling uneasily on his feet as if learning to walk again. A deep rasping sound crawled up his throat as he moved, yet his chest remained still, as if not breathing. George was quite sure he agreed with Frank's wife. This was a dead man walking before him.

The door crashed open. George turned back towards the hallway. He raised his hand, not even getting time to shout out a warning before they were on him. Norman had taken out his baton and was feverishly attacking without discrimination. The old woman fell to the ground, still staring at her dead Frank. George shouted warning after warning at the crowd. But it was useless. No one was listening; no one cared.

And in that instant, George snapped. He snapped like an overused elastic band. He snapped without thinking or considering what he was doing. It was almost like a reflex action. An 'act-first-think-never' kind of thing. The television man was still ranting, still asking what was being done. But George knew what was being done.

He was doing it.

He drew his own firearm. He aimed it, first, at the swearing banshee woman, now at the front of the crowd, no longer filming with her mobile phone, but still screaming and, seemingly, shaping those f-words at him.

And he fired.

ONE

Six weeks later

Geri stood statue still, holding the small bag of shopping above her head.

She was standing on Belfast's Dublin Road, once a busy part of the city, now a dusty ghost town. Paper littered the streets like leaves in autumn, dancing sprightly in the light wind. Shop windows lay shattered on the pavements, tiny shards of glass strewn across the road like crystal bread crumbs. A bloody palm print stained the nearby wall. A bright red anarchy sign barked angrily from another, staining a sharply worded government information poster with its messy, free-styled paint. Other posters, less controversial, simply advertised gigs that would never take place. Never to be attended by people most likely dead. A number of cars were dotted throughout the road, abandoned.

But there were no bodies.

No signs of death, in the normal sense of the word.

A light breeze caressed Geri's face, a red splash of hair falling over one eye. Her mouth and nose felt damp, but Geri still dared not move. She stood outside a small supermarket, staring into the face of a man wearing a balaclava and holding a gun.

"Did you fucking sneeze?" he asked.

"Yes, but it's j-just hay fever," she replied.

Her hands were shaking. A random tin escaped from her white Tesco's bag. It rolled along the ground, almost cheekily.

"Bullshit," Balaclava replied. His gun was aimed squarely at Geri. His hands weren't shaking.

"I get it every y-year," she stuttered, fighting against the tears.

"It's the fucking flu!" he yelled, voice dulled with the woollen muzzle. His eyes were wide and tense. He looked tired and out of shape, yet he was still the healthiest looking person she'd seen in days.

"It's NOT the fucking flu!" she yelled, tears breaking from her eyes. Her raised voice rang out through the empty streets, crassly. Like a laugh at a funeral. Disrespectful. Bold. Antagonising. "I've had hay fever since I was a child! I take tablets for it... they... they're in the back pocket of my jeans."

She looked him in the eyes, waiting for him to give her the go-ahead to retrieve the thin packet of tablets. Instead, he moved, slowly, around to face her back. She could hear his breathing in the still, dead air. It was steady – not laboured and wheezy and flu-ridden like most of the other people she'd encountered, recently. But she felt uncomfortably vulnerable with him staring, no doubt, at her arse.

"Okay, slowly reach into the pocket with your left hand–"

Geri reached down towards her back pocket.

"Your LEFT hand!" he corrected her, causing her to jump. "And QUICKLY. They're fucking everywhere, today."

She shot the offending right hand up into the air again, still holding the plastic bag. Another couple of tins and a bottle of water fell from the bag's grasp. They scuttled along the quiet street uncouthly, like a drunken brawl. Slowly, she reached her left hand into the back pocket of her jeans. She retrieved the flat packet of tablets, limply flipping them out of her hand. She heard the short slap as card hit pavement. For a moment, nothing happened. She reckoned Balaclava was probably examining the packet, most likely from a safe distance. She hoped he could fucking read, because her tablets were for general allergies. The actual words 'hay fever' were in small print at the back of the packet. She suddenly remembered she hadn't taken one this morning.

The sound of commotion cut through the silent air, disturbing their moment. It was quiet at first, as if in the distance. But, as she listened, Geri could hear it grow in intensity. Slow, heavy footsteps. A guttural moaning. Deceptively amplified within the stillness of the city. These were familiar sounds. Sounds that wouldn't have made much sense, two months ago. Back when it was reasonable to expect a person to die, then stay dead. Left to the mercy of relatives and clergy and the cold, pale hands of morticians. To be buried within three days, with family and friends mourning by the graveside.

But those days were gone.

"Hello?" Geri said, still standing very still. She was terrified to turn her head. Instead, she spoke, again. "Listen... can you hear them?"

There was no reply. For long, stagnant moments she remained where she was. She tried to stay as still as she could, shopping bag (now half empty) hanging over her head. She didn't want to be shot, but she sure as hell didn't want to be around when the footsteps reached her, either.

"HEY!" she shouted. "We need to get out of –"

Was he even there anymore? She listened more closely, still not turning around. The footsteps from town were getting stronger, closer. The moaning was getting louder. They were tangible, now. She could almost smell them. A cold, nervous sweat ran down her back, tickling her spine. Another light breeze caressed her hair, as if to gently remind her of the need to move. A car engine stuttered, some distance away. She turned, sharply, her eyes finding Balaclava firing up an old Ford Escort.

"Hey!" she shouted, dropping her bag and waving her hands in the air, as if Balaclava couldn't see her. "Hey! Wait for me!" she persisted, running towards the car.

The Escort was halfway through a three point turn, set to burn down the Dublin Road, away from the incoming footsteps. Geri ran towards it, throwing herself onto the bonnet, just as the car was about to speed off. She didn't know what the hell she was doing. She hadn't planned *any* of this. But she knew she had to do something. She knew she had to fight for survival in any and every way possible.

Balaclava yelled at her, his voice fighting against the angry revs of the worn-down engine. She gripped tightly onto the old car's wing mirrors, stretching herself across the entire width of the car. She suddenly realised she had very long arms. She also realised how very silly she must have looked, but she didn't care. Who was looking, anyway? Except *him,* maybe. And possibly a mob of very pissed-off dead people.

Balaclava's voice grew more agitated. From behind the steering wheel, he brandished his revolver, waving it at her threateningly. He looked in his rear view mirror, his eyes growing more intense. He glared at her, defiantly, revving the engine.

Geri looked him in the eye, pleading with him. He hadn't shot her on sight after the sneezing incident, so there had to be some small trace of decency in him. If he would only stop the car, allow her to climb inside. Just to get away from *them.*

The commotion was growing in intensity. More of them had appeared from the many streets running off the main road. They were closing in around the car from all directions. There was no way she could move past them, anymore. She had to just hang on, and hope for the best.

Her eyes were drawn to them, like car crash television. She could see them very clearly, now. Their sickly appearance, all coagulated blood and dark, hardened bile. Their shiny, sun-bleached skin. Some naked, others wearing the deathbed uniform of hospital gown or pyjamas. Some looked quite human, as if walking amongst the others in disguise. But their eyes were dead, their stares cold and indistinct. Their shuffling steps hit heavily on the littered road, like a slow round of applause. Their voices, a low moaning growl, pierced the quiet air like a football chant. Angry and nonsensical. Babbling with drunken exhaustion.

Balaclava was yelling, struggling to maintain his gruff, Derry accent over the grumbling of the Escort's engine and the incoming throng. He waved his gun at her. Still she clung on, literally for dear life.

The throng seemed to reach crescendo levels of fervour. Falling against each other, as if over excited by the prospect of new, warm and interesting flesh to explore. It reminded Geri of Shaftsbury Square on a Saturday night. Chucking out time for pubs and clubs. Bodies, everywhere, sniffing out fast food, hungrily. But, these bodies didn't want chips or burgers or Chinese takeaway. Their noses were exploring more taboo flavours in the air. The smell of Geri McConnell. The smell of her health. The smell of her pure, uninfected blood and sun-kissed flesh. The smell of her life, even though she, herself, was scared to death.

A sudden jolt of the car, but Geri still clung on. Tears rolled down her cheeks readily. She stared through the steamed up windscreen at Balaclava, pleading with him for help. She knew that if she climbed off this bonnet, he would tear down the road, away from her. She knew she would be left to the incoming mob. She clung to the bonnet, because she really didn't know what else to do. She didn't want to be left alone. She had seen, all too vividly, what had happened to others who had been left alone.

And then Balaclava lost it. He fired up the engine for real, this time, skidding away from the dangerously close voices. The car ran into a few bodies as it tried to negotiate the herd. Geri could feel their cold, wet, decrepit flesh press momentarily against her own. Still, she hung on, pressing her face against the bonnet's dirt and grime and gritting her teeth. She screamed, tears flowing freely. Her palms were sweating, and she thought she might be flung from the now speeding vehicle at any second. The wind and engine noise and their guttural moaning (they *were* everywhere, today!) filled her ears. The car took turn after turn, skidding nervously on the dry roads, mostly avoiding the aroused dead. Her hands slipped on one of the mirrors, but she managed to keep hold of the other. Her feet skidded on the ground, briefly, the noxious smell of burning rubber attacking her nostrils immediately. The road met with skin, the hot sting of tearing flesh causing her to screech in an almost banshee like fashion. She pulled her feet up, losing her grip in the process. The car came to a dramatic halt, and Geri felt herself freefall. She hit the road hard, a sharp pain running up her arm and shoulder. For a moment, she lay crying, her adrenalin so raw that she almost felt possessed.

Moments went by. Maybe she'd passed out, or maybe she just *wanted* to have passed out. She opened her eyes, looking around her. One of her ears was ringing. The other could detect the voices. The guttural ones.

DEFINITELY everywhere, now. She struggled to get up, reeling against her scorched, moist foot. It wouldn't touch the ground. She tried to walk, but ended up hopping. Her head was spinning. Her balance surprised her.

Balaclava had exited the car, now struggling with the lock on the door of a house in front of her. She struggled in his direction, cursing him as she moved. Yelling at him to stop. But she could understand why he hated her. Only a mad bitch would hang onto a car like that. A stupid, annoying, mad bitch. She was even starting to piss herself off.

Balaclava finally managed to get the door open, looking left and right before darting in and closing it behind him. Geri heard the door lock tight just as she reached it. She beat her bruised and bloodied hands upon it, yelling at the top of her voice. There were *other* voices, now. Drawn to the excitement, their footsteps getting closer. Panic ran through her blood like poison. She turned her attention to the front window, noticing how it was covered by a metal grill. She went back to the door, beating against it and screaming like the crazy bitch she truly had become.

They were almost upon her. She refused to look around, but she could feel them, smell them, almost taste their heavy, acrid stench in her mouth. *This is it,* she thought to herself. *This is your swansong, Geri-babes. Kiss your bye-byes,* as her mum used to say. *Rest in peace, you crazy, mad bitch.*

Geri closed her eyes tight, bracing herself for the inevitable embrace of a sweat-stained, flu-ridden death. She hoped it would be quick, painless. She hoped, but she knew that hope was not enough. Not anymore. Not when the odds were so readily stacked against her.

But then, when it seemed lost, the door opened, again. A hand grabbed her, roughly, pulling her through.

TWO

Balaclava manhandled Geri through the small hallway of the house, his eyes wide, and his gun hand ever threatening. He never spoke, instead keeping his head and mouth, purposely, away from her. He half dragged, half pushed her. Her torn foot was grating against the rough-fibred carpet, causing her to cry, and she hated crying in front of this bastard. They reached the small cubby hole under the stairs. He opened its panelled wooden door and threw her against the hoovers and brushes inside. She landed hard against her shoulder, scattering the various household junk. He closed the door, before she could even as much as take a breath, leaving her in darkness. A key turned, a lock clicked.

"You fucking bastard!" she called out, slamming her fist against the door.

From outside, she heard activity. Balaclava swearing loudly. Footsteps on the stairs and another voice, agitated, challenging Balaclava. An ensuing argument between the two voices, with only a few words made out. Words like 'flu' and 'girl' and, most worryingly, 'dead'.

Geri fumbled around in the dark, mouldy cubby for something that could be fashioned into a weapon. She found a brush shaft and gripped it like a gladiator, aiming at the door. It would be no match for a gun, but she'd spear the first bastard to open that door, then sprint down the hall...

(*to where?*)

Her heart sank when she considered the options. Back outside? Where the streets were becoming more and more dangerous, more and more populated by the sick, the dying, the dead and the...

She thought back to only a few days ago. When there had been four of them, none being people she'd ever known before the flu had struck. One by one, they had developed symptoms. Just like everyone else – the sneezing, the coughing. The temperature. The vomiting and diarrhoea. The mucus (oh dear God, the mucus!). And then the blood. Congealing with phlegm and excrement to gargle from every orifice. Draining their bodies from the inside out. Strangling and melting them. Stealing their breaths, their pulses, their lives.

But that wasn't all of it. Dear God, that wasn't even close. The bodies didn't stay down. Nobody ever could explain it properly, but some people on the TV had said the flu had mutated, evolved. Set up shop in the bodies of their victims, even hijacking basic functions. It was like the stuff of horror movies. First, their eyes opened. Then their limbs started moving. Finally, they were up and about, moving around and reacting to one another. Hunting together, like packs of tired, hungry dogs.

And that's what was outside for her. That's what was waiting, what the alternative to the cubby hole was. She'd seen it. She'd felt it.

But she'd survived it.

So, she wasn't going to let go, just yet. Heart racing, head pounding, Geri gripped the brush shaft even tighter and with more resolve. Staring at the door, she waited.

...

The man with the tattoos and piercings bounced down the stairs with purpose. His eyes were red and blotchy from sleeping. Charcoal eyeliner lended his face a gaunt, sickly appearance.

"Did you just throw some girl into our cubby hole?" he quizzed, brow furrowed with bemusement. He wasn't sure if the scene had been part of his dream (nightmare?) or if he'd really seen it.

"Yeah..." replied Balaclava. "I think she might be... sick."

"Sick?!" said Tattoo, with mock excitement. "As in, 'that's soooo sick, man' type sick?! Or, and let me be sure to articulate this in a manner most appropriate, FUCKING FLU SICK!"

"I don't know!" protested Balaclava. "She sneezed, so I –"

"SHE SNEEZED!" interrupted Tattoo, his whole face almost bouncing with disbelief and anger. "And you brought her here?! TO OUR FUCKING HOUSE?!"

He threw his hands into the air, dramatically. He'd known this idiot for long enough to know he wasn't the brightest spark in the plug. But this was taking the biscuit...

"I didn't have much of a choice! The bitch was hard to shake off. She was banging the door, and those bastards... they're everywhere, now! They would have found where we were, and then..." Balaclava's muffled cries broke off, reluctant to spell out the obvious.

"FUUUUCK!" shouted Tattoo, raising his hands above him, again, as if petitioning God. "FUUUUUUCCCCCK!"

Balaclava gave up mitigating for himself, setting his large frame down at a telephone table in the hallway. To the tattooed man, he looked like he was going to cry. Dampen his stupid woollen face with his clownish tears. But Tattoo had little pity for him. He had little pity for anyone who was an idiot. It just made him impatient, and when he was impatient he got irritable.

"Take that *stupid* thing off your head," he said, sitting himself down on the bottom stairs.

"It stops me from getting the flu."

"No it doesn't." Tattoo said, sighing.

It was a conversation they'd had many, many times before.

"It does. The news people said that you should always keep your nose and mouth–"

"The news people are dead," Tattoo said, shortly. "The scientists are dead, the police are dead, the fucking provos are dead... and all those idiots up at Stormont?" he asked, rhetorically. "That's right. Dead." He ran a hand along the stubble on his head, working the back of his neck as if a kink had developed. "So why don't you just take off the stupid fucking balaclava," he said, softly, "And tell me – *clearly* - how we're going to sort out this mess."

...

Minutes felt like hours. The darkness engulfed her, allowing little or no vision within the small cubby hole. Eventually, she gave up on the waiting game, considering the fact that they were going to leave her here for a while. Which sucked, of course, because Geri really needed a piss.

She groped around in the dark, looking for anything of interest. She didn't know what she was looking for or why. It was probably just a way to relieve the boredom (and take her mind off her bladder). It wasn't that she thought the cubby hole, under the stairs, held any treasures. Good God, she wasn't that deluded. She'd read CS Lewis as a child, but she knew it was fiction. Fairytales were made-up, right? And monsters weren't real, either.

(*right?*)

Her hands worked their way through all the familiars – the hoover, bicycle wheels, shoes, old tools and things that felt so... odd... that she really didn't want to know what they were. Eventually she found a tin. It jingled, as if full of coins. Instinctively, Geri reached inside, finding something smooth, metallic and what to her untrained mind felt bullet-shaped. She'd watched the movies. She knew what a bullet looked like, and she reckoned she'd know what it felt like, too. This definitely fitted the bill. Quickly, she shoved the bullet into the front pocket of her skinny jeans. It stuck out from the denim. She pulled her t-shirt down to cover it.

The noise of a key turning startled her. She threw the tin to the other side of the cubby hole, fumbled for the brush shaft and readied herself.

...

"Hang on a minute," Balaclava said, stepping back and aiming the gun toward the cubby hole. "Just in case she's turned..."

Tattoo sighed, unlocking the door.

"Are you ready?" he asked the other man.

"Yep," came the reply.

Tattoo pulled the door wide open, as if trying to surprise the girl. It ended up doing exactly the opposite, Tattoo himself surprised to find his jollies at the business end of a brush shaft. He stumbled back, the all-too-distinctive pain of being kicked in the groin descending upon his legs and abdomen, buckling him over.

Balaclava hesitated instead of firing, perhaps worried about hitting his friend. The second's hesitation was all that the girl needed, bringing the brush shaft crashing against his jaw with an almost feral force. The heavier man fell back against the hall wall, slamming against its magnolia naffness, dazed and confused.

The girl dropped the brush shaft to descend upon him, her long frame bent double over his short, stubby body as she struggled for the gun. Balaclava wrestled, bitterly, his eyes wide with panic as the threat of INFECTION clearly terrorised him. He began to scream like a girl. She was screaming too, their voices harmonising with each other, insanely, like some crazy death metal song.

But her glory was short-lived. The brush shaft that had caused him such red-faced, bulging-eyed and screw-faced pain became Tattoo's friend, swinging with vengeance to connect with the girl's jaw, cracking a tooth and knocking her off Balaclava. She tumbled, roughly, towards the kitchen door across the hall. Her lanky form sprawled half-in, half-out of the kitchen, face flat on the ground. She was out cold.

THREE

Some miles south of Geri's whereabouts, another young woman also felt trapped. The circumstances were different. The women, themselves, were *completely* different. This young woman had no captors as such. She also retained all of her teeth. Yet she still felt trapped.

Karen Wilson looked from the window of her flat, situated close to the top floor of one of Finaghy's tower blocks. The view was breathtaking – fresh blue sky stretching as far as the eye could see. A patchwork of flame-red brick and white, parched plaster mixing with chimney tops and roof slates. The greenery of gardens and sporadic colour of flower beds.

Hundreds of dead people. Walking.

A door opened behind her, causing her to jump. It was only Pat. Behind him trailed a wheeled suitcase, large and heavy, by the looks of the sweat breaking on his constantly furrowed brow.

"God, you scared me..." Karen said, pressing a single hand against her beating heart, as if to calm it.

"Didn't you hear the car?" Pat said without looking at her. He was a man of few words – she knew that already from the weeks she had spent under his care. Today, of course, he was a man with a mission, and it seemed like he'd accomplished it. He wheeled the formidable looking case into the middle of the room.

"Yeah, ages ago... What took you getting up here?"

"Lift's broke," Pat said. "I had to carry this thing up the stairs." He looked at her, briefly, adding, "It's heavy."

The lift had been the last thing that she'd known to work. Neither she nor Pat knew why, but it outlasted the television, electric, gas and telephone. As everything else ceased to function, the lift soldiered on, responding to every call like a loyal dog. Kicking into gear, metal rubbing against metal, cogs and coils grinding against each other like reluctant lovers. It was noisy, and, in a world where noise was as scarce as life itself, Karen had found comfort in that.

"Get everything you needed?" Karen said, keen to see what was inside the case. She suddenly noticed how she tailored her conversation for Pat, trying to sound more adult and serious. It wasn't the way she would have talked to her friends. It wasn't the way she would have talked to anyone, but then again, she wouldn't really have said much of anything to a man like Pat, before. She'd have considered him boring, truth be told, and maybe a bit uncouth.

"Pretty much," Pat replied, answering her question as economically as she expected him to. He stretched his back, pursing his lips as if strained. Sighing, he bent down again to the latch on the case and unzipped it. The sound of commotion, from outside, caused his ears to suddenly prick up. He looked to Karen, narrowing his eyes. "There's more of them, today. Don't you hear them? Made it harder getting around."

Karen listened more acutely. She could hear the slow, gruff rumblings from the dead. A gentle, bass-toned moan carried along to their perched view via the summer breeze. It came from the streets and gardens and houses below, as well as other flats in their block. Some of the dead were locked inside their homes, the result of desperate measures by crumbling authorities to quarantine the sick towards the end. It hadn't made any difference. Those quarantined died then got back up again, just like all the others. The only difference was that they were trapped in their own deathbeds, unable to get out.

"God..." she whispered, shuddering at the thought of more of them. She'd seen quite enough of the poor souls since it all kicked off.

Karen had holed up at her local church. It was where a lot of people had retreated to. After the authorities had crumbled, they sought the protection of *divine* Authorities. People were converting by the dozen. Overworked clergy hurriedly read scripture and recited prayers, rubber-stamping salvation as if they were on some kind of commission. The *men folk* (Karen often wondered why people didn't talk normally to each other at church) stood guard at the access points, brutally turning others away, when the building was overrun. Retreating when the dead came, locking up the doors and heavily grilled, security conscious windows. The *women folk* tended to the wounded, the dying. Mopping brows between simple meals and cups of tea. Tending to the needs of the *men folk*. But Karen didn't help out. Karen didn't do anything. Away from the chaos of the main church building, she found herself a small, quiet space. A forgotten storeroom, with nothing but a few dusty old bottles of coke, left over from the Sunday School Christmas party two years ago. She hid from the scared and dying. She closed her ears to the screams which inevitably erupted as infection spread and bodies refused to lie still. She drank out-of-date Coke and waited until everything was quieter, less frantic. And then she left, tired, hungry and scared, like a thief in the night.

Karen walked away from the window, towards the middle of the room, where Pat was. He'd finally opened the case. Inside was an assortment of tinned foods and bottled water, a chemical toilet and camping cooker. Underneath the rest, as if to be poorly hidden from the now extinct prying eyes of Customs and Excess, a couple of rifles and two handguns lay proudly.

"So much for decommissioning," Pat said with a trace of humour in his voice.

Karen smiled, nervously. She wasn't all that worldly wise, but she'd heard about all of that on the news. 'Decommissioning' referred to the recent move by various paramilitary organisations in Northern Ireland to give up their arms. The suspicion was that the arms given over were not the entire stock, that some weapons and ammunition had been stashed 'just in case.' Pat's find, of course, confirmed this.

"They look... more plastic than I expected. Will they work against those things?" Karen asked, innocently.

Pat lifted one of the rifles from the case, his eyes narrowing as he critiqued his find. He ran one hand across the barrel, doting on it as if it were a baby.

"Let's find out," he said, with no trace of humour this time.

...

Karen had never held a gun, never mind fired one. The same couldn't be said for Pat, though. This would have worried a girl like Karen in the old world, yet it strangely comforted her in the new world. She dwelled on that fact, on how things changed with perspective, as they took the long, gruelling stairwell from their top flat to the ground floor.

It wasn't that Pat looked in any way intimidating. To Karen, he looked not unlike a few of the *men folk* who had gone to her church. Po-faced and sincere. Suited and booted in a kind of quaint and fashion-free way. Okay, maybe the men in her church carried a Bible in hand, instead of rifle, but she reckoned they and Pat would probably have shared the same narrow view of the world that, oddly, made men like that loyal and dependable. You knew what you were getting with those kinds of men. And that was a good thing to Karen. She wondered if Pat, himself, was a godly man. But they hadn't talked of God or religion. They had only talked of the dead.

She could hear them, already. The recently quarantined, now joining the ranks of the moving, sniffling majority but unable to get out of their homes. It was unnerving to think that they would always be in there. Even when the block was secure and safe, the dead would remain amongst them. A constant taster of what was outside, like a free sample in one of those magazines you used to get.

The noise from beyond the doors was building as they drew closer to the entrance. It seemed that the recent activity of Pat's car journey had attracted them to the apartment block. When they reached the bottom floor and the view afforded them by the thick glass in the heavy wooden doors, they could see a small crowd starting to congregate in the car park. Karen's heart was beating hard and heavy. These things terrified her.

Pat took a moment to steady himself, clearly worn out by his second use of the stairs that day. Catching his breath, he checked his rifle.

"Careful!" whispered Karen, shooting him a dirty look.

"They can't hear you," Pat replied. "It's the flu, you see. It's blocked up all their sinuses. That's why they're always making that sound – trying to clear their throats. To be honest, I'm not sure if they can see you too well, either."

"How do you know all of this?" Karen asked.

"I don't *know* it," Pat replied, cocking the gun. "It's just a theory."

"I still think we should be careful," Karen said, pouting. She hated being patronised.

Pat seemed oblivious to her mood. Or perhaps he was purposefully being insensitive. Either way, he wasn't sporting any kind of bedside manner. She was nervous; she needed reassurance and comforting. He looked like a man who would grin and bear it, rather than let anything like nerves grind him down. Maybe that's why he had survived this whole thing for so long.

"Okay," he said, finally ready. "On three, I want you to unlock the door, pull it open wide enough to let one of them in, then shut it really hard."

"What if it comes for me?" Karen asked, a worried look spreading across her face.

"It won't," Pat replied, still checking his gun. He *really* seemed to like the gun.

"How do you know that?" she persisted. "Another one of your *theories*?"

He didn't respond to the rise, of course. His type never did.

"No," he said, simply. "Just trust me."

"What if they all get in?"

"They're far too slow and stupid. You'll be lucky to get one of them in."

"Why can't *you* open the door?"

"You know why," he said, patronisingly again. "I've got the gun, and I need to be able to use it quickly enough."

"What if you shoot *me*?"

"JUST –"

She had riled him. She hadn't meant to – she was genuinely scared. But she had worn him down with her constant OCD questions. That had been enough to make even a man as consistently deadpan as Pat lose it.

40

Karen must have looked startled because he immediately calmed down, even smiling a little to placate her. It wasn't the cuddly, fluffy grandfather-like 'there-there' she was looking for, but it was something. A gentle, paternal smile that she wished he would use more often. She needed more of those smiles in this world.

"Okay..." she said. "I'm going to do it..."

Pat nodded, readying the gun. His hands were steady, his movements controlled. He seemed rather pragmatic about the whole thing, as if he was about to hang a door rather than shoot up some monster.

Karen reached to unlock the door. Unlike Pat, her hands *were* shaking. Her heart was beating like a kanga hammer. She struggled with the lock, constantly looking out the window to check the status of the dead. Sure enough, just as Pat suggested, they didn't seem drawn to the noise. Not one of them flinched, morosely staring in the same direction they had been staring at for God knows how long. She could hear one of them coughing. She watched him spit and puke a thick gob of blood from his mouth. Karen immediately felt sick.

She stepped back from the door, placing a hand over her mouth.

"Are you okay?" asked Pat, sighing, gun still at the ready.

"Y-yeah..." Karen replied, trying not to heave. "I'm okay, just give me a second then I'll open the door." She steadied herself, again, breathing in deeply, then out once more. She had to do this right – for herself, more than for him.

She stepped forward and pulled open the door.

...

For a man like Pat Flynn, putting a clean hole through a slow moving target with an AR 18 would prove easy.

But this was not the kind of target he'd been used to shooting at through the years. No, his paramilitary 'career' involved more animated targets, regardless of how uncomfortable that had made him feel, at times. It was for this very reason that his current weapon of choice had been christened 'The Widowmaker'.

He hadn't always questioned orders. But some people just looked less *legitimate* targets than others. The young men kissing their wives and babies before going off to do a day's work. The fact that their day's work involved an army camp was enough to place a red mark over their heads. The middle-aged men, retired from their careers of service, yet still considered open game. One walking his dog to the chip shop to pick up a pastie supper. Another cleaning his car on a bright summer's day. And then there were the old men, polishing their medals up for Remembrance Day, quietly proud of patriotic service in decades gone by. But their loyalty was to an enemy state, and that made *them* a legitimate target, also.

Who was Pat to question orders? He hadn't been active in the early days, when the revolution had kicked off, but he did see what those British bastards had done to his friends and family when he was growing up. The 'legal' kidnapping and interrogation. The dawn raids on houses full of nothing but children and screaming mothers. Bloody Sunday, for God's sake! Surely the end justified the means? *It was for the cause*, they said. But, in the end, of course, he failed to see how any of it helped anyone but the politicians. The bloodshed on both sides of the divide. The killings by state and revolutionary alike. It didn't matter, in the long run. It definitely didn't matter now...

Except that it *did* matter. In a world full of death, overrun by death, it maybe even mattered *more*. Death begat death, and Pat was feeling even more tortured than before. He was far from a bad man. That's what

Father Maguire had told him when he'd wandered into church, one night, from the cold, dark, rain-stained streets of West Belfast. *This doesn't make you a bad man*, the priest had said. *But try telling that to the wives and children of those I've killed*, Pat had said. The brothers and sisters. The mothers and fathers. Every last one of them bent over the graveside, choking back raw emotion and salty tears. And try telling it to the ghosts of all the *animated* targets from twenty-five years of active duty – because those were the conversations that kept a man like Pat Flynn awake at night.

And as for those things outside, the poor bastards with bloody gore seeping from every gap in their skin, God knows what they felt anymore, if anything. Were they even human? They couldn't be – they were dead. He knew that much. Were they ghosts? What would Father Maguire call them? Of course, last time Pat had seen the good Father he wasn't saying much about anything. In fact, he looked just like the others outside. But Pat couldn't do what he was planning on doing now to a man of the cloth. Good God, that would make his pitch in hell all the more permanent.

He was going to shoot the next bastard that walked through the door, though. He was going to shoot it because he knew that if he didn't, there was a fair chance it would turn and do God-knows-what to the young girl standing opposite him. The young girl with her hands on the door handle, shaking. He was going to shoot it because he wanted to protect her, do something to make up for all the bad things he'd done (*for the cause*) over the years. The things that didn't seem to matter anymore on paper or in history but mattered a hell of a lot to those still living and breathing and coping with loss. Even if they were living through all of *this*.

Pat may not have been a bad man, but he was a determined man. As the shambles of a walking corpse came through the door, blood and gore hanging off its Sunday best like wet confetti, Pat didn't hesitate. He took aim with the AR18, looking down its black, polished barrel and pressing his finger against the trigger. He blew a sizable hole through its chest – various organs and bone spreading across the nearby wall like a tantrum in an abattoir.

The corpse was thrown back powerfully with the significant kick off the blast. It stopped at the very door it had wandered through, crumpling against the wood and glass like a broken bottle. It lay there like some 'down and out', almost looking confused, baffled by the shot. But it didn't stay down, and it didn't stay out.

The girl was behind him now, having cowered in the corner like a frightened poodle after opening the door. She was behind him, tugging on his shirt sleeve and pointing at the dead corpse clambering back onto its feet. It seemed ridiculous to her and frightening, and she wanted him to stop it. So, he shot again, aiming for the chest a second time. The second shot completely shattered the damn thing's entire upper torso, leaving almost none of its ribcage left. Diseased lungs slapped against the wall like oily pancakes. There was very little holding the thing together, now, its arms hanging off its rickety shoulders like a broken puppet. Still, it didn't stay down, hauling its mess of a body back onto its feet for a third time.

Pat was completely baffled. He looked to the girl who was staring back at him, both confused and terrified. He shot again. This time he aimed for the damn thing's head, a blotchy mess of dried blood and mucus that looked about as human as road kill. When Pat's bullet pierced it, almost at point blank range, the head all but exploded, a pink mist spraying across the doorway like strawberry milkshake. The corpse fell back against the door, down and out, again. But it wasn't for getting up, this time.

FOUR

Major Connor Jackson didn't take his eyes off the side window as the people carrier he was travelling in moved along the M1 motorway. They were en route to Portadown, a town some thirty miles south of Belfast. His driver was as monosyllabic as was to be expected, given the grim scenery. There wasn't much to coo at when driving along a post-apocalyptic motorway. A stalled vehicle here, a mini pile-up there. Foliage-clad fields with dead animals side by side with the living, the grazing. Wisely, the driver just stuck to what he did best, negotiating every obstacle before him with admirable calm and resolve.

The red stripe of dawn that had stained the sky as Jackson's journey began now blossomed into a rose-blushed skyline. The sun was almost fully in view, and Jackson wondered if it was going to be another glorious day. Weather wise, that was. Because nothing else was going to be glorious about today. Or any other day, for that matter.

Jackson wasn't normally a man given to maudlin thoughts. Not in recent years, anyway. Retiring early, he had spent much of his days fussing over his daughter's kids, playing the doting Grandpa. The only people who called him Major anymore had been the old boys down at the Legion, sharing little more than smutty jokes from

45

their days in service. Until this all kicked off, Jackson had been pretty happy. Killing time (and wasps) at his Donegal summer retreat from March to September. Kicking back and watching old movies in his Derry city terrace during the Winter. A suitable pub was never too far away, whether Paddy's Bar in Glenties or the Legion in the Waterside. There was always a beer tap or bottle of whisky on hand to pass the odd evening, with good company to go with it. And that was fine by Jackson. All he needed was something to distract him, something to bury the bad times, the dark old days of the primitive North, where he had played a most gruesome role...

He had been standing in the back yard of his Derry terrace when the call came through on his cell. He had come back to pick his daughter and the kids up, hoping to take them to his Donegal retreat. He knew the call was from the military when he read 'number withheld' on the cell's incoming alert. And when the speaker at the other end of the line, a young man named Harris, had addressed him as 'Major Jackson', his fears were confirmed.

They allowed him to return to Donegal on the premise that he called them when he got there. A secure number was provided, Jackson urged to call at a specific time to confirm his whereabouts. A helicopter would pick him up to take him to RAF Aldergrove. From there, they would travel across to London for a special briefing. Only, it didn't quite work out like that. With the flu hitting so furiously, and society quickly breaking down, Jackson found himself within a lock-down situation at Aldergrove. Weeks had passed without anyone telling him what was happening. Jackson watched as the television in his blacked-out quarters moved from constant news features on every channel to the po-faced debates, until eventually the Emergency Broadcast Channel was all that could be seen.

When the virus finally reached them, people inside the compound falling ill, Jackson was neither surprised nor worried. In a way, he was glad *something* was happening. But where in the old films he enjoyed watching, it had been women and children first, the military had different ways. As a Major, he was siphoned off to a special restricted section of the compound. Along with other high-ranking officers, he wiled the hours away, playing chess and drinking shots of whisky. Food and drink (including copious amounts of booze) were provided, daily, by men in yellow suits. All they asked for in return was some guidance, some advice regarding strategy on how to deal with the crowds of sick people constantly baying for medicine outside the gates. But what could you do when there was no hope, when there was no medicine, and even your own yellow plastic suit and cumbersome supply of oxygen couldn't stop the virus from reaching you. As their own numbers depleted, all the yellow suits wanted was light hearted conversation and an occasional shoulder to wallow on. These were dark days, and old men, old war heroes (or whatever these young men thought Jackson and his drunken cronies were) became important just for having lived life, just for having survived days that seemed more tempestuous than hell itself.

Eventually, against the advice of the other old officers, Jackson ventured topside to see what was going on. The base was in a mess, burnt up bodies of infected soldiers littering the ground like old, discarded bin bags. Most of the helicopters had been stolen, hijacked by deserters who bribed or threatened pilots to fly them to nowhere. Those still present and alive mostly wandered around in a drunken stupor. Fights broke out, unchecked, men pulling guns on each other over little more than lost games of cards. Others struggled with religious icons, crosses and bibles, to make sense of the new, torn world.

Few of the soldiers seemed to be acting reasonably anymore. The few that did, gathering around Jackson as if he were some sort of new Messiah, seemed clueless as to what to do. They told him what little they knew, how that burning the bodies of those who fell ill was the best way to ensure they didn't *come back like the others*. Jackson hadn't known what they meant until he took a look over the wall. Until he found dead people, instead of sick people, crowding the gates, walking and sniffing, spitting and scratching like prehistoric witches. He found himself suddenly thinking about his daughter and grandchildren, now that he knew the full scale of the situation. He wondered if they would be among the faces at the gate, or other gates like this. But the alcohol was doing its job well. His heart was tired, worn out, numb. No emotion could be rinsed from it.

Jackson remembered watching them, for hours, from the sentry box. The men came and asked him what they should do, what his orders were, but he just shook his head. "Do whatever seems right," he said, quietly. And they did. They shot the dead, threw grenades at the dead, doused the dead with flames. But they always came back. Thicker each day, the more attention the soldiers drew to the base with their violence. The dead were insurmountable, unstoppable. It seemed useless to oppose them in any way.

Some days later, two men wearing the yellow suits came to where the officers stayed, tired and sallow looking. They had removed their masks, no longer believing in the ability of such to protect them. They told the officers who had not ventured from their hiding place, most of them still cowering in the dark recesses of the base like the scared old men they were, that the majority of people were dead, that society as they knew it was gone. The provisions in the base were all but exhausted (including the whisky). Jackson nodded to confirm what they were saying – he'd seen it all with his own eyes. A choice was given to the officers, the more reasonable ones who hadn't regressed to drunken despair. Operations were still live at the Mahon Road Army Camp in Portadown. One man was needed to replace their previous officer, who had seemingly fallen ill with the virus and was currently under quarantine. There was enough fuel to get two men down there via car, a driver and one of the gathered officers. The others would be airlifted across to London, although no one seemed to know what was going on there. The pros and cons of both situations were laid out to the officers, but Jackson had been the only one to volunteer for the job in Portadown. London wasn't appealing to him anymore. God knew what it was like, over there. But he knew all too well what it was like at the Mahon Road. It was his old base, when he was active, and a part of him wondered what it looked like years later. The mission in Portadown suddenly reminded him of his daughter again, his grandchildren. It reminded him of the importance of family, and the love a man should have for his children...

He was still staring out of the car window when they finally pulled off the motorway, moving towards the Mahon Road. The Army camp was situated just outside of Portadown, one of the larger towns south of Lough Neagh. It was a place well known for its problems, torn apart by violence between Northern Ireland's two largest communities over the years of the so-called Troubles. Jackson recalled days gone by taking this same journey, as the car turned up the Mahon Road, towards the relative countryside calm of a post-apocalyptic hell. He could make out the gates of the heavily secured Army camp, seemingly unchanged since his day.

Apart from being surrounded by dead bodies, ten deep.

The doors opened, more yellow suits rushing out, these men also having abandoned oxygen, but seemingly more organised, and armed with automatic rifles. Over the car's engines, Jackson could hear the familiar ra-ta-ta of the gunfire as the men moved to clear the area. Several heads popped like corks in the hale of fire, the cold flesh and bone exploding, each body falling to the ground like sacks of spuds. The car suddenly squealed, Jackson's driver cutting through the thinned herd of dead, mercilessly. Several bodies hit the car as he drove, the collisions surprisingly light against the vehicle, as if the dead were literally filled with air. But Jackson felt scared. He felt tired and sad and scared, until the yellow suited soldiers moved back inside, and the gates were closed.

He was hurried out of the car and through the main complex. One of the men moving him seemed immediately more aggressive than the others, his suit stained with blood, as if he had been wrestling with the poor bastards outside, then scalping them like some Apache from one of the old Westerns. Jackson recognised him, even from his swagger. His name was Dr Miles Gallagher, and by the looks of things, he was still a man not afraid to get his hands dirty. He welcomed Jackson warmly as they walked through the base. Jackson hadn't laid eyes on him for years, and that was a good thing.

They moved through the more obvious parts of the base, travelling to an underground section that Jackson was all too familiar with. Eventually, he was out of his civvies and back in standard uniform, wearing an officer's shirt and trousers (both at least one size too big). He tightened the loop of his belt as he was led, gently, into a musty room littered with old files, beer bottles and cans of half-eaten food. The smell was atrocious, even compared to outside. A couple of men lay like dogs in the corner on worn, padded sleeping bags. Gallagher looked appalled when he saw them.

"Get off the ground," the doctor said sternly, shocking the two privates out of their bags and onto their feet. "There's an officer on parade." They stood to attention as Jackson was introduced to them, hands raised in salute.

"At ease," Jackson said, surveying them with little more than pity.

Gallagher looked at him calmly. He was just as Jackson had remembered him. Cold, unemotional, polite. Weirdly unaffected. "I'll bring you to the colonel, sir," he said, quietly. "He's not very well, you understand..."

"I was led to believe he had picked up the flu," Jackson said, a little nervously. "Is it... er... safe to visit him?"

"We have him under quarantine, sir," Gallagher said, again quietly. "We can still communicate with him, without any risk. Of course, the quarantine is just a measure to make the men feel better, really," he said, smiling as if amused. "That's all it really is. In reality, there's no way to avoid the virus, at this stage of the game. It's all around us, all over us, all through us." His manner was quite clinical as he spoke, regardless of the seriousness of his words. But that was the nature of Dr Miles Gallagher, the paradox of the man. He had started out as a medic in the Army, soon spotted in the Gulf War for his more eccentric interest in the art of interrogation, in the ways of abusing a man, ever so acutely, without actually leaving any physical evidence of such. It was a radical use of medical training, but Dr Gallagher became an asset to the Army because of it. Eventually he was moved to Northern Ireland, to the project which Jackson had also been assigned to – a covert operation known, simply, as The Chamber. Gallagher had been one of the most vicious bastards Jackson had ever known, back in the day. After the embarrassment of internment, the British were pushing for results, while demanding discretion. He was asked to be brutal, yet subtle – all at once. Dr Gallagher was certainly brutal, but he was also one of the most polite men Jackson had ever known, despite his merciless way of 'doing business'. Jackson wondered if the good doctor had mellowed any through the years, as the focus on interrogation faded and less aggressive duties resumed. He certainly hadn't become any less formidable looking, Jackson could see, still retaining his tall, lean and frankly creepy looking exterior.

They moved through to another corridor, equally as rundown and chaotic looking as the room they had just left. The Chamber was clearly only hanging onto operations by a very thin thread, the apathy of post-apocalyptic depression affecting the men and women here almost as much as it had affected those at Aldergrove. Jackson wondered if the colonel's failing health had been the final nail in the coffin for the survivors here, a stark realisation that even they could be infected, despite the base's notoriously stringent protocols and high security.

Finally, they reached a sealed door, Gallagher removing a key from his pocket and inserting it into the keyhole. He unlocked the door and glided it open, slowly, as if worried about disturbing someone inside. Jackson was shown in first, Gallagher closing the door behind him and locking it equally as carefully as he had opened it. Looking around, Jackson remembered the room from days gone by. It was an observation room. It looked out onto the interrogation rooms, three in total. Glass covered each side wall, as well as the front wall of the room, allowing the occupants to observe any of the three interrogations. But it was to the front wall that Jackson's eyes were drawn, noticing the unmistakable form of a very sick man sitting, regally, at a table.

"I'm sure you remember how to communicate to the room, sir," Gallagher said in a matter-of-fact way. Jackson walked to the microphone at the control panel. It hadn't changed a bit since he was last here. Still as minimalist looking as before, featuring the mic and huge red button. A small dial allowed the sound control to be adjusted. A nearby chair, also familiar from days gone by, beckoned Jackson. He sat down, facing the one-way window, knowing, from experience, that the colonel would only be seeing his own reflection when looking at the glass. Yet, his cold, hard stare seemed to be burrowing through Jackson's own eyes, as if he somehow could see beyond the mirror. As if, in the ongoing transfiguration from life to death, the colonel had achieved some sort of enhanced vision, a sixth sense that allowed him to see everything and everyone.

Jackson turned to look at Gallagher, who was standing by the door, facing the colonel as if on parade. "He's... already turned," he said, without pressing the red button.

"Not quite, sir," Gallagher corrected. "He's in the later stages of his illness, of course, but still able to talk. I've been just with him, before we got the call from the gate advising of your approach." Gallagher pointed again to the mic, as if Jackson had forgotten it was there. "Sir, if you please..." he said, as polite as ever.

Jackson looked back at the colonel, still drawn to his eyes. He hadn't noticed them blink since he had entered the room, as if the colonel was in some kind of trance. His hands clung to an old, bloodstained towel, now disused, as the effects of the flu were in freefall. Bloody mucus seeped from his mouth and nose, unchecked. He gurgled, as if choking. He spat on the ground beside him, clearing his throat. Jackson's hand reached for the red button, noticing how it lit up as he pressed it. The colonel didn't react, not seeming to hear the fuzz of the speakers kicking in.

"You may wish to turn the volume up a little louder, sir," Gallagher whispered. "The colonel's hearing is failing, you see."

"Of course," said Jackson, as he turned the dial, noticing the colonel suddenly looking around the room, as he heard his words.

"Hallo?" the colonel said, "Is that you, Gallagher?"

"No, sir..." Jackson said. "My name's Major Connor Jackson. I've been sent to... er..."

"Replace me," the colonel said, calmly. "It was me who sent for you, sir. Welcome to the Chamber."

"Thank you, sir," Jackson replied.

"Of course," the colonel said, picking up a clipboard from the mess littering the table in front of him, "I'm led to believe this isn't your first time at The Chamber. Bit of an old pro, you are. Duties alongside Dr Gallagher in the early nineties, it seems. Capture and interrogation of prolific IRA operatives... those were your specialities, weren't they?"

"Yes, sir," Jackson said. He reckoned that the clipboard contained excerpts from his personnel file. He knew what was in there, and felt a little uncomfortable at it being perused so liberally by the colonel, a man whom he had never met, in all his years of service. Those dark days seemed irrelevant to him, now. As if it were a different Connor Jackson detailed in that file. As if it had all just been a mix-up.

"Yes, sir, indeed..." the colonel repeated, as if he were a headmaster chastising Jackson. Jackson was a bit taken back by that, but said nothing. "However, seems you weren't always best pleased at the kinds of practices which went on around here," the colonel continued. "Retired from the Army after a certain incident involving –"

"Clearly, sir," Jackson said, interrupting the colonel and struggling to hold his cool, "there are things which a

54

man must do in a war situation which are questionable."
This was a dying man, he reminded himself. This wasn't
the time or place for debating the rules of engagement.
"I find I'm much more principled now, though," he said,
feeling the stab of bitter memories from yesteryear.
"What happened before –"

"This is no time for principles," the colonel said,
cutting over Jackson. "This is a time for doing what
needs to be done, in whatever manner the situation
requires. This virus, this fucking *flu* virus, needs to
be contained," he said, stressing the word *flu,* as if
marvelling at how something so trivial could cause such
chaos. "Strong leadership is required to make sure that
is what happens."

Jackson said nothing, feeling suddenly aware of the
cold-blooded doctor behind him, his narrow slits of eyes
seeming to bore into the Major's head. He wondered
why the colonel hadn't just passed leadership duties
over to Gallagher. After all, he seemed to want someone
to take over who fitted exactly Gallagher's profile.

"I'll do my best, sir," Jackson said, calmly but not
confidently. "Under your guidance, of course."

The colonel laughed. "I'll be dead within the day," he
said, a touch of anger resonating throughout his body in
the guise of a wheeze. "But I've left strict instruction for
my body to be *donated* to Dr Gallagher's project. Now,
please leave me," he said. "I don't have long left, and
I'm damn sure I'm not going to waste my final moments
on a prick like you."

Jackson couldn't believe the colonel had just said what
he thought he had said. He looked over at Gallagher,
his jaw hanging almost to the floor in disbelief. But
Gallagher looked back at him, almost smiling beneath
his benign expression.

"If you could come this way, sir," he said, gesturing
Jackson towards the door, as if he were a normal doctor,

an ethical doctor. "It's time to leave the colonel to his final rest."

Jackson moved out the door, knowing that the next time he returned, the man he had just been talking to would no longer be a man. In fact, he would no longer be alive, instead taking on the form of something that was, at best, imitating life. He was led to his quarters by Gallagher, where he was left to settle in. He had been given a modest room with the very basics a man required for life – a bed, a desk, a sink. On the wall was a single picture, a painting of a sunrise. It spoke of the only thing that Jackson could be sure of, anymore. That the sun would continue to rise. That the world would continue to turn. Nothing else was written in stone.

...

"Good, you're awake..."

Geri rubbed her eyes, too sleepy to notice that she was sloped over a chair, loosely tied. It was the tattooed man who addressed her.

"Oh, the rope was just to stop you from slipping off the chair," he said, smiling as if there were some kind of joke in that sentence. He was talking to her through a glass door. She'd come to while they were tying her to the chair, but she had decided still to feign unconsciousness. It seemed that, while pretending to be unconscious, she'd actually dozed off. *Typical, really*, she thought to herself. She always did love her sleep, even though she hadn't really had any for the last week.

Geri allowed her sleepy eyes to sweep her surroundings. She was in a glass patio at the rear of the house. It had obviously been an extension that was built fairly recently. They were popular for those kinds of terraced houses, offering some extra room and space to the rear of the house, where the gardens were often generously sized. The patio had been someone's pet project. Someone who was most likely dead... or undead... right now.

"It wasn't my idea," continued the tattooed man, palm pressed against the glass door as he talked. "But McFall thinks you're infected. This is your quarantine."

"I need to piss..." Geri said, uncouthly.

"Then piss," he replied. She had heard him being referred to by the other man as 'Lark.' It had struck her as a rather strange name. Strange name for a strange-looking man. "You're not *really* tied to the chair. Remember? It'll be easy to shake yourself free."

He watched her, almost leeringly, as if wanting to see her try that manoeuvre. But she didn't move.

Lark was still rattling on, though, like the insensitive lout he was. "I'm sure you'll find a pan in the cupboards that you can use," he said, "or you can use the sink – I think it still drains okay." He smiled, somewhat politely or ironically (Geri couldn't be sure which) as he pointed over to the small sink and cupboards next to the washing machine.

"Fuck you..." Geri said. She had decided he wasn't being polite, so why should she.

"Listen, I'm sorry about this," he countered, "but we need to know you're clean. Mc Fall said he saw you sneeze."

"It's hay fever. I already told him that."

"Sure, and if it doesn't develop into flu in the next couple of days, you'll be welcomed back into the house."

"I just want to leave..."

"Go back out there? Are you mad? Seriously, you're better in here. But I'm warning you, there'll always be one of us around, so don't try anything stupid."

Geri got up from the chair, feeling the muscles in her leg seizing up. She rubbed them, trying to ease the stiffness. Her wounded foot still hurt like a bitch, causing her to limp. She grimaced with the pain, setting herself down in the chair, again. She looked up at Lark, but he had disappeared back into the kitchen, it seemed. So much for someone always watching.

Her hand ran over the front pockets of her jeans. She checked for the bump in the denim – the bullet she had acquired from earlier still in her pocket. Again, she pulled her long t-shirt down to cover her pockets, smiling to herself. She couldn't believe those idiots had missed that one.

She rose from her chair, limping over to the generously glassed patio windows. It looked out onto a small garden that had once been someone's pride and joy. There were colourful flower beds, pepper-dash stones and an ornamental fountain – all landscaped to perfection. Yet, without tending, the garden was becoming wild. A mass of sombre-looking green weeds threatened the daintily coloured tulips. Grass sprouted up through the stones like hands from a grave. From the sky, the evening sun looked on like a powerless god.

Geri ventured over to the cupboards, wondering how best to take her piss. She fumbled through the cupboards, finding a sizable pan that should suffice. Nosily, she opened a couple of nearby drawers, finding nothing but scissors and plastic cutlery and other useless household items. She opened another drawer, noticing cotton wool, antiseptic, bandaging and waterproof plasters. She took the lot, throwing all the items into her new pseudo toilet bowl. Adding a roll of kitchen towel to the pile, she proceeded back to the white plastic dining table that looked out onto the garden.

She sighed, setting up her makeshift toilet behind the table. In the dim, evening sun, she undid the button and zip of her jeans, rolled them down and squatted to piss into the pot.

This is as bad as it gets, she thought to herself.

...

58

McFall stood looking out onto the street from the upstairs window. The light was dimming, evening's shadows moving in to throw a curtain over the day's events. He would be settling down to sleep soon, and it couldn't come soon enough. He felt knackered after all that had happened, all the excitement of the day's events. He promised himself never to go out there again, unless he really fucking had to.

Through the flower-patterned curtains, McFall could see a couple of the dead wandering aimlessly through the streets. It was the same story every night, almost as if they were on some sort of evening patrol, but they never seemed to cotton on to the fact that there were survivors in this particular house. And even when they did, just like before with the girl, it seemed to leave their minds like goldfish when you tapped their bowl – suddenly and momentarily riled before becoming quiet again. Tonight, they didn't seem to know he was looking at them, but he was still careful to peek from behind the curtain, nonetheless.

The house had been a great base for Lark and him for some weeks, now. Just how many weeks, he couldn't be sure. He'd found it pretty early on, pretty soon after meeting Lark for the first time. Was it three weeks ago? Four weeks ago? Hell, who was counting anymore, anyway? He wondered how long it would be safe to stay at the house. The longer they stayed, the more the dead seemed to multiply in number. He was worried that they would eventually sniff them out, and once that happened, he was sure it was game over.

But that wasn't his only concern. He had others, all scrambling for airtime in the WORRY section of his brain. First of all, there was the flu. Why he hadn't caught it, he couldn't be sure. Deep down, he knew it probably wasn't anything to do with his obsession with the balaclava, but he still wasn't prepared to take it off.

Every little helps, he said to himself, rhyming off the old supermarket slogan. But he could never be sure he was immune – people were catching it every day (if there even *were* many people left) and he knew he could just as easily be next.

And then there was the whole problem with supplies. Yesterday's run had, obviously, been very unsuccessful. What with the whole mess with the girl, he'd ended up leaving all the stuff he'd got in the boot of the car. And it was becoming so heavily populated with dead out there that he couldn't imagine it being safe enough to retrieve it any time soon. They had some stuff left from the last run, but only enough to see them through another couple of days. And who was to know how many more of those things would be walking past the window tomorrow, or the day after.

He thought back to his life before all of this had happened. He had been a taxi driver, and a damn good one. He worked long and hard and made good money. None of it mattered now, of course. His money was useless. The change in his pocket no better than the stones on the ground. His bank accounts no longer existed. Once mere numbers on a screen, his whole life savings had disappeared overnight – pretty much snuffed out at the flick of a switch. Twenty thousand odd quid blown like a faulty light bulb.

McFall considered, for a moment, what it was that made him rich now. He was healthy – that much was true. The flu hadn't touched him. Of course, he was never a man who took ill very much – there just wasn't time to be ill. Or maybe it was something to do with all the people he was coming into contact with. Hundreds of people sitting in his car every week. People from all walks of life, some coughing and wheezing and sniffing with colds and flus and God-knows-what. The school runs he did, the hospital runs – all of them without even as much as a sniffle from his seat. His body had most likely built up a resistance to all of the ills of Belfast, maybe even including this most recent flu outbreak.

But he wasn't taking any chances.

Still keeping an eye on the street outside, he removed his balaclava. He felt in his pocket for the small bottle of herbal remedy he carried with him. His wife had turned him onto this stuff when she'd heard he was going to be working as a taxi driver. She had said it would help keep the cold and flu away. It tasted like acid, but he mixed a few drops with his orange juice every morning and drank it down. He unscrewed the bottle, removing the small dropper. He squeezed out three small drops over the mouth and nose of his balaclava. It was a soothing, minty smell that came from the bottle, so he guessed one ingredient had to be mint. He didn't know what else it was made from. His wife had become increasingly bored with life, reading all kinds of nonsense in books and magazines. God knows *what* she had put in it! McFall screwed the dropper back into the bottle, sliding it into his pocket again. He slipped the rather pungent balaclava back over his face.

A noise outside startled him. Ducking to the side wall, he peeked, gingerly, through the curtains of the bedroom. Down below, he saw a couple of men struggling with the door of the car he had parked by the house. The one the girl had clung onto, earlier in the day, with groceries in its boot. One of the men held a small handgun and was aiming it, nervously, at a pack of dead that were moving, slowly, towards them from further down the street. McFall moved to change his view, still taking care to duck behind the curtains. From the other end of the street, he could see the couple of meandering dead he'd spotted earlier. They were wandering back towards the commotion, as if worried they might miss out on something really wonderful. It looked like the two men were hemmed in.

McFall watched as the two men continued to force the door of the car, eventually giving up. As the dead drew closer, both men jumped onto the car's roof. The man with the gun fired at some of them. His aim was poor, however, several shots flying wide of the incoming targets. Then he struck lucky, McFall noticing how one shot connected with the chest of a dead woman. She hit the ground almost immediately. To the surprise of both men, as well as McFall, though, she wasted little time before climbing back onto her feet.

Before long, the dead had surrounded the car and were grasping at the legs of the two men. They kicked and lunged out in panic. The one with the gun fired a couple more random shots, to little effect. Those who were shot looked stunned for a while, before moving back in for the kill.

One of the men was compromised, falling flat on the car roof as the dead managed to grasp hold of his leg. As McFall watched on, the poor bastard was dragged into the pack and onto the road. All the surrounding dead immediately closed in on him, hungrily, leaving the other man firing his gun and screaming the name of his friend – both in vain. Finally, as a last ditch attempt, he jumped off the roof of the car, grabbing his friend's arms and trying to rescue him from the closing quarters, but they grabbed him too, dragging both men to the ground and surrounding them like a pack of hyenas around prey.

But there was something new happening, here. Something McFall hadn't noticed before. Something that almost made him gag with disgust, despite the minty fresh feel of balaclava on his face. Sure, he'd known the dead to be aggressive. He'd even known them to tear at people with their hardened, rigor mortis fingers, or snap at them, like wild dogs, like feral beasts using every part of themselves to fell their prey.

But this was new. This was terrifying.

"Jesus..." McFall whispered to himself, unable to take his eyes from the gruesome scene. "They're fucking *eating* them..."

FIVE

Karen sat the pot of tea down on the coaster beside the milk and sugar. She set one empty cup where Pat was sitting, also laid out on a coaster, then another for herself. She then poured Pat a cup of tea. Only then did she sit down beside him at the table.

"It's the head," Pat said, staring into space. "You have to shoot them in the head."

"Uh-huh." She said, smiling. "Would you like a biscuit?" He looked up, as if to peruse the biscuits. Karen immediately jumped up, scrambling to throw some onto a plate for him to inspect. "Chocolate or Jammie Dodgers?" she said, setting the plate on yet another coaster at the table.

"Any plain digestives?" he asked, frowning at the choice on the table, "I'm watching my cholesterol, you see."

"No, but I could–"

"I wonder why it didn't fall when I hit its heart," he said, forgetting all about the biscuits. "I mean pretty much everything dies when you take out the heart... what's driving the thing if it isn't the heart?"

"Well, I –"

"And another thing; have you noticed that they don't breathe?"

"Well, maybe –"

"Sure they spit and choke and cough blood up, and stuff, but they don't seem to breathe. Maybe all the other stuff is just habit. Which is understandable, of course," he continued, "What with them being dead and all..."

Karen didn't respond, instead standing up from the table and reaching for the tissue in her pocket with shaking hands. She brought it to her face, choking back some tears.

Pat looked up at her, pulling his chair back when he noticed she was crying.

"Hey, I'm sorry. I –" he cleared his throat, looking embarrassed. Pat wasn't the kind of man who felt comfortable around tears or emotion, in general.

"It's okay, she said," Karen dabbed the corners of her eyes before flashing a very false smile at Pat. "It's just all this can be so –"

"Yeah, I know," said Pat. He wandered over to the large window, looking out into the night. Karen had lit some candles around the flat. It was pretty much the only light to be seen for miles, save for the cloud-clothed moon. *The lights had gone out in Belfast*, thought Pat, and it unnerved him more tonight than any other night.

He couldn't see any of them, now. If he were to listen really carefully, he might have heard the snorting and coughing of the ones trapped in the flats below. But they were relatively safe up here, and that kind of comforted him. Even if just a little.

He turned to look at the dainty girl at the table, sipping her tea politely. This world wasn't for her. She wouldn't survive it, unless she changed, adapted. He knew he would need to teach her a few new tricks in order to keep her safe.

Pat walked over to the small stash of weapons in the case he had recovered from earlier in the day. He retrieved a Heckler and Koch UPS handgun from the case, sizing it up.

"Tomorrow I'm going to teach you how to shoot" he said, looking at Karen, brandishing the handgun, "With this."

...

Pat rose early, waking pretty much as the sun poked its head through the cheap, thinly woven curtains of his bedroom. Of course, it wasn't his bedroom, per se. Truth be told, neither he nor Karen knew to whom their chosen flat had belonged prior to the flu. It was just empty and relatively safe. And that was enough to make it somewhere they could call home.

He rubbed his deeply set, tired eyes, sighed and pulled his stiff body out of bed. The years hadn't been kind to his bones, and he was certainly feeling the effects of the previous day's journeying up and down the block's staircase.

Pat opened the wardrobe, retrieving a dressing gown and towel. He moved out of his room, through to the bathroom, lifting a small bottle of still mineral water from the (ever-decreasing) stash in the hallway as he went. In the bathroom, he filled the small sink with the bottled water, then proceeded to wash his upper body as best he could. He emptied the sink before refilling it again, in order to brush his teeth. He opened the cabinet to retrieve some baby wipes, using them to clean his lower body. Finally, he took a piss, completing his morning hygiene routine for another day.

Coming out of the bathroom, he met Karen in the hallway. Her athletic body was also wrapped in a dressing gown, revealing all of her shapely curves. Pat felt embarrassed, all of a sudden.

"Morning..." he mumbled, dipping his head as he passed her.

"Morning," she replied, sprightly as usual, "Would you like a cup of tea?"

"Please," he answered, looking back at her, briefly. He watched her disappear into the kitchen area. As he retreated back into his room, he heard the clinking of cups and cutlery as Karen got their tea and breakfast on the boil.

From somewhere below, he heard the dead. They were also stirring, it seemed, although he doubted that they ever slept. Their low moans and constant, growling coughs harmonised with the whistling sound of Karen's boiling kettle from the kitchen.

Pat opened the curtains of his bedroom, looking out. There were definitely a lot more of them today. They crowded the entire greenery and car park immediately surrounding the block of flats. Their number spread out, fairly densely, as far as he could see from the bedroom window. It was going to make it almost impossible to move about without considerable danger. And that was bad news for two reasons.

First of all, there were provisions. What they had wouldn't last forever – and he wasn't just thinking about mineral water. Their tea-bags, biscuits, cereal and tinned goods were going to run out as well, and sooner rather than later. He reckoned they had about a week's worth left, but that was about the height of it.

Then, he thought about their plans for the morning. He had told Karen only last night how he intended to show her how to use the gun, but it would be both foolish and reckless for them to even consider opening the door on the ground floor of the flat when there were so many of the dead around.

He sat down on the bed, thinking things through the way men like him - pragmatic men - often did.

"Breakfast's ready," he heard Karen call, from the kitchen.

"Coming now," he replied, still going over everything in his head.

Karen stood, awkwardly, holding the Heckler and Koch handgun as if it were a hot coal.

They were in the 8th-floor corridor of the block of flats, just two flights down from their chosen home. At the far end from where they stood, a hastily sketched human-shaped target was taped to the wall. A few torches, taped to the walls of each of the corridors they ventured into, provided enough light.

"Is this the way that you point it?" Karen asked Pat, a strained look breaking across her face. Her forehead wrinkled, and her lips pursed in a way that made her look even cuter and more innocent than Pat had ever seen her look before. Even with a 9mm in her hands.

Pat gently corrected her pose, bringing one hand up to support the other as she aimed the gun towards the target.

"It's whatever is most comfortable for you," he said.

"Do I pull the trigger now?"

"Gently *squeeze* the trigger," he said. "Don't pull it too quickly."

Pat watched as she grimaced, closing both eyes before squeezing the trigger. Her hand shook, more with anticipation, as a round fired, noisily, from the gun. She immediately opened her eyes, staring at the target some metres away, excitedly.

"Did I hit it?" she asked.

Pat reached one hand across the barrel of her gun, lowering the weapon to point at the ground, snapping the lever onto 'safety' before he walked towards the target. He searched the white paper for any sign of a direct hit, finding a blackened chip out of the concrete wall above the target, instead.

"You were a wee bit high," he called back to her, smiling encouragingly. "Not bad!" he added, and he was genuinely impressed. They hadn't been at it for long, but it seemed she had a steady enough aim. He would just have to teach her not to be so frightened of the gun, to relax with it, and then she would be–

(a killer? Like you, Pat?)

He put the dark thoughts to the back of his mind. They were bubbling up again. Threatening to take over, to overcome him. Recently, before everything had kicked off, he had gone to see his doctor, just to get some tablets to help him sleep. Of course, the doctor – some young upstart fresh out of Nursery School - had only agreed to give him the tablets if he saw some counsellor. Pat had agreed reluctantly, at first, but soon found his bi-weekly trips to the clinic to be something of a God-send. Pat wasn't stupid enough to talk directly about the things he had done, or the things which were done to him, referring more to 'things he had seen', but he had always considered himself good at reading other people, and he was pretty sure that the middle-aged Englishman with the white hair and horn-rimmed glasses knew exactly where he was coming from. It made a difference to be able to talk about these things, get them off his chest. To talk about death. To understand death and his part in it. To mourn the dead, both the dead he had known and loved, as well as those who had been known and loved by others, but not him... But now... now he was suddenly surrounded by death. He was knee-deep in it. He was even teaching this innocent, young girl how to deal it out, and it was starting to eat away at him.

He looked at her as he walked back up the corridor. She was disappointed she hadn't hit the target. Her gun hand hung limply by her side as if ashamed of itself – ashamed for not being able to meet the target, of not being able to make a kill. Pat wondered if he was doing the right thing in changing her into something she would never have been, otherwise. A dark part of him even considered whether death, itself – her death – would be better than her *dealing* with death. Or dealing out death. But he knew, deep down, that he had to give her at least a chance to protect herself, a chance to prolong her life in a world where the dead were now the majority.

But there was another reason, of course. A reason much more personal to him. Karen was a rarity in every sense of the word. She had become precious to Pat, like she was his own child, and he had to protect what was precious to him.

This was something he had learned the hard way.

...

At precisely the same time, two days later, Pat and Karen were standing outside the door of one of the apartments in the block. They had cleared the two floors above them, already, pillaging each of the empty flats to fill their wheeled suitcase several times over. Pat's back was broken, dragging the case downstairs, each time, to their flat on the 10th floor, but the prize was worth it. They had managed to restock their own cupboards with enough tinned goods and bottled drinks to keep them going for at least a month. They had avoided the quarantined flats, of course, the blood-clogged sniffles vivid enough to discourage them from compromising the welded sheets of metal across their doors, and they hadn't met any nasty surprises along the way.

Yet.

"Okay, this is the last one for today," Pat said. "My back's killing me."

Karen stepped up to the doorway, her handgun at the ready.

Pat sighed, reaching across the barrel to lower the safety lever.

"Sorry," she whispered.

"It's okay," he said, smiling weakly.

Pat readied his own 9mm before bending forward, quietly, to open the front door to the flat. It wasn't locked, and that worried Pat. They'd had to break open every other flat, save this one. It certainly wasn't a good sign to find a door unsecured.

Pat reckoned that most of the block's tenants had shot through well before the worst had hit Belfast, leaving most of their belongings locked up tight in their flats. He had heard reports of rescue camps, during the height of the outbreak. Well after even the TV had stopped broadcasting anything besides the 'Emergency Broadcast Signal' that had become all too familiar. Of course, rumours were circulating that the 'rescue' camps were only slightly better than 'concentration' camps. He'd even met some survivors, along the way, who had broken free of the camps amidst reports of government-sponsored culling. That wouldn't surprise a man like Pat Flynn, when it came to the British government. In fact, it fitted in perfectly well with his political leanings, as well as his personal experience...

Turning to Karen, Pat raised one finger across his lips in a gesture encouraging her to move quietly. She nodded before moving to enter the flat, but Pat stopped her, choosing to enter first. A smell of rotting food and God-knows-what-else hit him like a smack around the head. It was pungent, weeks of neglect and shut windows creating something of a greenhouse effect with the sun's daily assault.

Pat checked behind him, finding Karen following closely, her handgun pointed to the ground. It impressed him to see how comfortable she looked with the gun, now. It was hard to think that only two days ago, she was holding it like it was a possessed thing or some kind of forbidden fruit. A good girl like Karen shouldn't look this comfortable with a gun, he thought, but it made him smile, nonetheless.

They moved through the hallway, quietly. It was the same layout as their own flat, so it was easy enough to navigate. They moved towards the kitchen, hoping to free up some tinned goods. The place was even more decrepit than they expected, more flies seeming to populate the area than Pat deemed possible. And then there was the smell... He slammed the door, tightly, turning to Karen and shaking his head.

"There's no way we're going in there," he said, "We aren't likely to find anything useable, anyway."

Karen nodded, turning to retreat out of the flat. Absentmindedly, she reached for the door to the bathroom on her way out, turning and opening the handle before Pat could stop her. The door slammed back on her face as the figure of a man lumbered out of the small room. His entire face was completely caked in bloody mucus. A quick glance inside the bathroom revealed a scarlet-stained toilet and more of those damn flies.

Karen fell back onto the ground, the dead man lingering over her, dangerously.

Pat did the first thing that came to mind, slamming the creature, hard, forcing it through the hall and open doorway. The two of them fell to the cold, tiled floor of the outside corridor. Pat struggled against the thing, his own handgun having slid across the corridor during the commotion. It was on top of him, somehow, and seemed much stronger and aggressive than he had thought it should be. With one hand, he held its face away from his as he struggled to reach with his other hand for his weapon. The thing's teeth were showing, rotting and slathered with the same bloody gore that leaked from its eyes and nose. Flies continued to crowd him, creating a terrifying din of desperate moaning with the annoying buzzing sound.

Pat fought against the damn thing, but it was every-where – Tearing, scratching and... trying to bite him. It managed to get its jaws over his sleeve, closing down upon his leather jacket. He could feel its hunger, its feral nature having completely taken over its brain and functions to make it the predator it had become. This creature was no longer the docile, disease-carrying pest it had been before. It was a hunter, now. A savage hunter.

A shot rang out close by, and Pat found his face completely covered in blood within an instant. Another shot, and then there was calm. The dead thing no longer bit against his jacket. It no longer dragged and scratched against his clothes and person. He kicked it away from him, as if it were a dead rat, and scrambled to his feet. He wiped his face, spitting to make sure none of the dead thing's blood had got into his mouth.

"Did I hit it?" said the voice from inside the flat.

Pat turned to find Karen, gun pointed towards the ground, just as he'd taught her. She looked almost scary in the pale light, wearing that little white dress that used to look so innocent to him, stained by a single speck of blood. Her face remained naive, questioning, even, as if she wasn't so sure she'd done the right thing. He realised, suddenly, that she *had* become a killer, that she *had* learned to protect herself, but she still remained pretty much the person she had always been. Maybe in this new world, where death was becoming a part of life, it wasn't so bad to kill. Especially if in self-defence. And especially if what you had killed was, in some strange way, dead already.

"Yep," he said, smiling as he cleaned his face with a handkerchief. "You hit it."

SIX

Although he was dead by the late afternoon, it was almost midnight by the time the colonel had turned. Gallagher was prepared for him long before that, of course, standing over the old man's body wearing a harshly scrubbed, yellow plastic suit, its thick material to act as protection against a potential attack from the late colonel, regardless of how unlikely such was. The colonel was stripped naked, lying on the floor, the desk and chair from the interrogation room having been moved to the back of the room to allow Jackson to view the situation more fully from the observation room. The dead man's arms and legs were tightly bound, meaning he would not be able to get up or grab anything.

"I think he's coming around, sir," Gallagher said, somewhat excited. "We can see the coating on his skin already fully formed."

"You mean sweat?" Jackson said, inquisitively. He sat, uncomfortably, at his chair by the red button on the other side of the glass.

"Almost, sir. But more than that," Gallagher said. "I've noticed this from other bodies I've examined. After death, a thick, clear mucus seems to emit from their pores, layering their skin *like* sweat. But, over time, it hardens – a bit like liquid latex – to provide some sort of preservative, some sort of protection against the ravages of time and the sun. It's really quite remarkable. Apart from that, I know little about it. I haven't sufficient equipment at my disposal to examine it properly. However, I would guess that it's made up of the substances our bodies already secrete during life."

Jackson remembered watching them from the lookout at Aldergrove, soon after the oxygen had run out and the surviving military gave up fighting them. Their numbers became thicker, attracted by the soldiers' constant to and fro at the gates. They were in various states of degradation, some of them ravaged more severely by the flu virus that had ripped life, brutally, from their bodies, than others. But, for most of them, you could tell they were dead. They were different to the living. They *acted* differently from the bodies of the living, or, indeed, the bodies of the dying. The sun's daily onslaught was merciless, as if some great pagan god were angry at their ongoing pillage of Great Mother Nature and all she had created. Its damaging rays took a gradual toll on them, regardless of the preservative Gallagher spoke of, and despite this, they seemed drawn to the heat, even energised by such. At times, some of them would lift their hands up, as if worshipping the sun or trying to grab it and pull it down towards them. One would suspect that they, in some way, fed off light in a similar, but less aggressive way, as they fed off flesh. But that would make them uncomfortably close to human, of course.

"So, they're more or less made up of the same stuff we are," Jackson said, sighing heavily. "Well, what makes them tick, then? Do they have a heartbeat, for example?"

"Good question, sir. They don't use their hearts anymore. In fact, they don't seem to need *any* of their inner organs. It's really quite curious." Gallagher stepped back slightly as he spoke. Jackson glared in through the glass, catching a flicker of movement from the colonel's hand. As he watched, the eyelids started to move. A long drool of phlegm sputtered from the colonel's mouth, like oil from an old engine, rolling, slowly, down his chin, as if to demonstrate Gallagher's next point. "That cough, sir. It isn't a sign of life, you understand. This isn't a resurrection you are witnessing. When they wheeze and spit like that, well, it seems to be their way of getting rid of disused, broken down organs, simply spewing them up along with the phlegm that still troubles them from their dying moments."

Jackson felt his stomach churn at that. He was beginning to resent Gallagher's running commentary. But another part of him was fascinated by the dead, needing to understand them better, to watch their every move, analytically. To make more sense of their wandering, like lost children. Their drive to seek out the living like the embrace of worried parents. The way they seemed to change, evolve over time. At first, simply lethargic – attacking only those humans foolish enough to engage them – but eventually actively seeking out their prey. He had noticed it all at Aldergrove. They would batter down the gates, as if becoming stronger, as if some sort of hunger or desperation had set in. But their faces were always drawn, tired, maybe even frustrated looking, as if they knew they would *never* be sated, no matter how close they got to humankind.

The colonel was rolling about on the floor now, looking as angry and frustrated as he had sounded during his last moments of life. A part of Jackson was glad to see the old bastard suffer so much, even though he felt bad for thinking it. This man used to be human, he reminded himself. Human like himself, his daughter, his grandchildren. He watched as Gallagher continued to study the colonel. His face was studious, bearing no signs of emotion, as if he had never known the colonel in life. He seemed unconcerned about whether he might contract the virus, working so closely with the body. Jackson found himself wondering just how much use all of this study could be. What would it help them achieve, down at The Chamber? Were they no better than the so-called 'experts' who used to argue 24-7 on television, expounding their ideas like new religions? Theorising, as if their self-indulgent bullshitting could do anything other than make them *sound* knowlcdgeable, when, in reality, they knew absolutely nothing.

The colonel's eyes suddenly flicked open, struggling against the harsh light. He looked sad, mournful, even, as if part of him were aware of his predicament. His body shook, vigorously, trying to free itself from its bonds. Gallagher approached, eyes wide and joyful, like a nurse delivering a new baby. "You're awake," he said, smiling. "Let's get started then..."

...

Lark unlocked the patio doors. He looked inside, finding Geri sitting where he had left her – same chair at the same tablc, wearing the same bemused scowl. He stood back, gesturing for her to get up.

"Okay, you can come out, now," he said. "Quarantine's over."

Geri glared at him, wordlessly, as she got up off her chair. She kicked over her piss pot, knocking the plate resting on top of it and its contents across the tiled floor. Then she walked through the doors to 'freedom'.

"We had to be sure you weren't infected!" Lark protested, throwing his hands in the air. "It was nothing personal, like..."

"*Nothing personal*?!" Geri retorted, bitterly, "Just like it was *nothing personal* when your fluff-headed mate there," and she pointed to the nearby McFall, "almost killed me on those fucking roads!?"

McFall shrugged his shoulders, saying nothing. He was sitting at the kitchen table, quietly emptying his revolver of bullets. Once finished, he rested the revolver on the table and stood up to make himself a cup of tea.

"Look, we were just scared, that's all –" Lark said.

"Everyone's fucking scared!" Geri interrupted, pointing a finger in defiance. "Doesn't mean you have to act like a cunt, does it?!"

"Well, what's done is done," persisted Lark, "And anyway, it's not like it was a cell you were locked up in. The patio's comfy enough, like."

"Comfy?!" Geri said, emphasising the word as if it were something foreign to her, "*COMFY*?!" She was getting more animated, pacing the kitchen like a wild thing. Lark was really wishing he'd just kept his mouth shut. "Does 'comfy' mean sitting in a fucking cold, damp room, sleeping on a fucking rug on the ground, LIKE A DOG?! DOES IT?!"

Both men looked at each other, then around the room. She was acting like a woman possessed. McFall simply continued making tea for himself. Lark just stared at the nearby wall, rubbing the stubble on his head. Neither of the two men seemed to know the right thing to say or do.

"Or does 'comfy' mean eating *nothing* for three whole fucking days, because you two fucking pricks are too fucking scared to even slide as much as a biscuit through the door?! DOES IT?!"

"Well, we –" McFall went to say, before being cut short.

"OR – maybe 'comfy' means pissing in a FUCKING pot on the FUCKING ground like some kind of refugee! Does it?!"

Lark stared at the overturned pot on the patio floor. He watched as the lurid yellow contents spread out in the grooves of the tiled floor. It was making him retch, a little, so he turned back to Geri.

She was in tears now, completely overwhelmed by the whole affair. She sat down on a chair by the table, burying her head in her hands. McFall, having returned to the table with his tea, moved suddenly away from her, again, as if crying were more infectious than sneezing.

"Listen, love..." Lark said, "We had to leave you in there for three days. That's all there is to it."

"Why th-three?!" she blubbered, her lanky upper body seeming to cover the entire table as she rested her over-tired head upon it.

"Because that's what they said on the news," McFall interjected, knowingly. "There's a... can't remember what they called it... but it's the 'period' between catching the flu to actually showing signs of having... er... caught it. Something like that, anyway..."

Geri continued to cry, her sobs becoming gradually less frantic. Lark noticed how tall she was and how red her hair seemed. Although he knew it wasn't possible within the brave new world they now lived in, Lark would have guessed that Geri had dyed her hair, such was the richness of colour. It should have been greasy, smelly, lank and sticking to her head, but instead it was radiant. Oddly, he found himself wondering if she'd found some shampoo in the cupboards of the patio. He also realised just how attractive he found her to be.

McFall, in particular, seemed embarrassed by her tears, scared even. Yet, in reality, Lark, too, was no fan of emotional outbursts like this. He certainly couldn't have boasted sensitivity as one of his strong points in the old world, and his tolerance for such certainly hadn't improved any in the new one.

But neither man need have worried, of course. Unknown to them, they were being played like fiddles, as the saying went. The sobbing stopped, giving way to gentle laughter. It was as much of a surprise as it was a short-lived relief to the two men.

Lark looked to McFall, baffled. The older man looked back, shrugging his shoulders the way he always did.

"Are you okay, doll?" Lark asked, smiling and moving towards her, carefully. He was beginning to think she was infected, after all, with some kind of 'Mad Cow' strain of the virus. He'd heard about that one on television, just before people began to be *actually* worried about the whole thing. A few comedians were, as was the norm, taking the piss out of the news reports, throwing a comedic twist on some of the tests that were being carried out on the first few victims. One sketch featured a man with antlers on his head scratching his chin and trying to decide what box to tick from a choice of different types of flu, including 'swine', 'bird', 'dog' and 'mad cow.'

Her laughing continued, getting louder by the second. It was as if she were watching the sketch that was playing back in Lark's head. He moved closer to her, rather tentatively (lest the Mad Cow symptoms present aggressively). Just as he was within reaching distance of her, she suddenly sat up, pointing the revolver which McFall had left at the table at both men.

"Jesus Christ," Lark said, stepping back and reaching his hands into the air, automatically.

He looked over at McFall, curious that he seemed uncharacteristically calm. In the short time he'd known McFall, he'd pretty much written him off as the most nervous, and perhaps useless, individual he'd ever met.

But McFall didn't move, seemingly unconcerned by the gun pointing at him.

"It's not loaded," he chuckled, "I took all the bullets out."

"Bullets like *this one*?" Geri spat, holding a shell in her hand for them to see.

"C-come on, now," stammered Lark, "Let's–"

"Shut up!" yelled Geri, switching to point the gun straight at him, "Shut the FUCK up!"

"Okay!" said Lark.

McFall moved beside him, starting to doubt himself, such was her venom.

"It *couldn't* be loaded," he said. "I'm sure I took the bullets out."

"A-all of them?" Lark asked, nervous sweat breaking across his forehead. He knew McFall was a useless cunt, but surely he wasn't *that* useless.

"Keys to the patio," Geri said, smiling.

It was an indulgently malicious smile.

"Oh, no," Lark said.

"Oh, fucking yes," Geri replied, grabbing the keys from his hand.

...

It had literally been weeks since Geri had enjoyed a good wash, and months since she'd been able to soak in a nice, hot bath. But both of these things had been made possible through the wonders of a camping cooker. Arduously, she'd spent the best part of the afternoon boiling up large pots of water before tossing the contents into the bath. A little bit of bubble foam from the bathroom cabinet put the cherry on top of what was going to be a very fine cake, indeed.

She lay in the water like a veritable Cleopatra, bubbles kissing her exposed skin like tiny fairies. Her eyes were closed, her lips open as she gently breathed in the wonderful Eucalyptus aroma from the foam bath. Thick clouds of scented steam escaped from the nearby open window. She watched the mist as it disappeared, remembering her science teacher's explanation of how water, when it got hot, converted to steam. She decided it was going to be her omen, her sign from the Great

Gods of Bathwater that things were going to change, that her boat was about to finally come in, as it were.

She picked up the little hand mirror from the side of the bath, noticing a layer of the steam had coated the glass. Carefully, Geri used her finger to write on its smooth, cold surface. She inscribed the words 'I will survive' in honour of her moment of random optimism. Smiling, she thought back to her eighteenth birthday. Being lean and finely featured had not always been welcome attributes to Geri McConnell. At school, other kids were constantly sniffing out weaknesses amongst their peers, like predatory cats. The corridors of her sixth form college were rampant with 'social Darwinism', as her old science teacher might have said. It was 'survival of the fittest' all day, every day, and being both tall (read 'gangly') as well as ginger (read 'freak') had very obvious drawbacks to a teenage girl's self esteem. But she had made it through to the other end of the year group, scoring moderately good results in her A-Level exams, despite the challenges brought by peer pressure. At her eighteenth birthday, she remembered hearing Gloria Gaynor's 'I Will Survive' and really *feeling* it. She *had* survived.

The healing water lapped against the superficial wounds on her shoulder and foot, soothing the now-dulled pain. She was practically dozing, such was her calm state. It was a little taste of heaven within the very pit of hell, but she reminded herself just how much she deserved it. Especially after all the shit she had put up with at the hands of those monkeys in the patio. She laughed to herself, thinking back on how she'd fooled them. The revolver *hadn't* been loaded. She had been bluffing, just as they had suspected. The bullet she showed to them was the one from her pocket, the one she had found in the cubby hole. She had tricked them. Sure, the gun was loaded now, and it had taken her quite a while to work out just how to do that. *Thank God for cowboy movies*, she whispered to herself, smiling.

Geri stretched her long body out, enjoying the fact that she didn't have to think or plan her next move. She was sick of all of that. From now on, she was going to live in the here and now. This bath, this bathroom, this house. That's as far as it went for her, now, and that's as far as it was going to go for her in the future. It looked pretty hopeless out there, anyway. The dead were everywhere, now, their tediously large numbers seemingly increasing by the day. It was becoming almost impossible to venture outside the house. In fact, she reckoned they would soon try to find a way in themselves. Sure, the house was locked up and secure enough with its heavy door and grilled windows. But there was the patio around the back. The wooden fencing in the back garden kept them out, for now, but it was only a matter of time before they were thick enough, in numbers, to command the brute force needed to break right through. And once through, the patio was just a big greenhouse, really.

But, no – she wouldn't think of those things...

(I will survive)

She would only think of nice things, things she remembered from the good ol' days. Things that made her happy. Things that made her feel like a woman, again.

Geri had been a pampered girl, in days gone by. Daughter of a financially shrewd entrepreneur father and school teacher mother, she grew up to be some kind of hybrid of the two, pragmatic and careful like her mother. Sharp-witted and loose-tongued like her father.

At the tender age of twenty-one, sick of the pampering, she'd set off travelling, Daddy's credit card in the back pocket of her jeans. Two years later, she returned, worldly-wise but forty-grand in debt. Her daddy dearest wasn't thrilled that she hadn't called her mother once in all of that time, caring less about the maxed-out credit card. Of course, none of that mattered then any more than it mattered now. Geri was welcomed back into the family home as if she'd never been away.

She set to work off the debt, insisting on such, regardless of how much her father protested. She worked for his company, learning the do's and definitely-do's of business, honing the maverick skills that her father was renowned for. Of course her quasi-supermodel looks made things a little easier for her. She flashed what needed to be flashed in order to get ahead in a world supposedly ruled by chauvinistic men but ultimately *overruled* by a sharp-witted bitch such as her. It was those days that she harked back to, even now. The days when she felt special. The days when she felt in control. The days when she felt sexy.

A casual wipe of the little hand mirror, now perched at the end of the bath, revealed the kind of woman she was now. A parched, poorly slept pallor glared back at her. Rings around her eyes and an under-fed jaw line made her look like some kind of overgrown EMO. She poked the big toe of her good foot over the water to knock the mirror off the bath. *Won't be needing that, thank you very much!* she thought.

A sound from outside startled her. It was the sound of an engine – most likely a car engine. It seemed to have stopped right outside the house.

Geri quickly pulled herself out of the bath. She grabbed the towel gown she had found in one of the bedrooms, throwing it over her still wet, soapy skin.

Unable to see clearly through the bathroom window, without drawing further attention to herself, Geri crept, carefully, into the nearby bedroom. She peeked out onto the street taking care to remain under cover of the curtains.

The sight which greeted her made her tummy flutter.

A police Land Rover was parked in the middle of the road, surrounded by the dead.

Her boat had come in.

...

Geri ran into the bedroom, slowing to a quick hop as her foot screamed at her. She pulled on her clothes as fast as she could. Once dressed, she speed-limped into the bathroom, retrieving the mirror that she had kicked onto the floor. She fumbled about, quickly, with make-up before rolling her hair into a towel and moving downstairs. All of this was done in just under five minutes, spaced between continuous peeks out the window to make sure her would-be saviours hadn't left.

Geri could hear muffled shouting from the patio, but she ignored it. She proceeded into the living room, opening the curtains, wide, and waving out to the Land Rover. There was no sign of life; the dead still completely surrounding the vehicle. She waved, again, hoping to catch the attention of whoever was inside the vehicle.

A single hand appeared out of the vehicle's nearest window, pointing, sternly, to suggest that Geri should move out of sight. Geri did as the hand suggested, ducking behind the curtains while still remaining transfixed on the scene developing before her eyes.

Before long, a formidable looking rifle with a long, black nozzle appeared out of the vehicle. It aimed at the nearest dead body, firing, silently, to tear a sizable strip along the top of the thing's head, sending it to the ground.

Three more bodies, as if drawn to the muzzle like flies around a light bulb, shuffled over to investigate. One of them reminded Geri of a work colleague, similarly dressed and styled as the woman she used to know. It unnerved Geri to think that those weren't just anonymous monsters out there, that they could very well be her friends, her neighbours... her family? A second and third blast took out Geri's work colleague with relative ease, the neat jets of blood from the falling body spraying the vehicle's familiar white pallor like pinstriping.

Another rifle could be seen protruding from the rear windows of the vehicle. It looked similar: long, black and shining in the sun. Just like the other, it flashed, quietly, efficiently disposing of several more of the dead, sniffing and shuffling around in an almost confused manner. Soon, the herd was thinned considerably, leaving the vehicle less densely surrounded. The two rifles disappeared back into the vehicle again.

Several long, stalactite moments later, Geri noticed the doors of the Land Rover open, two men appearing, one from the rear and the other from the driver seat of the vehicle. One of the men, heavy set and dressed in full riot gear, pointed to the door as he moved, quickly, through the crowd of dead, using his baton to clear his way. His partner, similarly dressed but of leaner build, followed suit, carrying a large bag on his back. Both men ran for the door.

Geri headed into the hallway, as directed. As she reached the front door, she realised that she hadn't got the key. She had never even considered that the door would be locked tight, thinking that she would be able to open it, easily, from the inside.

"Fuck fuck fuck fuck!" she chanted, like some perverted mantra.

The police were banging on the door, now, shouting. She could hear their voices. This would usually be an unwelcome thing, but with those two idiots in the patio being the only alternative to solitude, Geri was keen to get the boys in blue into the mix.

Not sure how to achieve that, Geri changed direction, heading for the patio. She fumbled for the patio keys, grabbing the revolver off the kitchen table as she passed it.

She opened the patio doors, nervously and excitedly pointing the revolver at the two men inside.

"Front door key. Where is it?"

"No way," said Lark, shaking his head, "We have no idea who–"

"It's the fucking police!" yelled Geri, her patience completely shot. "So give me the fucking keys, now!"

"How do you know who it is?" argued Lark.

"Because they look like the police, they shoot like the police, they dress like the police and they're in a fucking police Land Rover!"

"This is bullshit..." McFall offered, also not convinced.

"I swear to God, I will shoot you right now unless you –"

"Okay!" Lark yelled, seemingly fully convinced she would shoot him. "In the bottom drawer of the kitchen –"

She was gone before he even finished his sentence, taking care to close the patio back up again. She threw the patio keys on the kitchen table, still keeping the revolver in one hand, searching the bottom drawer of the kitchen unit with the other. Sure enough, she found a set of what looked to be house keys under some drying towels and dishcloths.

The banging continued, more frantically, now. The voices of the two policemen were becoming more panicked. Geri limped towards the door, groping for and trying each of the keys on the Yale-shaped keyhole.

Eventually one turned and she went to pull the door open wide, frustrated whenever it caught on the security chain. Swearing, she shut the door, again, undoing the security chain and pulling it open.

The next few seconds were a blur, Geri being knocked to the ground as a mass of police riot gear, dead grasping hands and panicked voices poured through the front doorway. Geri fell hard against the hallway wall, losing consciousness for the second time within a week...

SEVEN

Pat sat on the sofa, his 9mm sitting on the coffee table beside him. A damp, blood-stained cloth rested in his hand. He was leaning back, blowing out some air as if suddenly able to relax. His face was clean, and Karen could make out his furrowed brow, again.

"Doesn't look like you've been cut, or anything," she said, smiling.

Pat looked at her with no expression.

"It was trying to bite me," he said. "Did you see that?"

If she were completely honest, she had been terrified that he *had* been bitten. She had completed a first aid course recently, in preparation for some youth work in her church. She knew from the training that a bite would be one of the worst ways for infection to spread. He would have almost certainly become infected, were that thing to have sunk its teeth into him. A part of her realised, then, just how much she depended on the man on the sofa opposite her. Even though he was stubborn. She reckoned he didn't believe what those things were capable of, that his theories on them had been proved all wrong from this most recent encounter. For a man like Pat, a man who held steadfastly onto all his beliefs and ideas, through rain and shine, to have to admit to being wrong about something would not sit well.

But Karen felt something else, as well.

"Did you see *me* shooting it?" she exclaimed, excitedly, like a little girl after a fairground ride. Her heart was pumping, but not nervously. She felt strong and powerful, as if able to take on the world. She remembered reading comics that her brother used to like, when she was little. She had always been attracted to the female super-heroes. Crimefighters who wore heeled boots and super-sexy outfits. She used to tie her coat around her neck, like a cape, and pretend to be one of them in the playground. All the other girls would be playing with skipping ropes while she played 'super heroes' with the boys.

"Sure I did," Pat said, the hint of admiration spreading across his face. She knew he would have to give it to her. She had saved his life, after all. "You did really well, today," he continued. "Really, really well."

Karen beamed, lapping up the praise, regardless of how economically it was relayed to her. In fact, it seemed even more ingratiating coming from a man like Pat, who was so economical with words. She thought about the word 'praise' – what it meant. What it *really* meant. It was bandied around a lot in her church. They should all praise God for all the things He had done for them, all that He had given to them. But, if she were to be truthful, she never meant those words when she sang them. She thought back to the Sunday mornings during 'praise.' How some people around her, young people like her, seemed to so confidently raise their hands, close their eyes and squeeze out the praise. Some would cry, others would smile and laugh. But she could never do any of that. She would have felt too much of a fraud because, if she were honest, she just wasn't feeling it like that.

She lifted the handgun (*her* handgun), playing with it as she moved around the kitchen, aiming it at her reflection in the candlelit room's window. Pat had told her it was a 9mm. She studied it, noticing the words '9mm' were indeed inscribed on the jet-black barrel, beside the letters 'USP.' She decided she was going to keep it really clean, really polished, as if new.

"Careful with that," Pat warned. "It's not a toy."

"Don't worry, I've got the safety on," she said, waving her hand at him and pointing at the lever as if to say *I'm an old pro, now.*

"Well, just be careful..." he said, grumbling to himself like the old man he was.

When she held the gun, it made her feel confident. As confident as those people in the church. It was as though she were beginning to feel like more of an equal to Pat, no longer needing his protection. She even felt like his ally, since the incident in the flat, as opposed to a liability. Someone he could depend upon, perhaps discuss plans with and gain insight from. She felt like a different person altogether when she was holding the gun. She could imagine herself even wearing different clothes. Out with the cute dresses and flat pumps. In with the combats and DM boots.

"I want to shoot more of them," she said, suddenly.

Pat shook his head.

"Too dangerous," he said. "Plus, we really have no need to go outside again. Not for a long time." He pointed over to the opened cupboards, stocked to excess with tinned goods and bottled water. "We've only cleared a few floors and we have enough to do us for months. We should find enough in the other floors to keep us even longer."

"But I want to hunt them!" she protested, like a child begging to go to the park or swimming pool. "I'm a good shot – you even said so yourself. Come on! Let's go shoot some more. Even if just from one of the windows, lower down."

"No!" said Pat, quite sternly.

It unnerved Karen, a little, knocking her out of her excited tirade.

"It's not a game!" he continued. "Those used to be real people, you know. They aren't just dummies for you to take potshots at! They were people like you and like me. People with feelings and emotions and –" He stopped, suddenly seeming aware of himself. He stood up from the sofa, looking away from her. A heavy mood seemed to have descended upon him. Karen had never seen him as intense as this, and she didn't like it. "I'm going to bed," he said. "Make sure you blow out those candles."

And with that, she felt small again. The child in their 'adult-child' relationship. It was almost as if he were saying, 'You've had your fun, now get back into line.' And she didn't like how that made her feel.

Karen set her gun down, carefully, on the table. She walked, quietly, over to the sofa and picked up the damp cloth he'd left lying there. She tutted at the state it was in. It used to be pure white. She found herself wondering how she'd get the blood stains out of it.

EIGHT

"Miss? Are you okay? Miss?"

Geri was lying on the sofa, coming to. She could hear commotion in the living room around her. It panicked her, at first, and she almost jumped to her feet before being stopped by the stranger in the flak jacket and helmet.

"Just relax..." he said, easing her gently back onto the sofa. "You took a knock to the head, but you'll be okay."

Geri ran a hand through her still-damp hair. She hadn't had any time to dry it from her bath, earlier, and for some reason felt embarrassed by that. She could feel a plaster on her left temple, where she'd obviously fallen. A tender lump rose up from its centre.

"Thanks for letting us in," the young police officer said. "It's pretty wild out there."

Geri smiled back, shaking his hand gently. She was feeling a little nauseous.

"Least I could do," she said. "Good to see you still out there, doing something about that mess."

The cop looked momentarily uncomfortable, offering only a weak smile in response.

Geri winced, scrunching her eyes up as she let the wave of sickness pass.

"You okay?" the young cop said.

"Yeah, just feeling a little sick," she said. "I'll be okay. Making a bit of a habit of falling down, to be honest."

She looked to the other man, broader and older than the one talking to her. He stood by the window, looking out onto the street. His attention was on the dead and the dead alone. He had completely ignored her. It was almost as if he hadn't noticed her, and to a girl like Geri that was very bad manners, indeed. "Are they still out there?" Geri asked, slightly interested in the answer, but mostly to introduce herself.

"We got rid of a lot of them," he answered, still peeking through the curtains. "There are still a few lingering about, though." He looked at Geri, his face a lot more serious and less kind than his partner's. "They're dumbfucks," he said. His accent was gruff, thick like porridge. "After a while, they forget what they were doing, why they were doing it and move on. There were about thirty of them outside, five minutes ago, but now there's only about five or six of them left." He stood back, as if proud of himself.

Sure, he may not have been a 'people person', but Geri was still comforted by his presence. Stern, no-nonsense and built like a brick shit house. Wearing the uniform and carrying a gun. In a world like this, those kinds of specs would do a girl alright. The perfect double act, when paired with his calm, handsome mate. Her very own *Starsky and Hutch*. The complete package seemed to say *Just relax. Everything will be fine now that we're here.* And she wanted so badly to feel relaxed.

"The two men in the patio," the younger cop said, suddenly. "Who are they, and why have you locked them up?"

"Oh, them?" Geri laughed, genuinely having forgotten all about her two ex-captors. "They were here before me. They tried to lock me in there, thinking I had the virus, but I managed to get the better of them."

"I'll bet you did," replied Young Cop, almost flirtatiously.

Geri smiled, slightly embarrassed. She didn't know why she was getting on like this, like a starry-eyed little girl. She supposed it was the uniform. It didn't just offer comfort and security to her. It was more than that. Like many women she'd known, Geri had always been a sucker for a man in uniform. That and the sudden lack of anything even smelling like talent in this new fucked-up world she found herself to be in.

"So, what's the plan?" Geri asked, looking to both men in turn.

The two men shared a glance that unnerved Geri slightly. Smiling, the younger one reached his hand forward to help her up from the sofa.

"The plan is as follows," he said, placing his other hand on his partner's shoulder, "we'll let the big man, here, keep watch, while you give me a guided tour of the house. Preferably," he said, "with a cup of tea in my hand."

Geri smiled, accepting his hand to pull her up from the sofa.

"Do you take sugar?" she asked.

"Always," he said, smiling.

...

Lark stood up, nervously. He walked to one end of the room and then back. He repeated this action several times over, pacing like a caged animal.

He thought back to when things were a lot simpler and less fucking hazardous to his health. Back when he had worked the desk at Belfast's infamous Gen X tattoo shop, suffering little more than stoned sixteen year olds with false ID and a grumpy bitch of a boss. Of course, he'd often moaned about life then, too. That was his nature – glass half-empty and all of that shit. But he'd had it pretty good, considering, and a large part of him was starting to realise that.

He picked up a pan from the floor, aimlessly, then threw it back down, as if piping hot, realising it was the one that Geri had pissed in for three days.

"Fuck this shit!" he spat, kicking the cupboards under the sink just a little too hard and hurting his DM-clad foot. He really had thought he was doing the right thing by quarantining Geri. That's what they had said to do in the news, right? *Quarantine your family*, they said. *Quarantine your neighbours, yourself, even. If symptoms such as sneezing or coughing or prickly throats develop,* they said*, you need to QUARANTINE*.

Of course, towards the end, they sent the fucking pigs around, wrapped in yellow plastic and breathing like fucking Darth Vader, to do all the quarantining themselves. And that's what worried him about the two newcomers, because Lark had been witness to a couple of incidents where the 'quarantine' had been replaced by 'extermination'.

He'd been staying with a couple of mates. They'd been kicking back, drinking a lot of beer and smoking a lot of gear while the whole world went to shit. It seemed to be the best way of dealing with it, the only way of dealing with it.

Until one of them got sick, that was.

They never found out who it was who called the police, although Lark reckoned it was one of the bitches who were hanging around – no one seemed to know them too well. Either way, the cops came calling all too soon. A few of them kicked up a fuss. Anarchist types, in the street-understanding of the word, not too shy of fucking shit up when something needed sorting. They weren't too keen on the cops taking their friend away, so they put up a fight, some silly cunt deciding to pull the oxygen tank from one of the cops' back. It was maybe meant as a joke, when Lark thought back on it. Or a joke with a jag, at the very most. Just some pisshead mucking around, acting the big man in front of his mates. They were all pretty mangled by that stage, and probably not capable of very much in the way of a reasonable struggle. But the cops took it very seriously. Seriously enough to blow a hole right through the poor bastard's head with a Glock 17.

Lark had gone on the run after that, scared out of his wits. Life on the streets had been pretty bad, too. But he managed to keep one step ahead of both The State and The Dead, the numbers of the former dwindling as the latter grew. Of course, it felt like they had caught up to him, now. And he was really starting to get fucking scared about what might happen.

"If they're really pigs, I think it's time you took off that stupid fucking ski mask," he said to McFall.

"No way!" McFall countered, placing one hand on the mask as if defending his right to wear it. "It stops the infection!"

"It doesn't stop the –" Lark started before giving up and sighing. Another thought ran through his mind suddenly. "Look," he said, "we could be in real trouble here. What if they find the gear?"

"What gear?!" McFall asked, bewildered.

"The fucking –" Lark looked through the glass patio door, noticing Geri and the younger cop chatting and making tea in the kitchen. He continued, with a whisper, "The coke, you idiot. And I'm not talking cola, here."

"We have coke?" McFall said, excitedly.

Lark couldn't be sure if McFall was more excited by the hard drug or soft drink, but he wasn't for discussing it further. He watched as Geri and the cop (*were they flirting?*) finished in the kitchen, moving back towards the hallway. Neither of them looked in the direction of the patio.

"Where are they going?" whispered McFall, still resting a hand defensively on his balaclava.

"Don't know. Back into the hallway, it seems."

"What'll we do?"

"I guess there's nothing we can do," Lark said, dejectedly. "Just got to sit tight and see what happens.

...

They headed up the narrow staircase, laughing awkwardly at how tight a fit it was for a man in almost full riot gear.

"I should really just take this stuff off," the cop said.

"Kinda suits you," Geri said, facetiously, patting his padded back.

"Why thank you," he replied, turning to mock-bow and almost banging his head off the dangling light bulb in the process.

Geri smirked. He was being indulgently silly, now, and he knew it.

His little performance was either an attempt to make her feel more comfortable or an attempt to bed her. She didn't care, either way. Fact of the matter was, she hadn't had *any* positive male attention (being locked in the patio *really* didn't count) in quite some time, so she was keen to make up for lost time.

They made their way through to the largest bedroom, both immediately seeming embarrassed to have automatically found this room, in particular. The room's decoration suggested older and more conservative inhabitants than its current motley mix of Geri, Lark and McFall. To Geri, it smelled immediately like someone else's house. Floral wallpaper, poorly lined, covered the walls. A dressing table and drawers combo stood, sensibly, against one wall, the bed being perched against another. A generously sized window, clothed by thick, velvet curtains, looked out onto the main street. China dolls and other small trinkets and ornaments were dotted around the room, more dusty now than they had ever been allowed to be in the past.

The cop looked around, lifting random things up and setting them down again, whistling. He was probably feeling uncomfortable on his own with her, without his buddy to bounce one-liners off. Not that his buddy seemed the one-liner type. But men and boys were stupid that way. Geri would always have found the blokes she went out with to be one type, whenever they were with her, and another type when out with their mates. It kind of disappointed Geri, made her reluctant to trust a guy if she saw him being a dick with his mates. Especially if it was at her expense.

"Nice view," the cop said, eventually turning his attention to the window.

"Sure, if you like dead people," Geri replied, venturing a look out the first floor window, down onto the street.

A few of the dead were shuffling around aimlessly below. They were circling a nearby abandoned car, as if expecting someone to get out of it. She counted them, only noticing four where there had previously been six around the house. Several more were interested in the Land Rover, but less than before. What the older cop had been saying was obviously right, then. They did get bored and wander off. One of them looked way too young to be dead, maybe still a teenager. She knew it would sound stupid to say something like that, but to Geri, it seemed less fair for a younger person, or a child, to end up like one of those things. Older people were one thing, she reckoned, but a teenager or a child...

The dead seemed to be gradually forgetting about the Land Rover, paying it the same attention as they paid the house and just about everything else, including each other. Many of them were just simply standing there. Lethargic. Dreamy, even. Like willow trees in summer.

"What do you think happened?" the cop asked her, still staring out the window.

Geri was suddenly gobsmacked. She turned, sharply, to look at him. This one comment ruined everything for her.

"What, you mean you guys don't *know* what happened?!" she said, indignantly.

The cop seemed shocked by the question.

"Of course not," he said, defensively. "How would we?"

Geri laughed, sarcastically. She really couldn't believe she bought into their whole 'we're in control' performance.

"Because you're the fucking government!" she said, almost aggressively, "It's your job to know this kind of stuff..."

"We're *not* the government," he said, "We're just a couple of cops. We don't know anything more than you do..."

Geri stared at him, disbelief hanging from her face like a dead man's noose.

"Listen, I'm sorry!" he protested, hands outstretched, "Would you rather I lie to you?"

Geri thought about it for a second. She realised that a very large part of her may just very well prefer him to lie to her. To tell her things like (adopting a deep-sounding, 'official' voice), 'We've got everything under control,' or, 'We'll just phone through your whereabouts to rescue central,' or whatever. But she had to accept the reality that these were just another two guys who had stayed alive, for whatever reason. No more knowledgeable, it seemed, than the two buffoons in the patio. Regardless of whether they were cops or fucking robbers.

Sighing, Geri leaned her head against her hands, resting on the window sill.

"Where does this leave us now?" she asked him.

The young cop removed his helmet, running a hand through his dark hair. He moved away from the window, sitting himself down on the bed.

"It leaves us here, right now," he said, without a trace of irony in his voice. "We make the best of what we've got, and we try to survive."

"For what?" Geri snapped, "What's the point in it all?"

"What was *ever* the point in it all?" he countered, sharply. His pallor changed all of a sudden, all of the likeable goofiness from before gone. In the poor light of the bedroom, Geri could see shadows under his eyes. The faint hint of stubble suggested a day without shaving. He suddenly offered his smile, again, almost as an afterthought. It didn't seem that reassuring anymore.

"I'm sick of just making do," she said, tears glistening in the corners of her eyes, "Fucking sick of it. And I really thought when you guys... when the police came... it would change everything."

The young cop stood up again, moving to comfort her. She accepted his embrace, willingly, offloading the emerging tears onto his bulky, padded shoulder.

"I don't even know your name," she laughed, wiping her eyes with a free hand.

"George," she heard him say. "My name is George."

...

Lark poked McFall in the ribs, waking him from his slumber.

"What? Where are they?" he muttered nervously as he woke.

"Shhh..." Lark said, one finger over his pierced lips, "They're coming."

Both men sat upright on the plastic patio chairs as the formidable shape of the larger of the two cops came to the sliding glass doors. He fumbled in the keyhole, opening the door and quietly moving inside. He stood in front of the two survivors, riot gear still hanging off his familiar PSNI uniform. A bag was slung across his shoulder. He held his rifle in his left hand, which surprised Lark, who found himself wondering whether a rifle had to be made specially to accommodate left-handed users, the way guitars were.

For a moment, the man said nothing, simply staring at the two men sat before him. Then, with one fluid movement, he slung the shoulder bag onto the ground before bending, slowly, to unzip it.

Lark felt a cold sweat tickling his spine. He went over various scenarios in his head, all of them ending with him getting gunned down, or at best pulverised, as he attempted to overpower the huge man in front of him. He looked to McFall, the white of his friend's eyes popping out from under the ski mask like headlights on a dark road.

Suddenly, the cop produced a smaller, blue plastic bag and sat it down on the patio table. Pulling up a third chair, he removed his helmet and laid his rifle across the ground beside him.

"I don't know about you lads, but I'm parched," he said, smiling and producing three tins of beer.

McFall laughed nervously. It was an embarrassing laugh. High pitched and way too girly for a man to be proud of. The kind of laugh you would get a kicking for at school.

Lark said nothing. He simply accepted the beer, cracking it open, quietly. There was something very familiar about this guy. Something tangible, as opposed to him just looking like any other cop – scary, creepy or a bit unhinged. Lark searched his narcotic-stained brain for any recollection of this particular smart-arse cunt, handing out the beer as if he were some fucking student.

"I'm Norman, by the way."

The name didn't ring a bell. Not even with the face to go with it. His voice did, though. He couldn't quite place the 'whens' and the 'wheres' of it all, but he did recognise it. Mind you, it had that familiar 'cop' twang to it. Affected, but not affected enough to take away *every* trace of shit-kicking country-boy. And shit-kicking country boy was exactly what this guy was. He even looked like one.

"What's the matter?" the cop asked Lark. "Cat got your tongue?"

Lark had never really got sayings like that. Nonsensical phrases of days gone by that only your granny would look right saying.

"No," Lark replied, calmly, "I guess I'm just a little more careful, these days, with the people I talk to."

The cop thought on that, for a while, nodding as if in agreement.

"Not a bad way to be," he said, cracking his own beer open. "Careful, that is."

The comment was loaded, but Lark decided not to rise to the bait.

"Lark" he said, offering the cop his hand. "My name, that is."

"Lark?" said Norman, accepting the handshake. "That's a weird one."

"It's not my real name," Lark said by way of explanation, still keen to offer no more than was necessary.

"Fair enough," shrugged Norman.

He seemed well used to playing these types of games. The 'sizing up' game. The verbal pacing, as if they were two prize fighters in a cage.

The cop turned to look at McFall, yet still addressing Lark.

"So who's your mate in the terrorist mask?" he said, sniffing.

McFall seemed nervous. He smelt nervous, too. A warm waft of sweat passed by Lark, the ski-masked man clearly feeling the glare of the old blue spotlight.

He looked to Lark and then back at the cop.

"I'm not a terrorist," he said, completely deadpan, as if to a teacher at school.

Norman stared back at him for a second, blankly. He looked like he was going to bellow at him, release some cop tirade of menace, then cuff McFall right there and then. Instead, he erupted into laughter. It was very different to McFall's laughter. This was a belly laugh, the kind of laugh that only big men seemed able to produce. A laugh that needed a bit of welly behind it.

McFall looked bemused, looking again at Lark and shrugging.

The cop finally stopped, wiping his eyes as he calmed himself. "I'm sure you're not, mate," he said, "but it wouldn't matter a damn if you were, let's face it."

Lark didn't believe that for a second. If you looked the part, you were the part. That's the way cops worked. That's why people like him always got so much shit from them.

But another part of him took what the cop was saying and considered it for a moment, pretending it came from someone else. It was a solid point. Belfast had been chasing its tail for almost half a century, its people drowning in a quagmire of bullshit politics and religious foreplay. The bombs, the bullets, the masks. None of it mattered a damn anymore. God or Mother Mary or Mother Fucking Nature had called time on proceedings, and it no longer mattered what the hell you believed or who you believed it with.

Terrorism was irrelevant. Ireland was finally united.

United in disease.

United in death.

United in fear.

NINE

Karen sat down on the sofa of the flat that was beginning to feel to her like a prison. She sighed, pointedly. She looked over to where Pat was, quietly reading a book at the table and sipping on his tea. He hadn't noticed her sigh. She sighed again, this time louder.

Pat looked up from his antiquated reading glasses, still holding his book.

"You okay?" he asked, lifting the cup of tea to his lips and lightly slurping it down (that was *really* starting to grate on Karen).

"I'm bored," she replied, pouting. "This place is too small for a young –" Pat held her gaze, cup of tea still at his lips. "Oh, I didn't mean that in the way –"

"It's okay," Pat interrupted, setting his cup down on one of the coasters Karen had laid out on the table. "I know it's a lot easier for an old fogey like me to deal with not being able to get out than a young slip like yourself."

"No, it's not like that at all," Karen protested.

Pat simply smiled, looking back at his book. Why the hell it was so interesting, Karen didn't know. She squinted to read the title. It seemed to be some crime novel of some sort. Of no interest, whatsoever, to a girl like her.

In days gone by, Karen's main literary diet had consisted of a couple of magazines that she picked up at her local Christian bookshop or church, as well as the various trashy magazines that the newsagent stocked. She couldn't remember the last book she'd actually read. She remembered studying a few novels and poetry books in school, but she had never actually read for pleasure. Her friend had once lent her some 'chick lit' book – something about a young marketing executive in Dublin, or something. She had managed to get through about eight chapters or so of it, before deciding it was a little bit too steamy for a girl like her and politely returning it.

Karen got up from the sofa and walked to the window of the living room-cum-kitchen, a journey she had already travelled about seventeen times that day. She sighed again, this time not checking to see whether Pat had clocked it or not. This one was natural.

Looking down, her eyes met an all-too-familiar sight. There they were... The dead, as she and Pat referred to them. Ten floors down, they looked like the little action figures her brother used to play with when he was a lad. Loose-limbed and awkwardly posed. Every now and then, they'd move. Shuffling about, as if controlled by some drunken puppeteer. She hated them, all of a sudden. She hated every last one of them. She wished that some great big bomb could be used to wipe them all out, just like in the movies. She pondered asking Pat if he knew of such a bomb, but immediately decided not to. It was a stupid question, and she knew it. Born out of boredom, alone. Immature and scantily thought through. The kind of question that a man like Pat would laugh off, at best, or frown over, at worst.

"I need to get outside," she said suddenly, without even realising she'd said it out loud. She looked towards Pat, gingerly.

Pat looked over his glasses again, book still in hand, tea cup still at the ready.

"Seriously," she persisted, "I'm going mad in here."

"Well," said Pat, "you know why you can't go out." His voice was patronising. It wasn't dissimilar to the kind of voice that a young mother would use to tell a toddler off. It frustrated the hell out of Karen, and she felt her face reddening with rage.

"I DO know," she said, suddenly animated, "I'm not stupid!"

"Well, then, don't act –"

"Just shut up!" she shouted, looking at him sternly. "I'm sick of being patronised all of the time! I'm sick of being the stupid little girl, the... the naive one, here!" She beat upon her chest in complete frustration. "I've been practising shooting every day. I saved your life that time, remember?!"

"Yes, of course I remember," Pat replied, calmly. He still held his book aloft, as if planning on returning to read it once this little 'tantrum' was all sorted out. "But, I don't think any of that means you can safely leave the building."

"I know," Karen said, dejectedly, suddenly calm again. She returned to the sofa, setting herself down.

"And with all the food and stuff we have from the other flats –"

"I know!" stressed Karen, frustrated by Pat's common sense and annoyingly calm resolve. "I'm just bored and really claustrophobic, that's all."

She sighed loudly, looking over to Pat. He had returned to his book, contentedly reading as if it were a Sunday afternoon. Moments passed as she watched him read the way a dog would watch someone eat. She tried to will guilt onto him, force it down his throat with her tireless, melancholic gaze. She noticed him look up, clock her staring at him, then look back to the book.

She sighed again, this time even louder than before. Pat looked back at her, shaking his head and smiling when he noticed her still looking at him. She was trying to do her best puppy eyes.

"Wait there one second," Pat said, a resigned look drawing across his face. He removed his glasses, only used for reading, setting them on the side of the chair. He disappeared into the hallway, where Karen could hear him fumbling in the pockets of his coat. It reminded her of her grandfather, how he would fumble in his pockets for change whenever she had wanted a comic or some sweets. Eventually Pat reappeared, smiling. "Follow me," he said simply.

Karen paused, suspiciously looking at him like a girl awaiting a birthday surprise.

"Come on," he said, seeming quite upbeat for a man like him. "Seriously, you won't want to miss this."

Karen got up, following him towards the door of the flat. They exited into the main corridor of the tenth floor, moving along towards the stairwell. The corridors were getting dirty, grimy, and she made a mental note to clean them at some stage. That would pass the time, if nothing else. They climbed until they reached the top floor of the tower block. A maintenance door could be seen, at the opposite end. Karen had never had any reason to wonder what or where the maintenance door opened onto, but she was about to find out.

Pat tried a couple of keys in the lock before finding the one he needed. He opened the door into a small, dark storeroom. He proceeded through, looking back towards Karen.

"Come on, it's safe," he said, smiling mischievously at her as if they were doing something wrong. He reminded her, suddenly, of her brother when she had been young. He was always leading her to forbidden places. Big houses with long, winding gardens and foreboding gates. Quarries with steep, treasure-laden cliffs. Anywhere there was a 'No Trespassing' sign and the taste of danger.

She followed him, cautiously. Her curiosity had been pricked, that much was for sure, but another part of her felt more than a bit uncomfortable when he acted out of character like this. Karen suddenly realised that she knew nothing at all about Pat. Not really. And, for the briefest of moments, as she spotted a warning sign saying 'Authorised Personnel Only' that scared her. Maybe even more than the dead scared her. But then it was gone, again, and he became Pat the Protector. Pat the Provider.

(Pat the father?)

She had never really known her father. He had left her mother when she was a little girl, not even at school. She had vague memories of raised voices coming up the stairs at night. Her mother's high-pitched and panicked. Her father's deep and heavy. And then he was gone, and she never heard his voice again. In fact, she never heard *anything* about him, again. It was as if he had *never* been there. As if she had imagined him all along – some character in a movie of her life, as opposed to the real thing.

Pat pushed his way through a few discarded tools and boxes, clearing the way for Karen. Reaching backwards, he took her hand, gently leading her through the dark, musty room. His hands felt as lined and creviced as his face looked. Like dried-out newspaper left in the sun. Karen felt a weird, nostalgic pleasure in those hands. It reminded her of being smaller, younger. Of trips down town with her grandfather, the main paternal influence in her life, prior to meeting Pat.

They reached a metal ladder at the back of the small room, leading up to a trapdoor in the ceiling. Pat quickly climbed the few steps, unsealing the trap door to reveal the most beautiful blue sky Karen had ever seen. A warm wind blew through as Pat poked his head outside.

"Is this enough of the great outdoors for you," he shouted over the wind, smiling.

Karen laughed, deliriously, like a child at Christmas. She climbed, quickly, up the steps, accepting Pat's hand to help her out onto the roof of the apartment block. The feel of the wind against her face was mesmerising. It rushed through her light clothing, touching every part of her. Tickling the tiny hairs on her skin like a thousand feathers. The glare of the naked sun was delightfully blinding, the taste of fresh air alive in her mouth, nourishing her very body and soul while it filled up her lungs, again and again.

She drank it all up as if with a straw. She stood on top of the roof, closing her eyes and stretching her arms wide.

She felt almost free.

TEN

"So where have you guys been?" Lark asked, crumpling his fifth can of beer and throwing it onto the patio floor, "You know, since it got bad..." The can rattled along the floor to rest by the cop's shoe. Lark had thrown it with indulgent abandon. As if on the street, right beside the cop. As if to rile him.

Norman fixed Lark with a gaze that may have spelled a night in the slammer, once upon a time.

"We've been around," he replied, guardedly. He sat his beer down, forcefully, as if to make a point. As if to call time on the discussion before it even started.

"Around where?" pressed Lark, smirking. The beer was going down well. It was the first time in quite a while that he'd felt relaxed enough to drink. Ever since the last time he'd seen a cop, actually. Maybe this cop, but the jury was still out on that one and would probably remain out. There was no way to tell the difference between them, at the best of times, never mind when they were wearing those fucking yellow suits.

But he was feeling the boozy bravado all too common after can number four, and nothing scared him. Especially when it came to dealing with the pigs.

"Like I said, we've been on the move," said the cop, more sharply.

"Hey, any more booze?" McFall interjected, laughing nervously at the growing tension. He was clearly trying to lighten the mood, change the subject and keep things from blowing up. But Lark *wanted* things to blow up. He was in the mood for a row.

"Sure," said Norman in answer to McFall's question. But he held his eyes on Lark. The big cop was a player, that much was clear. Lark didn't even blink. It was like a test of resolve or strength of character. The two men, the chalk and cheese of humanity, searching each other's eyes and faces for signs of weakness.

Lark was keen to find out just what the fuckers had been *really* up to. He'd never trusted cops in the best of times. He knew they'd been up to *even more* no-good just before it had all gone to shit. But what were they doing now? Something about these two just didn't add up. They were too friendly, maybe. Too ingratiating. *Was there something they weren't saying?* Lark thought. Maybe. Or maybe he was just being his usual, miserable, pessimistic self. After all, they were hardly cops anymore, were they? Just a couple of blokes with guns and uniforms. All the rules and regulations they used to uphold were mere lines on a page, now. Those dead fucks out there, lumbering around Belfast today, could hardly care less about any of their rights or violations. The old law had no relevance to them. No potency.

"So, where's the other beers, then?" Lark said, finally blinking and breaking his stare.

Norman continued to stare at him, smiling in celebration of his little victory. In the end, Lark had felt threatened by him. He was big, strong and nasty looking. He could likely crush Lark with one hand. And with no rules or regulations to follow, no one to report back to or answer to, Lark realised that the slimmest bit of restraint left in this cunt was all but gone.

But there was something else.

Lark remembered *exactly* where he knew the cop from. Maybe it was the booze that had cleared the fog from his mind, sparking some circuit that had been made dormant through one too many snorts. Either way, he was sure where he knew this particular pig from, and just how much of a cunt he really was.

It was one of those nights where things weren't so easy to remember. A hell of a bender out with the lads. He was staying with Chalky Charley that night. An odious little twat who was only useful to know because of the amount of snort he seemed able to get his grimy little hands on. Lark had been kicked out of yet another apartment, having missed a couple of months' rent. He had trundled on home, only to find the locks changed and his stuff in bin bags on the road. Charley offered to put him up for the night.

The two of them were approaching Charley's place, when Lark noticed a formidable shape standing outside his door. A cop, still in full uniform. He was convinced now that it had been Norman.

"It's okay," Charley had said, noticing Lark's discomfort.

He'd strolled up to the cop in that way he often did. All gangsta-like. As if he was a six-foot-tall black man, as opposed to a five-foot dweeb. But that was always the problem with dealers – more often than not, they had an inflated image of themselves.

The two of them had a conversation. The cop got angry, though, and immediately started beating the shit out of Charley. Now, Charley wasn't much of a fighter at the best of times, but he went down hard when the cop started on him.

Lark didn't know what to do. He looked around, but there weren't a lot of people about. The few who did happen upon the scene quickly turned and walked in a different direction. No one wanted trouble. Lark sure as hell didn't want trouble, either. Eventually, he had to do something, though, because the cop looked like he was going to kill Charley. He was on the ground, straddling Charley as if about to fucking scalp him.

Lark had cursed to himself, moving closer to the scene.

"Look, man..." he said, "I think he's had enough. I'm sure he deserved this and all, but maybe leave him alone, now, eh?"

Norman had looked up at Lark, smiling. Lark noticed that Charley's blood was smeared all over his face and uniform. It was as if he'd been at a pie-eating contest, odds-on favourite to win. He drew his handgun, still smiling at Lark, aiming it at poor Charley's head. He held the gun there for long moments, before sliding it, slowly, back into his holster. He ran one hand into Charley's coat, pulling out a stash of coke in a clear plastic packet. Still smiling, still holding Lark's gaze, he slowly rose to his feet.

"Say no to drugs," he said to Lark, slipping the white powder into his pocket.

It had been him, alright. Lark could never forget the smile.

"The booze is outside," Norman said. "In the Land Rover." He slid the keys to the van over to Lark on the table. "Wanna go grab them?" he said, eyes still staring, face still smirking.

McFall looked uncomfortably at Lark.

"Seriously, mate," he said, quietly. "I'm alright for one. You needn't bother."

Lark ignored McFall, still looking at the cop. This wasn't about the beer. This was more than that. He lifted the keys from the table.

"I'll be right back," he said, getting up from his chair, a bit light-headed.

"You sure about that?" the cop said, eerily, just as he was about to leave the room.

Lark paused for a second. He considered turning around, checking the cop on his comment. Instead, he moved on through into the kitchen. The beer had gone to his head and he was feeling a bit woozy. He lifted the revolver from the table and checked it for ammo. There was only one shell in it. He picked up a few more shells from the ash tray on the worktop, quietly loading the gun. He smiled, thinking back on how Geri had got the better of them with this very gun. He almost respected her for that move. Almost.

She walked into the kitchen, now, the other cop behind her. Her eyes were red and moist as if she'd been crying.

"What are you doing?" she asked, seeing him loading the revolver.

"Beer run," Lark smiled, looking at the other cop, suspiciously, as he followed Geri into the kitchen. He checked Geri's puffed-up face with a single finger, still eyeing up the younger cop.

"Fuck off!" she said, ungratefully. She pulled away from him, her face turned up in disgust.

"Everything alright?" Lark asked her, casting a glance at the other cop.

"Yes. So don't touch me," she replied, backing away as if he were one of those diseased fucks outside. Truth be told, he probably meant less to her than they did. But that was fine. He didn't need her. He didn't need any of them. He just needed more beer.

Lark stumbled through the kitchen, brushing against the other cop.

"What's your problem?" he heard the younger cop muttering as he walked on through the hallway.

As he reached the front door, he could hear a single sniff from the dead fucks outside. He laughed, suddenly amused, then turned the key in the lock. He placed his hand on the front door handle.

Geri was suddenly behind him, placing her arm against the door to prevent it from opening.

"Think about this," she said, looking at him like she was his mother.

"Let go of the door," he said.

She didn't move her arm. She didn't say anything, either, simply fixing him with one of those 'disappointed' looks. An exasperated look, the way a teacher would look at a problem child.

"Let go!" he yelled, more aggressively, when she didn't respond.

She lifted her arm away, still glaring at him.

He said nothing, stepping out into the street, gun in hand.

...

McFall sat quietly, sipping the last dregs of his beer. He felt the eyes of the bigger cop burning into his head, but he didn't dare look up.

"Why do you wear that ski mask?" the big cop suddenly asked.

The cop was pissed, and his words were slurring. He'd had as much as McFall to drink, and McFall was sure as hell feeling pissed. Yet, unlike Lark, McFall didn't get any bravado when drinking. He just felt even more paranoid and nervous.

Sometimes, of course, that was enough to get him into bother. An angry outburst at the bar, aimed at some lad who was, supposedly, checking out McFall's wife (God rest her soul). An over-zealous reaction to someone walking past him on the way home. Or some bloke who looked at him funny whilst ordering a pizza in their local fast-food at one in the morning. These were the kinds of situations that got McFall into bother.

Yet, regardless of how many pints he'd downed, McFall was usually pretty good at choosing his fights.

And he wasn't for choosing one with this guy.

"I said, why do you wear that –"

"I heard you," McFall said.

"Well, then answer me," The cop replied, simply.

"Come on," McFall said, laughing, "what does it matter?"

"It matters because your friend thinks I'm hiding something when you're sitting there wearing a fucking balaclava!" he said, his voice slightly raised.

The other cop came into the patio, immediately catching wind of the tension. He was followed by the girl – both looking rather bemused.

"What's going on, here?" the younger cop said, looking at McFall. "I've just caught your mate on his way outside. You want to tell me why?"

McFall looked at Norman, who was glaring back at him with a 'don't tell teacher' look on his face.

"He...er... wanted more beer," said McFall.

"More beer?" the younger cop said, looking at Norman. "We have no more beer. You lot have drank it all."

"Yeah, that's what I told him!" Norman said, smiling over at McFall.

McFall looked at the older cop, his eyes filling with venom. His lips felt dry. He felt his face heating up under the mask. He immediately stood up, kicking the chair away rather aggressively. He pulled the mask back over his mouth, as if now meaning business.

Norman started laughing at him.

Ignoring the drunken cop, McFall moved straight out to the kitchen, pushing past the others. He stood by the kitchen table, calming himself. Then he looked through the hallway towards the door his friend had left through.

He hoped to God he was okay out there, but he didn't dare follow him.

Lark reckoned the herd had thinned a little since he'd last looked out. From the garden of their house, he could make out three of them, standing near the Land Rover. They were staring at their own feet, doing very little of anything. They looked almost human, for a moment. Like bored teenagers hanging out at night. But then the moonlight caught their faces, and they began to look far from human and more like the monstrous parodies of their former selves that they truly were. After a while, one of them noticed Lark and started to wander towards him with about as much enthusiasm as a whore in church.

Lark laughed at the thing, drunkenly. "Come on, ye bastid," he slurred, raising his handgun. He aimed, rather confidently, and fired the first shot. The bullet struck gold, capping the poor fucker on the eye, shattering half its cheekbone in the process. It fell back, hitting the ground with all the grace of a donkey doing ballet. Lark laughed at it, strolling over and squeezing his DM boot against its head. He could feel his boot grinding through the flesh as if it was dried mud. It repulsed Lark. He took his boot away.

"Fucking stupid..." he mumbled at the dead fuck, bending down to aim his gun at its head, point blank range. He was interrupted by another one of them, reaching forward as it approached, grabbing Lark's gun arm. "What the –" he muttered, heart leaping with shock. "Are you trying to save your mate?!" he said, laughing out loud.

The thing didn't reply, of course, simply reaching with its other hand in the general direction of Lark's throat.

Lark surprised it by head butting it sharply, drawing blood and fuck knows what else from its feathery-skinned nose. The thing stumbled back, Lark first splitting its brain with his second shot before cocking the revolver's hammer and finishing its mate on the ground with his third.

He looked to the Land Rover. It was close, but he wondered what lay behind it and to its blind sides. He was full of gusto, full of the drunken bravado that made men climb walls far too tall in order to impress their mates or girls walking by. A hidden voice from below the reverberating warmth of his drunkenness told him to be careful. But he ignored it. Mocked it, even. He took another step towards the vehicle, jingling the keys in his hand to antagonise and whistling...

The door to the house suddenly opened. He turned at its sound, finding Geri standing there, looking at him, leaning against the door. To any man, the sight of her long, lean frame would have been welcome. But to the beer-goggled Lark, it was more than that. She looked every bit like the *Red Sonja* he'd loved to perv over as a lad.

"There *is* no more beer," she said. "Come back in; they were just pissing around with you."

"How do you know?" he said back.

"Cos I'm a girl," she said, wryly. "And I know how stupid and childish grown men get when they're drinking."

Lark laughed, turning just as a third and forth dead fuck wandered around from the other side of the Land Rover. He raised his gun and aimed. He held his aim for a while before lowering the gun. Spitting on the ground, he simply turned and walked back up the path towards the house.

"What's the point, anyway," he said sulkily as he passed her.

He noticed her shaking her head as she closed the door behind them.

ELEVEN

He awoke having never remembered falling asleep, still wearing his clothes, lying on top of the slim bed of his modest quarters. Jackson's eyes moved around the room, finding the sunrise picture glaring back at him. It was a ridiculous joke to him, now. This reminder of a past, where the rise of the sun each day meant something. Now it was meaningless. Now he didn't even know whether it was night or day, nor did he care. But that was the way things were, down in The Chamber. Time was of no interest. Clocks were all but ignored. The dead had stolen the show, leaving life, and all that represented life, as some sort of half-arsed warm-up act.

Jackson ran a hand over his bearded face, clearing the cobwebs, as it were. He hadn't washed in days. There just didn't seem to be a point anymore. He pulled himself off the bed, stretching his tired, sore bones, before reaching for the bottle of vodka on the desk. They had run out of whiskey, so this old poison would have to do. He swigged it indulgently, shaking his head after gulping a sizable quantity of the liquid down. His throat burned, the vodka's sour taste rinsing through his lethargic body like a kick to the head. Jackson screwed the lid back on the bottle, tucking it into his coat pocket. He pulled the door open, wandering out into the hallway of the small compound.

He heard the sounds of the others from the main control room. They seemed to be in high spirits, and he quickly followed the noise down the corridor to see what all the fuss was about. When he got to the control room, he noticed a number of wall monitors, previously blackened and, frankly, unnoticeable to him beforehand, now displaying various images.

"What's going on, private?" Jackson asked, still feigning the charade of authority.

The private looked up at him, as if happy to see him. "Major Jacko!" he cried, throwing his arms around him. He was clearly drunk, and Jackson pushed him gently away as he pulled up a chair alongside another of the men, less inebriated. The second man handed him a beer, but Jackson refused it, retrieving his vodka instead.

"We managed to get the monitors going," the second man said, merrily, pointing to one particular screen showing a shopping centre. "We're taking bets on who's going to win, that poor bastard with the cricket bat, or the crowd of dead approaching him from the arcade." Jackson watched as the silent fight ensued on the black and white monitor, the man hitting out, viciously, against the undead horde as half of the soldiers cheered him on. The other half sang out, though, as a young dead woman grabbed him from behind, sinking her teeth into his neck like some vampire.

"Jesus," Jackson said, unable to take his own eyes away from the scene. He forced himself to look somewhere else as the fight continued, some of the men throwing down their crudely constructed betting stubs, angrily, as the man on the screen became completely overwhelmed. As the rowing over bets continued, Jackson cast his eyes over the other monitors. They seemed to be displaying different locations, some more recognisable than others. He wondered why there were cameras at all of these spots. What new project had The

Chamber been cooking up since his resignation? His eyes were drawn to one monitor, on the far left hand side, displaying the front of a flat, its door completely boarded up.

"You can change the picture for that one, if you want." The slightly less drunk soldier said, still smiling, having obviously won the bet.

"What are these?" Jackson asked, standing to his feet and retrieving his glasses to get a better look.

"Surveillance cameras," replied the soldier.

"Yes, I can see that, private, but where are they watching? And why?"

A voice from behind answered for him.

"They are part of a special project we were working on following your retirement, sir." It was Gallagher, his voice immediately silencing the men's frolics. Jackson immediately felt inferior, his own entrance having had little to no effect on the men. He turned to address Gallagher, finding him still dressed in the yellow plastic suit, doused in blood as if he'd been at a riot in a butcher's shop. "The aim, at first, was to maintain surveillance on several key suspects. Without their knowledge, of course. Worked very well, sir. We were able to gain insider knowledge on the extra-curricular activities, shall we say, of several key representatives from the paramilitaries. Such information helped us to secure a ceasefire, sir. We simply blackmailed each of these men to ensure they played ball with the British and Irish governments. Of course, we took on other projects after that. Once the peace process was secured..."

Jackson looked at the screen, already having blanked out Gallagher's voice. It wasn't that he doubted any of what the doctor was saying. The Chamber's work was every bit as effective as it was questionable. Operating with free rein to do as it saw fit, results were achieved all too readily. But Jackson was drawn to something else, something that reminded him of his old life, of Derry and Donegal. Of his family. He brushed over the image of the struggling man, almost invisible now against the throng of starving dead. He moved back to the still image of the flat, noticing a strand of tape hanging off the door. He walked closer to the screen to get a better look.

"This is one of the quarantined flats," he said. "I remember a house down from me, in Derry, getting similar treatment just as things got bad. The cops put yellow tape across anywhere they boarded up. Seems they only got started on that one."

"Here, you can probably look inside," the more sober private said, setting his beer bottle down and fiddling with some controls on a nearby panel. The screen flicked to the inside of the flat, throwing up images of each room as the private worked. It looked no different to other flats, largely untouched by the madness outside, almost looking hospitable. As the private continued to change the display, showing each room, separately, Jackson noticed a dark shadow move, suddenly, across the screen.

"Good God," Jackson said. "Did you see that?"

"Where? Which room?" the private asked.

"The bedroom," Jackson said, siding over to the private. "Move back to the bedroom. There's someone moving inside there..."

"Probably one of the dead, sir." Gallagher said, from behind. His voice sounded disinterested, as if this was all trivial compared to whatever savagery he had been up to with the colonel's body, earlier.

"No," Jackson said. "Look closer." As the private returned to the bedroom, they watched as the shadow moved across the room, again. It moved as if with purpose, as if in full control of its movements. It lifted something from the floor. Gallagher moved beside

Jackson, now intrigued. The room fell silent, everyone staring at the screen, mesmerised. The private worked with the controls to achieve a close-up.

The image became clearer, more defined...

...

They looked small from the roof top. Less demonic, perhaps, and more human. You could make out their clothing, their hair colour, their arms and legs, even. You could see them walking, then stopping. Shaking their heads, as if tired. As if human. But you couldn't see their faces. The decay, the starkness of their dead, bloodshot eyes. And you couldn't hear much of their breathless moaning, the comforting whirl of the blue-sky, cloud and wind whipping up enough of an air show to drown out their voices.

Pat sat quietly on the rooftop of the tower block. Thinking, dreaming, reflecting. Looking up to the sky and down upon the dead.

Although it was late morning, Karen hadn't stirred from her room, as yet. He had gotten up early, as always, but she wasn't there to pour him some tea and make him some breakfast. He was quite embarrassed to admit it, but he had become quite accustomed to her fussing around him. He missed her when she wasn't there.

Beside him lay his 'Widowmaker' rifle, this time with a scope attached. He fumbled in his pockets for a pair of binoculars, lifting them to his eyes and checking along the ever-increasing sea of bodies outside the tower block for one particular one he had seen earlier. He had noticed it wandering about amongst the others, but then lost it again. He would find it again, though, despite their number. Regardless of how indistinct it was from the others, in every way.

Every way apart from one.

It was wearing a uniform. A police uniform.

Pat recalled the speech he had given to Karen only the previous day. About how those bodies, below, once belonged to people. People like him, people like her. People who once cared for their wives, their families, their friends. People with lives and loves and passions. She had wanted to shoot more of them, but he wouldn't let her. But now, on the top of the tower block, more than ten floors from the ground, he was going to break his own rule.

Pat didn't know exactly why he felt the need to shoot the cop. A part of him wanted to do it indulgently. A gratuitous act of petty vengeance. A hark back to the old Pat. The freedom fighter. The prisoner. Yet, he was also wise enough to know this was hardly a revolutionary thing to be doing with his time. For another part of him, the therapy of (re)killing it might have come from having a target that was already dead. Legitimate, then, in every way. A way of taking life without *really* taking life. Or maybe, were Pat to look really hard beneath the quagmire of his damaged heart and mind, the desire to shoot came more from Pat actually having a chance to put the poor bastard out of his misery once and for all. He'd taken the lives of a lot of men in uniform through the years, as part of his 'armed struggle.' Men who may or may not have deserved it. So, maybe now he could make up for at least one of the lives he had taken, giving something back where he had taken it from...

(give a life, take a life, give a death, take a death)

In all honesty, Pat didn't know what was making him do what he was doing. Probably a mixture of all of the above. And none of the above. A potent cocktail, flaming at the neck like a petrol bomb. Damning. Calming. A toast to the old days and the new days, waiting to be drunk thirstily, like some dare at a stag-do.

He lifted the rifle, aligning the scope to the horizon. He lay down on the rooftop, getting himself within comfortable view of his target. He took aim, his steady hand sure to keep the cop's head well within the bullet's radius. He fired once, keeping his eye on the target, satisfied to see the cop's head explode, quietly, in the scope before the body sank to the ground.

Pat immediately pulled himself to his feet. He removed the scope, quickly putting the rifle back onto safety and sliding it into his bag. He left the rooftop as quietly as he had entered it.

...

On reaching the flat, he noticed Karen standing by the window, looking out at the dead. She seemed to be becoming more and more infatuated by them, and it was beginning to worry Pat. He knew what cabin fever could do to a person, having shared smaller spaces than this for weeks on end with other operatives during IRA assignments. It took real strength to find your own space where space wasn't available, and he didn't know if Karen had that strength.

"Where were you?" she asked, without turning around.

"Just on the roof," he said, innocently.

"What were you doing up there?" she asked.

"Not a lot," Pat replied. He quietly stashed his bag behind the sofa. He suddenly noticed how untidy the place was. An opened tin of fruit sat on the coffee table, next to a mug of coffee. Neither had a placemat under them.

"That's funny," Karen said, still without turning to look at him, "because I heard shooting."

Pat sat himself down on the sofa, running a hand through his hair to flatten it down. He looked at Karen, noticing how unkempt she looked. She was still in her pyjamas and dressing gown. It didn't look she'd even had as much as a wash since getting up.

"Are you okay?" Pat asked.

"Yes," she said, turning, finally to look him in the face. "Why?"

"You just look a little..."

"Ropey?" Karen asked, without humour.

"Well, I wouldn't quite put it like that..." Pat backtracked.

"Just doesn't seem much point in worrying about how I look, does there?" she said. "Why bother when I'll never get out the door."

"Come on," Pat said, tiring of this same routine. "Don't be like that..."

"I'm not being like anything..." she said. "I'm just telling the truth. Aren't I?"

Pat stood up, walking over to the counter to make himself some tea. He noticed the worktop hadn't been wiped; spilt coffee granules peppered across the bench like soil. It reminded him of his childhood, suddenly. Innocent days spent hunting caterpillars in the garden.

"We've got to keep positive," he said. "We don't know what will happen in the future. One day all of those things outside might weaken, even die..."

"They already died," Karen said, without humour. "That's the thing. And when we die, we'll be just like them."

"You don't know that –" he countered.

But she interrupted him, "Of course we know that. In fact we can be sure of it. It's the only thing we can be sure of. Death used to be the only thing we could be sure of. That's what they told me in church. But now... now we can't even be sure about that, anymore."

Pat noticed she had been crying. The tears had dried on her cheeks like old cellotape. He went to comfort her, but stopped himself mid-motion. What could he tell her? How could he convince her to keep her spirits up, when she was pretty much telling the truth? He realised that she had grown up very quickly since he'd known her. And grown more cynical with it. But it didn't sit well with him. It didn't make him proud to see her mature. She no longer saw him as the father figure, the one who could protect her from the scary monsters. She no longer trusted him, doted on him, even. He realised that he had been depending on her to keep *him* stable, to distract *him* from all that was going on. He needed her as much as she needed him. That's what gave him purpose.

Pat simply sidled up to Karen, hands in pockets, looking out at the dead. They were so small, so insignificant from so far up. But they surrounded her like a moat. And she seemed reckless, now, unpredictable. Like Princess Karen of The Tower Block, able at any minute to unravel her hair and let it down for them to touch, feel.

For them to climb.

The reality of their existence was hitting home to her. He would have to watch her even more closely, now. Because, for Pat, this could be a life. This could be *enough*. Yet, for her, it had become little more than death.

From that moment, he realised that this tower block was no longer a haven.

It was a prison.

And he had to make sure it was locked up tight.

TWELVE

"Three cans of soup – mushroom, no less. One bottle of water. Half a pound of sugar, some powdered milk and... an out-of-date block of cooking chocolate." Lark listed the contents of the almost-bare cupboard with a hint of irony in his voice. He smiled, once done, stepping away from the kitchen cupboard as if to invoke applause. But no one applauded. The two cops, McFall (still wearing his balaclava) and Geri sat around the kitchen table, wordlessly. Each of them nursed a cup of weak tea, drained from one bag in a full pot. "That's it," he said as if to encourage the credits to roll on his little performance.

"That's it," George repeated, flatly.

No one spoke for a while, all five survivors sipping on their tea. McFall burped loudly, somewhat ruining the contemplative moment they had all shared over a bare cupboard.

"Sorry," he said, smiling, weakly.

Geri glared at him.

"Well," said George, before clearing his throat, "we're going to have to do a food run, then."

"What, out there?" McFall said, shuffling in his chair, nervously. Geri glared at him, again. This time shaking her head.

"We have to," George said, politely. "It's not like we have any choice in the matter." He looked to Lark, who was still standing beside the opened larder, as if lording over some failed magic trick. "Where's the nearest supermarket?" he asked him.

"Tesco's," Lark replied, "but I'd say it's been completely pillaged. I think it was one of the first places to be raided."

Everyone looked to their cups, again, trying to think of other options.

"What about the off-licence across the road?" Norman said.

"I think we need more than just booze," replied Lark, shortly. George reckoned he still hadn't got over the previous night's run-in with the cop.

"Yeah, but a lot of offies do more than just booze, now. There could be biscuits, crisps, tinned foods in there, as well. There'll definitely be soft drinks. Water, even."

George looked around the room, hoping for other thoughts on the idea.

"I guess it's as good a call as any," Geri said, clearly in agreement.

George looked to the other two. McFall didn't seem that interested. The talk was clearly making him nervous. For someone who chose to appear so intimidating, with that ridiculous mask, George couldn't get over how cowardly he was when it came down to it. Every mere mention of the dead seemed to ooze fear from him in waves of heavy-smelling sweat. His main interest in this most recent proposed encounter would be in steering well clear of it.

He looked to Lark next, the less predictable one amongst their number. He knew that no love was lost between the tattooed man and his partner, Norman, but would they be able to put their differences aside and work together for the greater good, as it were? Or would he need to keep them apart like warring children...

(Lark, sandpit. Norm, swings).

A sudden realisation dawned on George – he was playing Sergeant for the first time in a long while. Order had broken down during the whole end-of-the-world thing, meaning that what police remained on the streets worked outside both regulation and rank. Although some troops were drafted in from both the UK and south of the border, they, too, stopped playing by the rules fairly swiftly. Some more swiftly than others, of course. Soon, having a gun and wearing a uniform offered little hope to anyone, least of all the civilians of Northern Ireland.

His mind travelled back to that final quarantine he'd been on. The little girl. How her mother looked at him as if he had the power to do something for them. How he caged them both in, like wild dogs. That might have been the last time he'd tried (and failed) to act like a Sergeant, to act like it meant anything to be in the force or to wear the uniform. But it was hardly a glorious moment.

George suddenly felt short of breath, heating up as if in that suit again. The girl looked over to him, concerned.

"Are you okay?" she asked.

"S-sure," he smiled, unconvincingly. "I just choked on my tea."

She smiled back at him, seeming to have bought his excuse.

"So, it's decided, then?" George said to the others.

He stood up before anyone had replied, suddenly feeling sweat break across his back. He could sense the eyes of his partner on him. He excused himself from the kitchen, moving out into the hall and quickly up the stairs towards the bathroom. He feigned a cough, as he went, but it wasn't his throat he was worried about. His chest felt as if it were going to explode. He was heating up under his collar. He stepped into the bathroom, locking the door behind him with a shaking hand. A bottle of mineral water stood by the sink. A couple of chemical toilets sat in the bath, unused. He inserted the plug, emptying half the contents of the water bottle into the sink. He tore at his collar, loosening his shirt and removing it, roughly. With cupped hands, he cooled himself with the water. Finally, he sat back on the toilet seat, breathing deeply.

These bloody panic attacks were getting worse.

A knock at the door disturbed him.

"Everything alright?"

It was Norman. His partner knew he had been faking. He knew what was really wrong. But George still felt the need to play along with his own facade.

"Yeah, just choked on my tea," he said, repeating the original lie as if it would make it more believable.

"Just as long as you're alright," said Norman, moving away.

He was a man who had many faults, but disloyalty wasn't one of them. George couldn't count the number of times that his old partner had saved his hide, especially in the last while, when things had got way too bad for a cop like George. A cop who liked to follow the rules, do things by the book...

(a cop who had killed, firing upon innocents)

George put the dark thoughts to the back of his mind, marking them with a 'do not disturb' sticker. He sat up, lifting the bottle of mineral water and drinking deeply from it. He threw some more water on his face from the sink and then looked into the mirror.

"Come on, he said to himself. "Get a grip..."

His eyes were circled by black rings, sharply contrasting his pale skin. His hair stuck to his head as if glued to his scalp. He looked like shit, but he didn't care. Everyone looked like shit. Especially in this house.

A sudden flicker of more beautiful eyes flashed before the mirror in front of him. They were not his, nor the eyes of anyone he had known or loved. They were the eyes of the little girl he'd quarantined. The Eastern European girl from the flat in the tower block at Finaghy. He wondered if it was her ghost. She had been preying on his mind, in his sleep, ever since he'd met her. If she *were* a ghost, some restless spirit trying to 'find itself' in a world where to be dead meant very little, George thought that she was a *beautiful* ghost. Big, oval shaped coals looked out at him from the mirror. Rich, dark brown, like chocolate. Bordering on black. And then she was gone again, and his tired eyes were in her place. Ragged pieces of tired jelly, no more beautiful than his guilt.

He pulled his shirt back on, creasing the collar down. He rubbed his face, looking back in the mirror. He spotted the emblem on his shirt, running a hand over the raised embroidery. He still had a job to do, he thought. More so than ever.

THIRTEEN

They spent most of the morning preparing for the outing to the off-licence. After more aimless talking back and forth, Lark and Norman finally volunteered to be the main players. George took point by the first floor bedroom window, intending to provide covering fire with a scope fitted to his HK33 rifle.

"You ready, mate?" Norman shouted up the stairs to him.

From somewhere on the first floor of the small two-up-two-down, George's voice replied.

Norman next looked at the tattooed man beside him, somewhat outrageously dressed in George's full riot gear and carrying a revolver.

"Looking good," he said, smiling.

Lark just sneered in reply, like a huffy child.

"Okay," Norman said to Lark, "I'm going to do most of the legwork here. You just stay the fuck out of my way and get over there as quick as you can."

Lark simply nodded, seeming ambivalent to the baiting within Norman's words. Norman couldn't tell if he hadn't heard him properly – those riot helmets can be a bitch on the old audio – or if he was intentionally ignoring him. He preferred the former, of course. Ignoring someone like Norman was considered *particularly* bad manners. Like red rag to a bull.

The nut with the balaclava came out to the hall. He looked at Norman, awkwardly, before patting his friend on the back.

"Good luck," he said warmly to the other guy, eyes falling on Norman again, quickly and uncomfortably.

"Okay, let's go," Norman said to Lark, looking at Balaclava and shaking his head. He hated cowardice in a man. It was so undignified, so embarrassing for all concerned. Maybe Balaclava had some reason to be scared, some huge overriding issue or experience or parental bullshit creeping in from his previous life. But Norman didn't care. In a broken down world, a desperate world like this, everyone was on a level playing field. It was survival of the fittest, the strongest, the scariest. And Norman intended to survive.

There seemed to be more of the dead around than normal. He didn't know why, though. In fact, Norman couldn't see any kind of pattern to their behaviour. Sometimes they were lethargic; at other times they were aggressive. Sometimes large in number, at other times wandering around in ones and twos, as if lost. In a way, Norman thought, they weren't a hell of a lot different from what they were before. They were still fat, thin, old and young. Only, now they were *dead* and fat, thin, old and young. Of course, for Norman, there was no need to study them or understand them. He saw no need for touchy-feely bullshit when dealing with them. You just needed to be ready for them and then kill them. He had no problem with that. When it came down to it, in order to survive he had no problem doing just about anything.

Their street rolled down a hill, just like many streets off the Lisburn Road. Tall, angular houses faced their row of two-up-two-downs, shielding them from the sun. The off-licence across the road stood on a corner, forming a crossroads. It seemed out of place, to Norman, like a priest at a brothel. Shifty looking. Embarrassed.

Dark, grated windows frowning in the shadows, as if hiding some shameful secret.

He watched Lark bolt across the road, towards the off-licence. The boy could sprint, Norman had to give him that. Of course, God knows what he was wired up on. Speed? Ecstasy? Coke? There had to be something flowing through his veins. Norman hadn't scored a hit in days, and he was feeling all the worse for it. His bones felt tired, lethargic. He was weary and feeling every second of his age. He made a mental note to go through the house, when he got back, and find a little of whatever Tattoo was no doubt hiding.

The first threat was taken out by a shot from above. Literally. Norman watched the corpse fall before he even got near it. The damn thing looked confused, disappointed even, as its neck split in two, pieces of cartilage spreading across the road in a bloody mess. Norman looked behind him, up at the window, catching a glimpse of George. He raised his thumb in thanks.

He worried for George, of course. Since he'd joined the force, some years back, Norman had always been his partner. And, to be honest, he hadn't liked George at first. He wasn't like Norman. George had been career-driven from the very start. Keen to get ahead, score some stripes. A big fan of paperwork (his own and Norman's) and 'touchy-feely' policing. He went far because of it, of course. And he was a good Sergeant, Norman thought to himself. Knew when to turn a blind eye – even when he didn't agree with what was going on. He was bloody soft, though. Needed looking out for. Especially in this new world. Especially since...

Another attacker, this one an old lady, reached for him. He could tell her age by the night dress and wrinkled skin. She had caught him off guard, grabbing the padded arm of his jacket and busily trying to sink her teeth through. Norman laughed. She must have been the hungriest bitch out there. She had no teeth, only gums writhing, trying to find a grip. Hair sprouted from her head like sun-stroked grass, yellow and parched. Her misty eyes showed little expression, hanging in her head, motionless, as if she were blind. It was a pathetic display. Norman kicked her away with his steel-toecap, raising his rifle and pumping two rounds through her frail old head. It split apart like a rotten tomato, flesh, hair and gum slapping against tarmac like projectile vomit.

Norman looked over at Lark. The silly bastard was still outside the door to the offie's, struggling with the lock. One of the dead challenged him briefly, but the tattooed man dealt with it quickly and efficiently, raising his Glock 17 to blow a clean hole through its head, dropping it to the ground like a heavy bag of shopping. It didn't seem to bother him, either, and Norman immediately felt himself respecting the man a little bit. A lot more than his cowardly mate, that was for sure.

Before long, Norman was by Lark's side, flanking around the man as he worked the lock, picking off the most dangerous of their attackers with further flashes from the muzzle of his own HK33. They fell immediately, the closeness of range only making their wounds all the more fatal. A couple more shots from the first floor bedroom put paid to another few, thinning their numbers even further.

"Hurry up!" shouted Norman, impatiently.

"It's fucking locked from the inside!" Lark said, somewhat irritated.

"Well, just blow it open, then!" Norman said, demonstrating just how by blasting the cheekbone of a young dead girl in front of him. She crumbled to the ground, reaching for her missing face as if angry or shocked, Norman pumping another round into her for good measure.

The big cop heard Lark firing once, twice, before kicking the door through. Both men quickly moved inside, before shutting the door then searching, desperately, for a suitable barricade, finally working together to push a large display of Alco-pop against the entrance. It would hold the crazies back for a short while.

Once the door was secure, Norman turned around to properly survey the shop. The windows were partially blackened out, meaning visibility was poor inside. Norman pulled a torch from his pocket, switching it on to shed light on the situation. It was an old-school off-licence. Minimum decor, no frills. Defiantly untidy. In fact, the place was a fucking mess. Smashed glass littered the floor, the reek of alcohol heavy in the air. A single body lay across the counter, its head having exploded, messily, over the back wall. Several spent rounds of ammunition mixed in with the glass on the floor. Another body could be seen sprawled across a stack of six-packs. It, too, was without a head.

"I guess someone got here before us..." Norman said.

"No shit, Sherlock..." Lark muttered under his breath.

Norman let it pass, simply pressing the torch across his lips to silence the other man. He had heard something. No, maybe it was something he *felt*, more then heard. Something beyond sound, yet intense enough to feel like sound. This was another sense. A sense of danger, honed by years of policing.

He moved slowly through the shop, taking care not to stand on the glass. Everything was stained. Tarnished, unusable. He wouldn't put his lips to any of the bottles or cans left on the aisles. It was as if some huge dying monster had ripped the roof off and puked its bloody guts up all over the place. Norman had only seen this kind of mess once, before, when he'd been first on the scene of a brutal bomb blast. Bombs were vicious things, of course. Unapologetically messy.

Halfway across the spacious shop floor, Norman looked back to find Lark closely following him. He pointed to the storeroom door, further through an archway towards the back of the room. If they were going to find anything usable, it would be in there. Of course, Norman was convinced that there was *something else* in there, also...

Both men approached the storeroom from different sides, covering each other as if on automatic pilot. They seemed to have put their differences aside, suddenly. Forced to work together in order to stay alive together. Team bonding with guns. Norman reached the store first, slinging his rifle around his shoulder and choosing his Glock, instead, to investigate. He didn't want to create a bigger mess than he had to. The place looked fucked up enough already.

Lark was beside him, looking over and reaching for the handle of the door. He seemed to be waiting for Norman's signal.

Norman nodded, raising the torch's light towards the door.

Lark pulled the door wide open, and Norman stepped into the room, weapon drawn with one hand, torch spilling light from the other. Inside, several of the dead turned to stare back at him, almost as if they felt intruded upon. Their empty eyes reflected the unforgiving light, cold and devoid of any feeling or emotion. A swarm of flies circled the room, excited and overstimulated. On the floor was the body of what seemed to be a soldier, given the rifle and backpack nearby. Several of the dead crowded around him, on their knees, each dipping their hands and mouths into the middle of the man's open stomach as if bobbing for apples. A long string of bloody sausages spread out along the ground, Norman realising that they were, in fact, the poor bastard's intestines.

"Fuck me," he heard Lark say, before gagging.

The dead didn't even hold his gaze, seeming immune and ambivalent to the torchlight. They greedily turned back to their meal like starving dogs. Norman watched them eat, for a while, unable to take his eyes off the scene, as if it were a car crash. Their faces were strained and feral looking, focused solely on the task of devouring the camouflage-clad body on the floor. One of the dead wore similar clothing, as if he, too, had once been a soldier. Norman noticed his arm was missing, the ragged remains of his sleeve hanging from his torso, as if ashamed.

For Norman, the scene had added poignancy. His brother had been a soldier for years. He had been just like Norman, even looked like him. Their mother had often referred to them as 'two peas in a pod.' They were both messers in school. His brother was the more sensitive one, though. Too big for his own skin. Constantly aware of himself. He left school as soon as he could. Joined the Army, because it seemed like the only job that would have him. He had been recently drafted to Afghanistan, and Norman suddenly wondered if he was, ironically, safer there than he would be here.

Norman raised his handgun and fired repeatedly until every head in the room was bloody pulp, flesh splashing violently around the walls like a bomb at an abattoir. There was no protest from any of them, each body falling limply to the floor, some jittering quietly as if slightly annoyed at having their meal disturbed. Within seconds, the job was done; Norman waited until every body fell completely silent . He went to leave but was halted by another sound from the cursed room. Norman stopped, turning slowly towards the noise. In the midst of the bloody chaos, he could see a small shape, scuttling along the back wall. He strained his eyes, shining the torchlight again, able to make out the body of a little girl. She was naked, blood coating her smooth, pale skin like red paint. She was licking it from her fingers, as if it were strawberry sauce, staring up at him as if she'd been caught stealing. Her innocence seemed, somehow, preserved. Even after her life, and everything that made her alive, had left her, there was still that one quality, that one dynamic at play. Innocence. She looked at Norman as if trying to melt his heart, trying to make him less cross with her for the naughty things she had done. She scuttled away from the torch beam, as if playfully. As if it were some kind of game. Norman could almost have sworn he could make out a smile on her face.

He fired two shots through her skull, her little head exploding more dramatically than the others, as if more delicate. Once done, Norman stood at the doorway, handgun still smoking in his hand. His head hung low. He dimmed the torch quietly, reverently. His mind travelled back to the tower block at Finaghy. To flat 23. To the little girl, probably scuttling around there, every bit as (un)dead as all the other quarantined. He wished he hadn't done that. Of all the many questionable things he had done in life, that quarantine, that visit to the tower block, was what Norman Coulter regretted the most.

He stepped out of the storeroom quickly, turning to look at the other man who was still bent double, retching. The smell in the shop was almost unbearable. Rancid flesh, pickled by spilt alcohol. And now the fresh puke of his fellow survivor. He could almost taste the virus in his mouth. Everything here was contaminated.

"Let's just get out of here," Norman said, pulling the other man's arm as he made for the door.

FOURTEEN

Pzzt. "We have the target area in sight, sir. But the area is heavily populated with hostiles. There's no way we can land." *Pzzt.*

Jackson held the radio mic to his mouth. "Circle the tower block. See if there's any sign of life."

"The target's reacting, sir..." Gallagher said, tapping the screen with a long finger nail. They were still watching the quarantined flat on the monitors on the wall. "It's moving more quickly," he said pointing at the image of the shadow on the screen as it got over-excited. Unfortunately, the target, as Gallagher called it, wasn't reacting the way they had hoped. In fact, it seemed the 'target' was hiding.

"Damn," whispered Jackson. He ran a hand through his greasy hair, turning and fixing Gallagher with a stressed look. The good doctor was far from stressed, of course, with a look resembling amusement etched across his long, pale face. "Any ideas?" Jackson asked him.

"I suggest, sir, that your plan is solid. Have the helicopter circle the building a few more times. There may be a number of survivors in there. Drawing them out could be used to our advantage..."

Jackson watched as the young, bedraggled private at the control panel switched views.

"This one is from a camera looking unto the flats," he said. "You can get a good view of our boys' approach."

They watched as the helicopter continued its orbit of the tower block, all eyes glued to the array of screens on the wall, showing a variety of angles. Jackson began to wonder how they got those cameras all fitted without the locals noticing, without anyone questioning the alleged maintenance work being carried out. Of course, having worked for The Chamber, he knew how easily they negotiated such seemingly impossible barriers. And how brutally.

...

Pat was in a dark room, sitting on a chair. He was wearing a white shirt, once ironed to perfection by his wife, now stained by nervous sweat. His hands were tied behind his back. A light shone down on his tortured but clean face like the moon itself – bright, sombre, sinister. Shadows filled the walls, dancing as if part of some hellish puppet show.

A man moved towards him, another man pulled him back, whispering something in his ear. The first man came towards him, again. Pat could hear his heels scraping the floor, as if being dragged.

"We have your wife, Patrick..." the man said, his face completely hidden under the shadows of the light. His voice was smooth, like velvet, and perfectly intonated. Melodic, almost soothing, and polite to a fault. "She'll be charged for resisting arrest. Oh, and assaulting a member of the armed forces. Let's not forget that, of course."

Pat spat in the direction of the voice's face. The man said nothing, but a charge of electricity raced through Pat's body, rinsing out pain that made him cry out involuntarily. Sweat and urine spread across his skin, the sudden attack of dampness making him feel both hot and cold at once.

143

"Leave her alone, you –"

"Now, now, Patrick," the first man said, leaning closer. Pat noticed his silhouette was tall, lean. "You play nice with us, and we'll play nice with you. And your good lady wife, fine looking woman that she is..."

"You SCUM!" Pat yelled, trying to shake his hands free from the chair. It was no use. He shook the chair, frantically, growling like a mad dog, such was his frustration.

The second man drew closer now, moving out of the shadows. He sighed as he looked at Pat.

"Just tell us what we need to know..." he said to him, his deeper voice lending a serious tone to his words. "Please tell us, Pat. For everyone's sake..."

"Fuck you," Pat said, simply.

"Okay..." the first man said, walking back towards the door to the room. Pat could hear him muttering something out in the corridor. There was the sound of a struggle as someone else was dragged into the room by a pair of other men. "Just sit him down there," the first man ordered them.

"Who's there?" Pat asked, still unable to see anything beyond shadows and silhouettes.

"Daddy?" a voice said, nervously.

"Sean?" Pat called. "Sean, is that you?"

The second man came closer again. "Tell us, Pat," he said, his voice shaking with either anger or frustration. "Tell us, or God knows what's going to happen to the boy."

"Daddy, don't tell them nothin'!" Sean protested.

"Okay, that's enough," said the first voice. They bundled Sean out as quickly as they had bundled him in.

"Wait!" Pat called, irritably. "Where are you taking him? Sean! SEAN!"

But Sean was gone, the sounds of his voice fading. The two men hung in the shadows, as if building momentum. As if allowing what had just happened to digest, to sink in. Then they both came closer to Pat again, their feet dragging across the floor even slower than before.

"One last chance, Pat," the lower voice said, drawing close to his ear.

"We could make him disappear..." the more polite voice whispered, dramatically.

"You –" Pat said, tears rinsing from his eyes in anger and frustration. He could hear the two men continuing to talk to him, continuing to reason, but he wasn't taking it in. He was too angry, too feral. Their words were garbled, their sounds soaring in volume as he sat there, tied to the chair, in that darkened room, crying like a baby. The words were nonsensical, now, mere jibberish, speeding up as if on fast-forward, rising in the air, circling around him, racing through him. He could hear it everywhere, as if it were some sort of machine, now. Relentless, frightful. Loud and obnoxious.

His eyes flicked open. Pat was lying on top of his bed in the flat, still dressed. But he could still hear the sound of the babbling voices, insidiously close to him. It penetrated the silent room like some kind of huge engine. He realised it wasn't voices he was hearing. This was something else.

Karen appeared at his door, hair all over the place and face spotty. She was talking to him, shouting at him, but her voice was lost under the deep monotony of the other sound. She ran back out, leaving the door to Pat's room swinging in the sheer excitement of the moment. Pat followed her out into the main living area of their flat. She was standing at the window, her window to the world, looking out upon all that was forbidden to her. The blinds were wide open. When she saw him, she started pointing. Her lips were moving, but the words were still lost in that all-consuming noise. It was like some kind of silent movie playing out before him. As if he were still dreaming.

Pat followed her gaze, finding the source of the noise. A helicopter hung in the air, right outside their flat, the face of the pilot staring in at them. It was a green military helicopter and Pat immediately recognised it as the standard RAF Wessex, often used to transport the Army to and from operations in Northern Ireland. His heart sank as he spotted it, a cold sweat splashing against his spine like the very electric they had used against him all those years ago. He felt a sudden rage swell up within him, his hands immediately reaching for the bag behind the sofa.

"Get away from the window," he spat at Karen, but his voice was as uselessly silent as hers. She looked at him, baffled. "NOW!" he stressed, but she still looked confused. He unzipped his bag, retrieving his AR 18 rifle. He quickly clicked the thirty-round mag into place.

But Karen was yelling at him, her words lost in the deafening noise of the helicopter. She was rushing to him and grabbing his hands. She fought him viciously for the rifle. She sank her teeth into his arm, the sharpness of the bite tearing Pat's skin as if she was a wild dog. As if she had suddenly turned into one of the dead. He wrestled with her, trying to shake her off, surprised at how strong she was. How determined. The noise of the rotaries was even louder now that they drew closer to the open window, Karen still hanging off his arm, tears breaking from her crazed eyes like drunken piss. But he couldn't let her deter him. He couldn't let her get her way.

Pat shook his rifle free with one arm, grabbing Karen's neck with the other. He pushed her away from the window, quickly grabbing the rifle with both arms to bring the butt of it across her face. She hit the ground, hard and fast. Turning the rifle, Pat opened fire on the helicopter a slow hail of bullets rattling out the open window. The helicopter immediately turned, evasively, several shots piercing its shell as it retreated.

And then it was gone. As the noise receded into the fresh, cool air, Pat could make out the incessant crying of the girl on the floor. She looked up at him, her face damp, bloodied. Her sobs were aimed at him, angrily. It was as if she was howling at him like some angry, wounded wolf.

There were times, Pat thought, when you had to do a terrible thing in order to do a good thing. A moment of evil for the greater good. He had held dear to this theory all through his service with the IRA. Even during interrogation. Even when they took his wife from him, his son... Even when the so-called 'peace process' had pissed all over his efforts from a great height whilst lining the pockets of the politicians – the people who he thought had been 'representing' him. The people who he had trusted to stand steadfastly against the empirical corruption of the British government. The people he had lost so much by protecting... To Pat, they hadn't found peace. Not real peace, on their terms. They had traded their integrity for a pay packet, for more power, more responsibility. They had made a mockery of him and people like him. They had made a mockery of his family, his boy... and all the people he had done terrible things to, in the name of 'the cause'.

Pat unclipped the rifle's magazine, mechanically and without thinking. He slipped it all back into the bag as if to hide it. He sat down on the sofa, and he waited for Karen to stop crying. His face was hard. Heavy.

"What did you do?" she asked, still damp. Still on the floor, like a broken doll. But she knew what he had done. And Pat thought for a moment that she knew that he *would* do it. A part of Pat considered that she knew it all along, but needed to test it, in some way. To test him.

"I helped you," he said. "I kept you safe."

She stared at him, face saturated with tears and anger. But something else was there, something new. There was hate in her eyes. He wondered if it was hate for him or hate for herself. Or hate for both of them and the world in which they now inhabited. He felt very sorry for her. She looked *beyond* broken, now. It was as if this helicopter thing was the last straw, and her back was now shattered.

He suddenly wished he had blown it out of the sky. He hoped he'd at least nailed one of the crew with his shooting. Those fuckers deserved what they got. They had a lot to answer for – stealing a young girl's hopes like that.

She lay on the floor, keening. Her long, sequinned skirt glistened in the sunlight. There was a stain in it that looked like blood. Her blood. The innocence that once radiated from her hung out to dry like dirty washing. This was her moment of transformation, thought Pat. This was her butterfly moment. When her young, spotty, innocent face would take on a harsher, older pallor. And it was for the best, Pat decided.

For the greater good.

"They aren't the good guys," he said quietly and calmly to her. "They never were."

...

"Wessex Two, what's your status?" Jackson said into the mic. Banging his other hand on the table, he barked to the private operating the monitor control panel. "I want a better picture of who that is firing!"

Pzzt. "Minimal damage, we think, sir. We're okay. Going to do an evasive circle of the city. Give us a chance to check our readings more closely." Pzzt.

Even Gallagher appeared excited. Not nervous, of course. But definitely excited. "Roll in camera three,"

he said to the private. "That'll give us our best view."
The private obliged, moving the camera as detailed
by Gallagher, seemingly ignoring Jackson's agitated
orders.

Jackson reached for the bottle of vodka on the table.
He poured the dregs down his throat, shaking his face
as it disappeared. He felt himself hating Gallagher,
intensely. This inhuman calmness of his. The constant
undermining of his authority. He felt the booze swell his
anger, sober logic dissolving like a tablet in water.

"What are you doing?! I need that picture!" he yelled,
dropping his empty bottle to the ground.

"And I'm getting it for you, sir," the private said,
continuing to close in on the image of the man firing.
The man's face became more and more visible on the
screen.

"Okay, capture that image, private," Gallagher said,
ever calmly. "We have our man, sir," he said to Jackson.
As they watched, the private fed the image into some
computer system on another one of the monitors. He
proceeded to flip through various suggestions of who
the suspect would be. "We were working towards a full
database of offenders, sir," Gallagher said. "We only
managed to get halfway through the project, but you
never know what might pop up."

But the seventh choice of name immediately struck
fear into Jackson. A man he had encountered before,
back whenever he had worked for The Chamber's
interrogation project alongside Gallagher.

"What do you know?" Gallagher said, laughing
sardonically. "If it isn't our old friend, Patrick Flynn!"

Jackson could hardly take his eyes off the screen. He
suddenly felt hot, sweaty, as if the image were literally
burning a hole through him.

"Never thought you'd run into Patrick again, did you,
sir?" Gallagher beamed, as if delighted. "How long ago
was it? Ten? Fifteen years? "

Patrick Flynn was a well-known IRA operative, serving time for various offences. Gun running was the worst they had on him, but they knew he was up to his eyes in it. His case was a particularly gruesome one. The Home Secretary was turning up the heat on The Chamber, threatening to pull funding if they couldn't get results. Gallagher, of course, was only too happy to try all kinds of new techniques to draw the information they needed to close the latest 'peace deal'. Something juicy to blackmail the politicians. But Pat wasn't playing ball. He was a veteran member of the IRA, so they knew that he was likely to have a lot they could use. But he didn't want to talk, no matter how hard Gallagher tried to rip the information from his tortured body and mind.

"I'd love to meet with Patrick, again..." Gallagher sighed, as if reminding himself of an old friend. "We have unfinished business."

"No way," Jackson said, suddenly. "I'm not going to do this shit anymore." He threw the mic from his hand.

"That's what you said back then, too." Gallagher pressed him. "But in the end, you did what had to be done." The private was working through an onscreen file as they spoke. Jackson watched, nervously, as the various details of the case displayed on the monitor before all gathered in the room. The times and dates of each interview. The methods used by Gallagher to 'interview' the man.

"They had my –"

"Your daughter, sir," Gallagher said, finishing Jackson's sentence for him. "I'm sure no one here is judging you. You did what you had to do. Who's to know what those terrorists would have done to your little princess," he said, smiling, paternally. As if genuinely concerned about Jackson's well-being. "Would you like to sit down, sir? You look very unwell, all of sudden."

"You son of a bitch," Jackson yelled. "They used me! They knew I had a reason to do what I did! But you! What reason had you?!" the computer screen continued to flick through the file, all eyes in the room fixed on the digital images that were downloading. They showed various pictures of Pat Flynn, his wife and his son, Sean Flynn. One image was taking longer than the others to load. It had the tagline 'LR' labelling it.

"Do you know what 'LR' stands for?" Gallagher said to the private at the control panel.

"N-no, sir..." the private answered, nervously. The tension was dampening the room with a thick, heavy smell. The smell of unwashed men sweating. But Jackson knew that Gallagher wouldn't be sweating.

"It means 'last resort'," he answered, merrily. "And the good Major was the man who initiated this particular action. It was intended to break the suspect, to the point where he would be more susceptible to my methods." He looked back towards Jackson. "Did it work, sir?" he asked, as if needing to be reminded.

"Fuck you," Jackson said. His eyes watched as the dreadful image was downloaded.

"Indeed," Gallagher said. The image continued to appear more fully on the screen. "Did it give you pleasure, sir?" he asked, drawing closer to Jackson. He extended two fingers, shaping his hand like a handgun and pressing it to Jackson's head, "To shoot a young boy in cold blood?" the image finally loaded, flicking onto the screen and causing a sudden intake of breath around the room. The body of a young boy, hardly sixteen, slumped against a chair with a bullet wound in his head. Jackson couldn't look at it. He pushed Gallagher away, reaching for a Glock on the table. Gallagher stepped back, steadying himself, looking right at Jackson as the barrel of the Glock travelled towards an imaginary crosshairs on the doctor's forehead. He didn't seem to be afraid. Even under threat of death, this callous bastard had nothing to give, nothing to share.

But Jackson felt a sharp pain stab him, as the sound of a silenced shot sliced the air, the private at the control panel firing upon him purposefully. He fell quickly, his own handgun rattling along the dusty floor of the control room to land at Gallagher's feet. His breathing became quick, his heart pounding in his chest like a hammer. He felt himself lose consciousness, fading out of the room like an old record. Everything was spinning around him, his eyelids starting to fall, as if heavy. The last thing he saw was the face of Dr Miles Gallagher drawing close to him, as if concerned.

FIFTEEN

"So, there was nothing you could take?" McFall asked.

They were sitting at the kitchen table again. Lark looked at the ski-masked man, shaking his head.

"Did you hear anything I just said?" he asked, mouth agape. "You're a fucking dick, man..."

"What?" McFall said, looking hurt. "I was just asking, like. I thought you might bring a few tins back for me..."

"Some poor bastard over there got his guts ripped out!" Lark shouted, slamming his fist on the table, "and all you can think of is ... what?!... your next beer?"

"Look," George interrupted, "he's right. He may not be the most sensitive bloke in the world, but he does have a point. We do need to get more food and drink. And quickly."

"But where from?" Norman said. "Every supermarket, every off-licence in town's likely to have been ransacked."

"We have to think creatively," Geri added. "He's right, all the obvious places will have been hit hard early on."

"Canteens," McFall said, looking around the room uncomfortably. "You know, school canteens and the like."

George tilted his head in consideration.

"Probably a better shot than a supermarket, that's for sure..." he said.

"What about other houses?" Geri said, "Like next door, across the road. That kind of thing."

"Oh, and there's a load of stuff in the car outside, too," McFall offered. "The one I drove on the day I –"

"Nearly killed me?" Geri spat, shooting the ski-masked man a dirty look.

"For the danger you'd be placing yourself in," George said, ignoring the tension, "I don't think there'd be much payback."

"Warehouses," Norman said.

George looked at him, quietly weighing up the pros and cons of the suggestion.

"They'd be in the edges of the city," Norman continued. "Less likely to be hit as much as the more central and obvious places."

"Probably onto something there," McFall said.

"How are we for fuel?" George asked, seemingly considering the suggestion from all angles.

"Not great," Norm replied. "But we could grab some on the way, maybe."

The five survivors thought about the proposal for a second.

"We have to do it," George said, sighing. "What's the alternative?"

"A couple of spoonfuls of mushroom soup. Chocolate for dessert," Lark offered helpfully.

"Okay," George said. "We need to get some sleep before we do this. We'll leave tomorrow at dawn." He got up from the table, making for the door to the hallway.

"Wait, who leaves?" McFall asked.

George stalled, turning around.

"We're going to need as many people as possible to get the job done fast. The Land Rover can take four of us, easily. There'll still be loads of space for the supplies. We may even find another van or something, to take more back with us."

"Y-you'll need someone to stay here and mind things," McFall stuttered.

George thought for a minute, rubbing the stubble on his chin. It reminded him to add razors to his shopping list.

"Okay," he said, shaking his head. "If you want to stay behind, then stay behind." He kept his eyes on McFall, noticing how embarrassed he looked by his own cowardice. The poor bastard was constantly on edge, constantly on the defensive. Retreating further and further into himself, like a snail with a shell. George wondered if the balaclava was more to do with terminal shyness than any hope of shielding him against the virus. His mind was brought back to the yellow suit and oxygen mask that he had worn. How they had helped to keep him separate from the world around him, a world going to hell. How they had made it easier to do the things he had done. He was glad when they had run out of oxygen and the suits became worthless, pointless. He was no longer that man in that suit. This was a fresh start for Sergeant George Kelly, and he was going to make the most of it.

Suddenly there were chocolate eyes staring up at him from within McFall's balaclava. The eyes of a child, a child still locked in a flat somewhere in Finaghy. A child that haunted him. George blinked, rubbing his own tired, red eyes. When he looked back at McFall, the man stared back nervously. No more chocolate.

He looked at his watch, realising, mercifully, that it was late. It was time for bed.

...

The sleeping arrangements seemed to revolve around Geri being the only woman in the house. She had the

155

pleasure, therefore, of her own room, while the others had to sleep in either the remaining small bedroom or downstairs. Lark ended up bunking in with McFall in the smaller of the two bedrooms, while the two cops spread themselves out between the kitchen and living room.

It made Geri feel safe. She was surrounded on all corners, her bedroom the furthest part of upstairs. She had the pleasure of knowing that if those things ever got into the house, they would have to get through the cops, then McFall and Lark, before she would be dealing with them.

Geri pulled the duvet over her tired body, snuggling into the comfort of an old teddy she'd found in one of the other rooms. She used to have one of her own, simply called Bear, and she often had to check herself from wondering what became of it. It was the epitome of selfishness to concern herself with the fate of a teddy bear, come the apocalypse.

She was hungry, the growl of her belly hoarse and uncouth over the stillness of the night. The sounds of hunger were uncannily like the sounds those things outside would make. Geri thought about that, for a moment, wondering to herself if the dead, themselves, were the very definition of 'hunger.' Hungry for flesh, sure, but also hungry for life, for the very thing that had been taken from them. Did they think, she considered, that in devouring the living, they could get one step closer to life themselves? Was it like some fucked-up version of purgatory? Either way, she hoped to God that she and the others would find food tomorrow. Otherwise, she would be seriously tempted to consider placing McFall on that fucking camping cooker he was so obsessed with fussing over. He did seem to be the weightiest amongst them. Well, maybe apart from the formidable looking cop. But, let's face it, no one was going to try and eat that scary bastard.

Her tiredness felt heavy, forceful, as if it were tying her to the bed and blindfolding her. She couldn't fight against it any longer. She simply had to give in, allowing sleep to take her into its dark domain. She was under in seconds.

Her mind refused to rest, though, eventually weaving through her hopes and fears to create a vivid dream. She could see herself standing on the street, wearing nothing but her t-shirt and pants. A sea of hot blood lapped at her ankles. She seemed strangely unaffected by it. It was as if it couldn't get to her, couldn't reach her for some reason. All around her, the friends, family, lovers she had known in the old world were drowning in the sea, blood staining their hair, faces, skin like thick sauce. They called out to her, and she tried to reach for them, but the sea cruelly beat against her hands, forcing her back with its ferocity.

She turned, suddenly, to find George standing beside her. She tried to call out to him, asking him to help those around them, but he stood stoically still, the body of a young child resting in his arms as if asleep. As she watched, the child's eyes began to open. They were beautiful eyes, and they made Geri smile. But then the child reached for George's throat with its tiny hands, pulling his exposed skin towards its mouth and biting through like toffee. Geri was screaming at George, warning him of the danger, but he just stared at her, as if this were part of his destiny, as if to reject it would be futile.

She woke to hear a hammering at the door. Her heart immediately leapt into her mouth as the cobwebs of sleep cleared. She realised it wasn't part of her dream. This was *actually* happening. The knock came again, harder and faster than before. It made her jump every time it hit. Was it the dead? Suddenly riled into a murderous fervour? Beating the door down and climbing through to devour them all in their sleep?

She climbed, quickly, from bed, pulling on her t-shirt and jeans and leaving the room. Moving into the hall, she spotted Lark standing in the landing. His profile cut a sinister shape in the dark, tall and lean, like the Grim Reaper himself, revolver in his hand. He was looking down the stairs, towards the front door. He looked up when he noticed her, dark rings circling his eyes as always, his face tired and dishevelled looking.

"What's going on?" she asked him, but he raised a finger across his lips to silence her.

She quietly joined him at the top of the stairs. She followed his gaze, focusing on the door at the bottom of the stairs. It seemed so weak to her, all of a sudden, and she wondered how they depended upon it to keep the dead out. It was literally bouncing with the force of the knocks against it.

She saw the bigger cop, Norman, moving towards it from the downstairs hallway, his own gun in hand. He cast a glance up the stairs. Lark shook his head, clearly advising the cop not to open the door, but Norman just smiled mischievously.

They watched in horror as Norman reached forward to unlock the door and pull it open. His large, bear-like arm reached through the crack in the doorway, dragging the panicked figure of a man into the hallway. Once through, Norman forced the door closed again, locking it up tight.

"Bad idea," Lark whispered, melodramatically.

...

He looked young, even with the facial hair and dirt coating his skin like tar. His face was blackened, the dirt

158

and grime of a dying city hardening around his mouth like soot. He obviously hadn't washed or changed his clothes for weeks. A large overcoat wrapped around him, soiled and re-soiled as if it, too, could speak candidly about the adventures they had no doubt shared together, the hell they had gone through. His eyes were full of fear, his scrawny, malnourished body cowering in his seat rather than sitting.

The others surrounded him at the kitchen table, the newcomer perched at the end, as if attending some bizarre interview. Norman took the lead, the cowering man seeming to look to him as the one he knew best, the one who had plucked him from the very pit of hell itself. And that was going to make Norman a man to fear or respect or thank, or all of the above.

"What's your name, son?" he asked, fixing him with a sharp, no-nonsense stare. It was obvious how intimidating the bigger man's presence could be in this type of situation.

"P-Paddy," the newcomer answered, stuttering and looking around at the others quickly.

"And how did you know we were here, Paddy?" the big cop continued.

Paddy was shaking. He was trying to find the words, but they didn't seem to be coming.

"We're not going to hurt you, Paddy; we just want to know what happened to you," George offered, trying to offset the other cop's more direct approach at questioning. He seemed almost embarrassed by the good-cop, bad-cop routine. It was very obvious, very stereotypical. But it appeared to be working; the shell-shocked survivor at the table seemed to be comforted by his words. Still he cowered, though, shivering in the coolness of the night.

George asked McFall to make a cup of tea. Paddy stared at the ski-masked survivor as he rose from the table.

"You needn't worry about him, son," Norman laughed, "He's not as scary as he looks. Quite the fucking opposite!"

But McFall said nothing, quietly draining the same tea bag he had used many times already into a half-filled cup of hot water from the camping cooker. He sat the cup down beside Paddy, who literally jumped as it tapped the table.

"Jesus," McFall said. "Steady on, lad. It's just a cup of tea, like."

"Leave him alone," Geri said. "He's obviously been through a lot."

"It's o-okay," Paddy said in a quiet whisper. "I know I'm getting on like some bloody weirdo. But it's pretty bad outside. Does things to a man, being out there for too long."

"Where were you, exactly?" Norman pried, further, trying to get the conversation back on track.

Paddy lifted the tea cup to his lips with trembling hands, gulping the contents down greedily. Once drained, he sat the cup down, looking to McFall as if an orphan asking for more.

"None left, mate," McFall said.

Geri glared at him, kicking his shins.

"Ah! What was that for? There *isn't* any left!" he protested, childishly.

"Just start from the beginning," Norman said to Paddy, assertively, clearly tiring of the nonsense bouncing between each of the other survivors.

"Alright," said Paddy calmly. He seemed to have got his gusto back rather quickly, almost as if the tea McFall had poured for him had been magical. "I'll tell you what it's like out there," he said. "But it's not going to be easy listening..."

...

"I was a school teacher before all of this happened," Paddy said, allowing himself a sardonic chuckle at that. "Even though I can hardly remember a thing about those days. How long ago it was, how good I was. I can't even remember much about the school I worked in or the kids I used to teach." He looked up from the empty teacup he was fumbling like a security blanket. "Everything changes when you've been there..." he said.

"Been *where*?" asked Geri, reaching her hand forward, placing it on the young survivor's shoulder.

He looked up at her, tears gathering at the sides of his eyes. "At the camp," he said, softly, as if it were a secret. "The Rescue Camp."

A silence descended upon the table. It was a reverent silence, but also a fearful silence. Pretty much everyone gathered had heard about the camps, some even knowing people who had sought help at one. But none of them, until now, had known of someone to return from one alive. This was history in the making. A new breed of history. The whole room was immediately hanging on Paddy's every word. The air was thick with anticipation.

"Which camp were you at?" George asked, his voice breaking a little when he spoke.

"Craigavon," Paddy said. "Near the lakes. About three hundred survivors were trucked in there, at the end. They had built it to cope with the evacuations of the bigger housing estates. I was one of the first to arrive. At the time I got there, there weren't very many people around. The camp was just opening, and although it wasn't anywhere near as good as they were making it out to be on the posters and on the broadcast channel, it wasn't *all* bad. They had plenty of food and water for everyone. Warm bedding and shelter. And it was safe, too. There were armed guards, everywhere, wearing those yellow suits."

George and Norman exchanged a glance. It was a knowing glance, and Geri wondered what connection there could be between them and the camps.

"They patrolled the area, keeping everyone in and... the dead out. I remember waking up to the sound of shooting more than once in those early days."

"Was there any medicine being given out?" Geri asked, "you know, like they promised on the posters?"

"I didn't see any medicine," Paddy said. "There were doctors, of course. At the start, it was hard to tell them apart from the guards, though. They all were wearing the same yellow suits, you see. And none of them spoke very much to you. Some of the doctors took folks away, during the early days. Especially the old and disabled. We never saw them again, but no one seemed to complain.

"Eventually, we didn't see the doctors much, either. Only the guards, and even their presence became less intense. They just told you where to go to get food and water, where to dump your waste or get washed up, and pretty much left you to your own devices after that. Some people asked for the medicine, but the guards just told them it hadn't arrived yet."

"How long were you there for?" George asked.

"A few weeks. A couple of months. One day bled into the next, so it was hard to tell. There was nothing for people to do, so most just slept the day away, waking up for the food drops. At one point, they brought us books and toys for the children to play with. But then more busloads arrived, and it was difficult to find any space to read or play anymore."

Geri felt like asking Paddy about the people she knew, her family and friends, even, to see if he had met them or knew what had become of them. But she thought it would be selfish to ask those questions, and she knew that, by the look of him, his tale was about to take a rather nasty turn for the worse.

"So, was that when things began to get worse?" George asked. "When the others arrived?"

Paddy fixed his eyes on George as he spoke. He suddenly began to weep. Silently and rhythmically. His head bowed, and his shoulders shook, like some kind of wind-up toy. It was all rushing back to him, Geri thought. Events that had stuck in his mind more vividly than his previous life, or job. She considered, for a moment, the power of 'experience'. How one event in your life could overwrite everything that had gone before it and would happen after it. For a moment, the brilliance of that scared her.

"Things got a *lot* worse when the others came," Paddy said, almost in a whisper. McFall offered him a tissue, and he took it, blowing his nose quietly before continuing. "They were bringing too many people in. I could hear the guards complaining about it to the doctors. Some of them even tried to turn the trucks away, but when it looked like a riot might start, they were left with no option but to open the gates and let them in. The dead were everywhere, then. We could smell them all around us, circling us like hungry dogs. They had completely surrounded the camp, meaning it was very difficult for the trucks to get in and out. Eventually, they just stayed there, parking in the perimeter fencing surrounding the main camp. Before long, there were too many trucks, meaning the guards couldn't open and close the perimeter entrance to allow any more to get in. And that's when things got *really* messy. You've got to remember, there was absolutely no space left, then. People were rammed in like sardines in a tin. We were sleeping standing up. The sewage system had broken down, and..."

163

Paddy broke down and started crying openly.

"Hey," Geri said, reaching her hand to sweep some hair from his forehead. "It's okay..." He looked up at her, smiling weakly through the dirt on his face. She could see that his teeth were almost yellow, and for a moment it turned her stomach. She felt immediately ashamed. The poor guy had been through hell and back, and here she was obsessing over his personal hygiene.

"The smell of the place," he continued swallowing hard. "It was almost unbearable. The guards were leaving us more and more to our own devices. They dropped food off once a day, but it wasn't enough. People started going hungry, then fighting over what was being thrown at us. At first, the guards intervened, even shooting a man dead who was fighting with some little boy over lumps of bread, but... pretty soon they stopped caring. And that's when it got even worse."

Geri wanted him to stop. She had heard enough to convince her that pretty much all hope was shot of civilisation, as she knew it, returning to normal. This was the very edge of the cliff, as far she could see. And there was no way back. Humanity had changed forever. But Paddy continued, McFall fetching him a little more tea even though he had claimed, earlier, that there was none left. From the smell emitting from the cup, Geri could have sworn he'd added a nip of vodka to it, as well.

"Eventually, the guards and doctors started fighting amongst themselves," he said, "Some even left through the gates in one of the trucks. Those that stayed were more interested in protecting ourselves than helping them... so the food stopped arriving just as regularly. And –"

"You said 'them'..." Norman interrupted, suddenly.

"W-what?" Paddy asked, seeming confused and nervous all at once. Geri felt him pull away from her.

"Just there," Norman said. "When you were talking, you used the term 'ourselves', referring to the guards, and 'them' referring to the survivors..."

"Oh, for God's sake," Geri protested, angrily. "Let the man speak, will you? This isn't a fucking interrogation!" She felt like they could lose Paddy at any time, and in so doing would lose their glimpse into a world none of them knew. He was right. His story *wasn't* easy listening. Not to her, anyway. But it still needed to be told.

"Just saying," Norman muttered, clearly a little surprised and miffed by her impertinence.

"Please," Geri said to Paddy, "just continue. Ignore him. Ignore them all."

Paddy looked to Norman for permission to continue. The big cop nodded, raising his hand in the air, dismissively.

"Well, where was I?" Paddy asked.

"You wcrc talking about living conditions in the camp," offered Geri.

"Right," Paddy said, rubbing his head as if to shake the memories out.

"Well, we were becoming more like animals by the day. The fighting got worse. The weak, the old, the ill simply wasting away, with few people actually caring for them, anymore. Things went sharply downhill. Some people were starting to develop symptoms, sneezing, coughing... the guards moved in right away, shooting them in cold blood and then... then... d-dumping their bodies over the perimeter fence." He reached for his cup with a shaking hand and downed the contents in one go. "T-t-they stopped sending any more food to us. People were killing each other just for scraps. Things got worse, all sense of decency breaking down in the camp. The guards moved in one day, not even wearing the protective gear anymore. They had been drinking... They took the younger girls from the camp, dragging them away from their parents to do God knows what. But no one cared. Everyone was too weak, too sick to care..."

"So, how did you get out?" Norman asked.

"A few of us went for the guards the next time they came in. They were drinking a lot by then and were getting careless. We managed to get past them, some of us making it to the perimeter fence trucks. We found one still with the keys in the ignition; we slammed it through the doors, breaking them down and..." he paused before finishing, "The dead were pouring through the broken gates as we left. But we just kept going, we just kept –"

"Hey," Geri said. "It's okay. There was nothing else you could do."

Paddy just put his head in his shivering hands, continuing to weep quietly. Geri wrapped her arms around his small body, as if he were a child. A silence fell on the table, everyone digesting in their own way the words they'd just heard.

"What happened to the others?" Norman said, no emotion in his voice or face. He seemed strangely unaffected, and Geri wondered why. Surely he couldn't be that cold inside? Surely even he had a heart that could melt at such a harrowing tale? She suddenly felt very angry with him. He couldn't be a good man, she thought, if he didn't feel *something* after hearing a story like that.

"We got split up," Paddy said, almost defensively. Geri could see Norman raising an eyebrow as he spoke.

"What do you mean?" he asked, still prying.

"Some of them wanted to travel to the docks, take a ship over to Scotland. I wanted to see if there was anything left of Belfast."

"So you left a relatively safe bus, filled with other survivors, who you had just been through hell with, to come... here? I'm sorry, son, but none of this adds up to me."

"W-what do you mean?" Paddy asked, looking to the others for back up. "I saw you coming and going from the house. I was hiding in a car down the road, and I –"

"You were spying on us?" Norman quipped, chuckling slightly.

"No! It wasn't like that!" Paddy protested.

"I think Paddy's been through enough," Geri said, defusing the situation.

"I-I just want to –" Paddy said, rising to his feet and then stumbling.

Lark jumped from his chair to grab hold of him as he fell. "I've got you, mate..." he said, propping the man up. He helped him through the kitchen, into the hall. He turned to the other survivors at the table. "I'll take him upstairs to the spare bedroom," he said. "McFall and I can sleep somewhere else tonight."

Geri was surprised by Lark. It wasn't like him to be so altruistic. Not since she'd known him, anyway. He'd certainly come on a lot from the days of locking her in the patio. It gave her hope to see that even a man like Lark, a man who seemed as selfish as they came, could be moved by such a story. He was human, after all, underneath all of that rough exterior. But the cop... he was still sitting at the table, his face heavy with cynicism. It angered Geri all of a sudden.

"I'm off to bed," she said, shaking her head.

"Okay, night, love," Norman called after her.

"Fuck you," she muttered under her breath.

"What was that, love?" she heard him call after her as she slipped out of the room.

...

Norman sat at the table, alone. All the others were sleeping, George in the living room and McFall curled up in the corner of the patio. But Norman couldn't sleep. His mind was still working, working as if on a case.

George had always said he'd make a good detective. He had a good nose for bullshit, and that was half the battle when it came to detective work. Unfortunately for Norman, the other half was paperwork. And that was why he never made detective. In fact, that was pretty much the reason Norman never got above constable.

Back in the day, the old days of RUC-style policing, paperwork wasn't just as important. Norman had learned to dodge it, getting some of the women in the office to sort out as much as he needed done, enough to keep the boss-man off his back. They would never have suspected that he couldn't read or write, but they knew he hadn't got what it took to make the Sarge exams.

It wasn't that he couldn't read at all. He could read some things, the important things. And he learned to look for other clues when it came to other stuff. Like the pictures around the text. Or signs, symbols. The teachers in school hadn't had much interest in him. He was too big, too stupid for any of the other kids to do anything other than avoid him. Eventually, he learned to use his size to his advantage, ruling the playground with a rod of iron. People wouldn't dare make fun of him, anymore. He made sure of it.

He thought of the story he had just heard. How it didn't make sense to him, how the scent of bullshit was heavy on young Paddy's tongue. Norman knew there was more than met the eye to him. He just didn't have the evidence to call it, though, and he knew George was too soft for his own good to listen to him. That lad always saw the best in everyone.

Lark appeared in the kitchen doorway, snapping Norman out of his daze.

"Thought you'd gone to bed," the cop said.

"Just tucking your new mate in," Lark smirked.

Norman allowed himself a chuckle. "How is he?" he asked.

"As crooked as you are," Lark said. It took balls to say something as candid like that to a man like Norman. But, as he was beginning to realise, Lark was a man who had large ones.

"How do you mean?" Norman said, still playing his cards safe.

"Oh, come on," Lark said, laughing. "You spotted the bullshit as quickly as I did."

"Maybe..." Norman said.

"Well, this might help, then..." Lark said, sliding something across the table at him.

Norman stopped it with his hand, finding a small, passport-sized ID card.

"What's this?" he asked, studying the card.

"What does it look like?" Lark asked.

Norman looked at the card, spotting various words on it that he couldn't understand. His eyes were drawn to the photograph. His eyes narrowed as he studied it more closely.

"That's your man," he said, finally.

"Bingo, Einstein!" Lark exclaimed, facetiously. "Now, don't you see what this means?"

"Well..." Norman stalled, not quite sure what the connection was.

"He was lying!" Lark said, excitedly. "He wasn't staying at the camp, he was fucking running it! Look at the ID card again."

"Oh yeah," Norman said, none the wiser. There were numbers, words, symbols on the card. He recognised the logo as one of the new governmental agencies set up to tackle the epidemic. He joined the dots, realising what Lark was concluding. "The slimy wee –"

"Yes, exactly," Lark said, finally having the cop on the same page as him. "He was fucking doing that shit to people, not having it done to him. We can't trust him, man. He's bad news."

"So what do you want me to do about it?" Norman asked. "Let's face it, none of us are saints, are we?" He thought of his own role in the quarantines. The yellow suit that *he* had worn.

"Come on, man!" Lark protested. "This is fucking different! The things they do at those camps, haven't you heard the rumours?"

"Sure, but that's all they are. Rumours," Norman countered.

"Rumours which he practically confirmed," Lark pressed. "That little story of his was practically a signed confession. We need to get him the hell out of here."

"No way," Norman said, waving his hand and throwing the card back. "I'll be watching him like a hawk, but I'm not going to turf him back out there. No way."

"Jesus," Lark said, throwing his arms into the air. "I'd have thought that you, of all people, weren't fucking soft."

"I'm not a fucking animal!" Norman yelled, suddenly angry. "So put this thing out of your head and go and get some sleep! We've a lot of fucking work on tomorrow, and I could use your help with that, rather than this bullshit." Norman could see the other man staring at him, baffled. But he held his ground. He wasn't going to be the local hard man. The 'go-to-guy' when it came to doing something unsavoury. Not anymore. This was too serious a situation for that kind of thing.

Lark looked disappointed. Deflated.

"Listen, I'm glad you told me, though –" Norman offered.

But Lark wasn't listening. "Forget it," he snapped, grabbing the ID card and storming off.

Norman watched him leave, slamming the kitchen door in his wake. *Stupid little prick*, he thought, blowing some air out of his mouth. *What did he expect? A lynch mob? A witch hunt?* But the young punk hadn't been too far off the mark, of course. Were he looking for any of those things in days gone by, he would have been talking to the right man. Norman thought on what he would have done with that information, of how it would have played out a lot differently for young Paddy even mere hours ago. The Norman-Of-Old would have wasted no time in confronting the newcomer, literally beating the truth out of him. But even his interrogation around the table had been half-arsed. More like a fucking quiz. He just seemed to have lost his oomph.

Of course, he knew exactly why this was. His mind travelled back to the off-licence and the little girl licking the blood of a dead soldier off her fingers. The events surrounding flat 23 came flooding back as well, somehow interlinked, as if both girls were the one and same, somehow intertwined in their undead quest to haunt him, to pine for his guilt.

Norman Coulter made a decision, right there and then, at the kitchen table. He would try to be a good man. He would try to treat people fairly, to act in a manner that was at least half appropriate for a man wearing the uniform. He owed it to George. He owed it to himself, to the badge on his shirt.

He also decided to right his most heinous wrong, the only wrong he could address in this new and broken down world. Tomorrow, after the supply run, he was going to visit flat 23. He was going to open up the flat, and put a bullet in that little girl's head.

...

Geri closed the curtains, blocking out the sun's rise to allow her tired eyes to close. She couldn't believe it was dawn. She was far too tired for it to be morning. She pulled off her t-shirt, then kicked the skinny jeans from her legs, awkwardly. She made a mental note to try and find some new clothes at their supply run later. Those jeans might walk out of the room on their own, if she had to wear them much longer. But, for now, she needed sleep. And lots of it.

She slipped under the covers, her body almost screaming with tiredness. She drifted off very quickly, Paddy's story of the Great Outdoors flashing around her brain like dim lights, unable to keep her awake. She felt herself beginning to dream again, the images and words mixing together, Geri finding herself acting out some of the highlights from Paddy's story at the camp. At times, she was a guard, and the survivors morphed into a herd of dead fucks. She lifted her rifle and blasted them mercilessly. And then she would be a survivor, scrambling to get out of the camp as a crowd of yellow-suited giants chased her with a huge net, as if she were some kind of animal.

She woke with a start, immediately finding herself staring into the dark face and wide, piercing eyes of Paddy. The covers were removed from the bed, and she suddenly felt cold. Paddy was spread across her, in the poor light, like a huge bear, his old, ragged coat cloaking them both like huge, dark wings. She thought that she was dreaming, at first, closing her eyes and then opening them again. But he was still there, his hands gripping her wrists tightly to hold her down. She tried to struggle, but he held her fast, his breathing intensifying, his breath heavy with alcohol and rotting gums.

She went to scream, but he placed a hand over her mouth silencing her. She tried to kick him, but his naked legs were pressed against her own. She was pinned down and completely helpless.

She looked to the door, finding it closed tight. She looked to the window, but the curtains were pulled right across, allowing only a little light into the room. She could hear the dead outside, their occasional moan croaking against the ever-decreasing morning chorus of the birds.

Paddy's eyes looked sad. Sad but desperate as he moved one hand over her throat to hold her while the other reached below his waist. She could feel the warm, moist tip of his penis as he worked it near her legs. She struggled, her eyes almost popping out from her face, but she was still unable to move. She felt as though she couldn't breathe, even though her airways weren't fully restricted. She tried to scream again, but her voice was dry and hoarse and only a pathetic squeak left her mouth. She could smell the coat, now, its mixture of the city's sweat and piss storming her nose like heavy smog. And then he began to press against her, the attempted penetration causing her bladder to weaken, the hot trickle of urine soaking her legs as he continued his assault.

The door opened, Paddy turning towards it quickly. Geri followed his gaze, finding the unmistakable silhouette of Lark standing in the doorway.

"What's going –" he began, but Paddy was off the bed in an instant, standing by the side as if embarrassed.

"What are you fucking –" Lark said, more angrily. He reached for the man, grabbing him by the overcoat, realising that he was completely naked underneath. He shook him like a tree, punching him squarely in the jaw to send him across the room, tripping on the end of the bed. Geri scrambled to cover herself with the damp, pissy duvet. Tears were streaming down her face, and she could hardly breathe.

"Get him out of here!" she screamed at Lark. "GET HIM OUT!"

Lark grabbed the other man, lifting him from the ground once again by the lapels of his overcoat. He head butted him, the attack more out of sheer anger than to immobilise him, but it both scared and bloodied Paddy.

"I didn't m-mean –" he began before being interrupted by Lark.

"Shut up!" the tattooed man bellowed in his face. "Shut the fuck UP!"

...

Lark felt more angry than he'd ever felt in his life. He dragged the scrawny shambles of a man out of Geri's room by his greasy hair. He threw him down the stairs, following him as he rolled, kicking him with his DM boot at every opportunity. Blood stained the walls. Paddy was crying like a child. Curling himself into a ball like a dog being beaten. But Lark continued to kick him vehemently.

George came running out of the living room, just as they reached the front door.

"What the hell?!" the cop began.

"He's leaving," Lark said, abruptly.

"What do you mean?" George said, his eyes heavy and hair ruffled, as if he were still waking up.

"He fucking tried –" Lark began, before checking himself. "Listen, he's not who he says he is... He's a liar. He's lied to us all."

"Wait," George said, putting his hand on the door to stop Lark from opening it. "What do you mean? What's going –"

But Lark pulled the revolver from his jeans, pointing it confidently at George.

"Move away from the door," he said, his voice shaking with anger. "Move away now, or I swear I will kill you..."

George moved away immediately, sensing Lark's anger. He was out of control. More unpredictable than ever.

Lark opened the door, immediately catching sight of the faces of several of the dead.

"P-please," Paddy said, blood seeping from his mouth and nose.

"Shut up," Lark said, lifting him and throwing him out the door. He slammed the door behind him, watching through the glass as the panicked survivor picked himself, quickly, from the ground.

"You better be able to explain yourself," George said, his voice almost shaking with shock at what he'd just witnessed.

But both men turned to see Geri looking down the stairs, wrapped up tightly in a long dressing gown. She was shivering, as if having just got out of the shower.

"He tried to attack me," she said, flatly. "If it wasn't for Lark –"

George stared at her as if she had two heads. He looked at Lark whose own head was bowed, as if ashamed. As if the attack was a slight not only against the attacker, but him, too.

Geri came down the stairs. She looked out the glass pane in the door. A cry erupted from outside. She continued to stare, unflinching. Lark moved his arm to gently lead her away from the view, but she remained where she was.

"I want to see this," she said. "I need to see this."

Lark handed George the revolver. The two men stood, quietly, respectfully, as Geri watched the dead tear her attacker apart.

SIXTEEN

"How many of them are there?"

It was Geri asking the question. George was looking out the living room window, full riot gear donned and rifle by his side.

"Six," he replied. "Fairly well spaced out." He turned to address the others, Geri and Lark in front of him, Norman eagerly standing by the front door. "Norman, you go first. Clear the way. You two follow only when it's safe to do so, when Norman has the back of the Land Rover open."

Lark exhaled, heavily.

"Deja-fucking-vu," he said to Geri, but she heartily ignored him.

Norman was out the door in seconds, his heavy frame moving with surprising agility. He raised his rifle, taking out the first of the dead quickly and quietly, a flash of the muzzle being the only sign of his approach. He moved around the perimeter of the vehicle, taking others out with similar ease.

George waited until he saw Norman open the back of the Land Rover, only then patting Lark and Geri on the back.

"Go now," he whispered.

As Lark ran, he noticed several of the dead crowding around a mangled corpse on the ground, feeding. He could make out the coat belonging to Paddy, but nothing else looked like him. In fact, nothing else gave away any clues that the carcass on the ground was human. It could have been any freshly-slain meat lying there.

Lark tried to take his eyes away from the scene as he moved towards the vehicle. Geri didn't seem interested at all. She was limping a little, perhaps still recovering from her torn foot on the first day they had met. Lark turned to help her into the Land Rover as Norman kept them covered. George moved next, nodding to McFall as he left, the door to the house slamming, loudly and uncouthly.

"Fucking tit couldn't just close the door," Lark mumbled under his breath, "Has to fucking bang it, let everyone and everything know we're here..."

But Geri said nothing. She was lost in a thousand-yard stare that seemed to speak buckets of what she had experienced the previous night. Lark didn't know what to say. He was good at using his fists, his feet, but not so good when it came to using his mouth.

George moved towards the front of the Land Rover, clambering in without incident. Lark could hear him shutting the door, but could see only the back of his head from the rear of the vehicle. He was fairly familiar with the set up of these Land Rovers. Pretty much similar to the ones he'd got more than a few drunken trips to the slammer in, after one drunken brawl too many outside the pub. *Halcyon days*, he thought to himself.

Soon, the Land Rover was kicking into action, moving fairly speedily onto the main Lisburn Road. They were heading towards the M1 motorway and the nearest available warehousing, just south of Belfast. The journey was fairly uneventful, Lark almost being lulled to sleep such was his level of exhaustion. He realised he hadn't really slept for the last few days. He had developed a kind of insomnia, it seemed. A tiredness that could never become sleep, always seeming to float around his mind, just beyond reach of sleep. Like something important that he had forgotten to do.

Geri sat facing him, head in her hands. Her red locks fell through her fingers like spaghetti. She was beautiful, and he suddenly realised he was falling in love with her, despite her absolute and obvious hatred of him. Despite the ridiculousness of falling in love in a world like this. But that was always the way with Lark. He seemed to always go for the hard-to-get types, in the hard-to-reach places, at the wrong times. Which, for a no-mark like him, meant pretty much all of womankind. Or the sane ones, at the very least.

Finally, they reached their destination. Being somewhat out of the way, they didn't expect much trouble. But George shouted into the back, advising them to stay put until he and Norman checked things out, first. A few minutes later, the back of the Land Rover opened, George standing with his riot gear intact and rifle by his side. He didn't seem too stressed, which was a good sign.

"Warehouse is clear," he said. "Plus, it's completely untouched. Good call, Norman," he said, smiling and patting his colleague on the back.

George took the lead, HK33 rifle ever at the ready, with Norman at the rear, as the survivors all moved towards the nearby warehouse. For Lark, someone who'd been on the streets since it all went down, moving from place to place, it was weird to see somewhere so untouched. In the city centre, pretty much every shop had been raided. Debris and waste littered the streets. Stalled cars sat jagged-edged along every road, some with infected bodies inside, resurrected but unable to climb out. But here, approaching the warehouse, it seemed to be literally spotless.

It got Lark to thinking that the flu may not have

spread everywhere. The people on the TV said it was airborne, and even Lark knew that was bad news. But who's to say it ever reached any other countries? With the UK and Ireland getting closed down pretty quickly, no one could be sure exactly what was happening anywhere else. Early signs suggested it *hadn't* moved through Europe, or across to the USA, but when the TV switched to Emergency Broadcast, and the phone lines failed, there really was no way of telling. Even the internet stopped working after a while, when the communications companies broke down. And that was definitely a bad sign.

"Through that door," pointed George, rifle still at the ready. "That's where I saw most of the stuff we need."

"How much is in there?" Geri asked.

George smiled in reply. "A lot," he said.

Lark opened the wooden door into the main warehouse building. His eyes lit up when he saw the full reality of what lay in store for them. A storeroom the size of a football pitch, stacked to the rafters with various colours of cardboard boxes, full of all types of things. This place must have supplied most of the major supermarkets; all the usual suspects, when it came to tinned foods and pretty much everything else, was present and accounted for.

"What's that smell?" Geri asked, seemingly only slightly impressed.

"Probably the dairy and meat locker," George said, pointing to a metal door in the corner of the store. "I'm guessing that's where the refrigerated and frozen goods were kept." A damp patch surrounded the metal door, suggesting the cooler had defrosted.

"Okay," Norman said, from the back of the group. "Let's load up as much as we can."

...

Geri found the task of helping out to be therapeutic, distracting her from the foul reality of what had happened to her earlier. She was determined not to let that experience beat her, overwhelm her. She was stronger than that, better than that. And there was no time for wallowing or reflecting on what it all meant. It was best to think that it simply meant nothing. And, for all intents and purposes it *did* mean nothing. *He* meant nothing. A stranger she never really knew, nor would know. Unimportant in the grand scheme of things.

The priority, now, was to secure as many bottles of water and canned goods as possible. Of course, Geri couldn't help but pilfer a few things for herself, as well. 'Womanly essentials', as she referred to the items she shoved into her own shoulder bag, and that seemed to be enough to stop the gents from prying any further. Once done collecting her 'womanly essentials', Geri helped load up the less heavy boxes into the Land Rover. They say that many hands make light work, but Geri thought it had probably more to do with the limited space they had in the back of the Land Rover. It filled up pretty quickly.

"Weren't we thinking of taking another van?" she said to George and the others, pausing to crack open a can of Coke which she'd liberated.

Norman looked around, seeming to recall the plan but having since forgotten about it. His eye went to a nearby white van, parked by the corrugated door of a nearby smaller warehouse.

"That one could do the trick," he said, pointing, then proceeding to move towards the vehicle.

"Careful," warned George.

"It'll be okay," shrugged Norman as he strolled over. "This place is deserted."

As the others watched, nervously, the big man searched the vehicle for any signs of life. He reached for the handle of the van's door, looking surprised as he found it to be open. Geri started to get nervous, wishing she hadn't reminded them of the plan. Norman jumped up into the front cab of the van, poking his head in and having a good root about. He appeared, shrugging, hands in the air.

"Nothing here," he shouted over. "I'll check the back and see how much stuff is loaded up."

He proceeded around to the back of the vehicle, out of sight of the others. Lark, bored of watching, returned back to the task at hand, loading the last of the boxes that would fit into the Land Rover. Geri was about to follow suit when a sudden shout startled her.

"What is it?" she said, turning to George.

George didn't answer, instead dropping his box and running towards the van as fast as he could. Geri followed, Lark calling after her but remaining where he was. She reached the van just as Norman stumbled out of the back of it, holding his hand. It appeared to be wounded, bloodied. His teeth were clenched as he looked up at the two other survivors approaching.

"You okay?" George asked him, drawing his own hand gun from its side holster.

A dead man wearing company uniform emerged from the vehicle, stumbling towards Norman.

"The bastard fucking bit me!" Norman spat, still holding his hand.

George wasted no time at all, offloading two shots into the thing's head from his HK. It fell, nothing but a scarlet stump remaining where its head had been. The thing jittered on the ground pathetically, a hoarse rasp of gas escaping from its gore-stained corpse as it seemed to 'die' again. This time for good.

"Let me see that," George said, walking towards his colleague to examine the wound. But Geri backed away. She knew whatever was going to come from the wound couldn't be good.

181

She ran back towards Lark, still rooted to the same spot he had been in before.

"What's going on?" he asked.

"He was bitten," she said, "by one of those things."

"Jesus," Lark said, rubbing the stubble on his head. "He's fucked."

"Maybe we can quarantine him, see what –" Geri started.

"You KNOW what will happen," Lark interrupted. "And with the other cop messing around with the wound, there's a good chance he'll go the same way as well."

Geri looked at the other survivor, wondering if his very obvious discomfort with the cops was colouring his thinking on this whole thing. It was an easy way to wash his hands of them, be done with them once and for all. But he didn't *seem* to be taking pleasure in it. In fact, quite the opposite seemed true. It also didn't help that deep down she knew he was right in what he was saying.

"What would you have done if I had started to show symptoms when you had me locked in the patio?" she said suddenly, not quite sure why she wanted to know. Maybe it was to try and put herself in the same position as the cops.

Lark just looked at her. His face said it all.

"Fuck," said Geri.

"We have to leave," he said, quietly. "Now." He quickly closed the back of the Land Rover, moving around to the front. Geri climbed into the passenger seat. Lark looked like he was about to follow her, until he seemed to think of something else.

"What's wrong?" Geri asked, impatiently.

"They'll follow us. In the other van," he said.

Geri looked out to the scene, noticing George and Norman still fussing over the wound. They didn't seem to know what they were planning.

"Wait one second," Lark said, grabbing the other rifle from the Land Rover.

"Wait! What are doing?" she shouted after him. For a moment, she thought he was going to shoot them. He walked halfway towards the van, rifle in his hands. He aimed, but instead of firing in the direction of the two men, he fired a volley of silenced shots at the van itself, taking out the front wheels and windscreen. She watched George and Norman jump at the noise of the breaking glass and blown out tyres.

"What the hell do you think you're doing?" one of them shouted at Lark. In response, Lark aimed the rifle at them, both cops immediately hitting the ground. Lark fired, anyway, his bullets striking the corrugated fronted door of the smaller warehouse. He hurried back to the Land Rover, still watching the two cops, while gesturing to Geri to fire up the engines.

Geri did as she was told, shuffling over to the driver's seat and turning the ignition.

"Fuck, you could have killed them!" she said as Lark jumped into the passenger seat beside her.

"Just go!" he said, throwing the rifle into the back, staring at the two cops.

George was on his feet as Geri was kicking the Land Rover into reverse gear. She could see him through the windscreen, making out a baffled expression on his face, as if he couldn't believe what was happening. She hoped to God that he wouldn't look hurt or disappointed. She couldn't bear seeing that look draw across his face. Geri turned her head to reverse, and in doing so, betrayed George as brutally as was possible.

"Shit!" she shouted, in frustration, banging a hand on the dashboard of the vehicle.

"Go, go, go!" Lark was screaming in her ear.

She turned the vehicle, quickly, changing gears with one hand, before pressing her foot hard against the accelerator. The Land Rover sped out of range, allowing Geri and Lark to look up, again.

"I can't believe we just did that," she said, shaking her head.

But Lark said nothing, his eyes glued to the wing mirror as they pulled further away.

...

Geri stuck to the main roads as much as possible for the short journey back to Belfast centre. There were fewer of the dead there. For some reason, and she feared she knew just what that reason was, they were sticking to the more densely populated areas.

Or the areas that *used* to be more densely populated.

The walls along the road were almost uniformly covered in 'flu' posters. Advice of what to do in the event of contracting the virus. Phone numbers to call and emergency helplines. Pictures of beautiful young women wearing headsets and smiling, as if they would *enjoy* talking to you about your death plague. They were the early warning signs, of course. The huge, hastily painted slogan 'Stay away, diseased bastards' hammered out more recent thinking on the infected.

Geri wondered just how many people were left now. She recalled Paddy's story of the rescue camps. How much of his story she could trust, she would never know. She remembered how some of her friends had tried to find out more about the camps, gathering at designated areas as prescribed by the Emergency Broadcast. But it all seemed just a little too wartime, for Geri. And she wasn't the countryside type, anyway. She was a city girl, born and bred.

Just as well, really.

Now, of course, the city seemed as still and barren as the countryside. Concrete jungles without any monkeys. Blocks of cement and red brick, poised against the skyline like dirty pieces of Lego. Belfast was the land of the dead, pockets of the fuckers constantly wandering the streets, as if having lost their keys. Stupid shadows of their former selves.

Or so she thought.

"Jesus," Lark said. "Check that out..."

Geri followed his gaze, slowing down a little to take in the scene. A pack of dead fucks were pacing, awkwardly, closing in on a single male. The poor bastard was hemmed in, and the dead seemed to be working together to keep him that way. They stumbled around, menacingly, like a gang of drunken sailors from some old movie. Their prey was panicking. Looking for a way past them, but they closed ranks wherever he found a spot, trapping him against a wall, closing in for the kill.

It was the first time that Geri had seen them working together. They normally acted randomly, passionately and selfishly. Now, it seemed as if they were following some kind of pack mentality in order to trap this poor bastard, hem him in.

"Keep driving," Lark said, glaring at her as she slowed the Land Rover. "There's nothing we can do for him. He's fucked."

"We're all fucked," she whispered, pressing her foot against the accelerator and moving on before the scene reached its inevitable conclusion.

...

A few short miles from the house, Geri looked at the fuel gauge.

"Christ," she said, slapping her hand on the dashboard.

"What?" Lark said, looking out the window for some incoming threat.

"We're out of fuel."

"We're nearly there. Just try and freewheel the rest of the way."

"Easier said than –"

The Land Rover engine started sputtering as if tired. The sound reminded Lark of an old person coughing. It wasn't a good sound.

"Fuck me," he said, putting one hand to his mouth, nervously, "that doesn't sound too healthy." All he could think of was that poor bastard back up the road, facing off against the new-improved-smart dead. He looked around, the empty streets glaring back at him blankly. He couldn't see any of the bastards anywhere close by. But that could change very quickly.

The Land Rover chugged to an abrupt stall, Geri freewheeling it, finally, close to the nearby pavement. It gave one final cough before the engine fell dead. Geri pulled the handbrake on.

"What now?" she asked, looking to the other survivor.

"Fucked if I know," lark said, his voice frustrated.

"Well, where are we?" she said, seeming annoyed by him.

Lark looked outside, trying to get his bearings. They seemed to be on the Donegall Road, quite close to their Lisburn Road house. Several of the dead were already moving towards them, attracted to their sudden appearance. Lark reckoned they could probably walk, or run, the remainder of the way home if not for the dead, obviously, and the fact that they desperately needed the supplies in the back of the Land Rover. Plus, a reinforced Land Rover wasn't something to throw away frivolously. Not in a world like this.

"Make sure your door's locked," Geri said, checking her own side.

Lark did similarly, even though he didn't expect their intellect to have developed to the point of negotiating locks. Mind you, he couldn't be sure how far they would develop. Or what new tricks they would learn, over time. He thought back to the poor bastard on the road, fending off the herd of dead. *You're underestimating them, Larky-Boy,* he corrected himself. *Bad move.*

"Listen, I know this area," he said. "There's a petrol station just up the road. I can see its sign from here."

"Well, I'm not getting out!" Geri said.

He looked at her, finding very real fear in her pretty face. It suited her, oddly, lending her a Celtic princess look that appealed to his inner Alpha-male. Lark felt for the very first time that she was looking to him for protection. Sure, there was *that-thing-they-shouldn't-speak-of,* but even then he was second choice; Lark was pretty sure she would have preferred Georgey-Porgey-Piggy to happen upon that Paddy bastard. With no other options in sight, though, Geri seemed willing to go with Lark for safe-keeping. *It didn't mean much,* he thought to himself, *but it was something...*

"Wait here, then," Lark mumbled, swearing under his breath. He retrieved the HK rifle from the back seat, checking to make sure it was loaded. It had half a magazine left, following his trigger-happy firing back at the warehouse.

"Be careful," Geri said, and he wondered if she meant it. He hoped she did. After all, he was doing this all for *her*. He wasn't a likely hero – God knows, no one would call him that. But something between them was beginning to click, and he couldn't ignore it. He had to stoke it, like a dying fire. Nurture it, feed it. This was Last-Chance Saloon, after all. Lark had never enjoyed much luck with ladies when there was a planet full of them. Now, with only one around (that he knew was alive) he reckoned he'd have to work a hell of a lot harder to stand any chance of getting his end away.

He opened the door quickly, stepping out into the surprisingly cool summer air. It was cloudy, and the surrounding houses cast a shadow over the road ahead. He could see the dead closing on him, less organised than the ones he had just witnessed, but threatening all the same. He smacked the nearest one across the face with the butt of his rifle, sending it stumbling back into its mate. Both of them fell to the ground, making what seemed like grumbling noises. Lark moved quickly across the road to avoid the main pack.

The petrol station wasn't far. He slung the rifle across his back, deciding to run for it. A number of the dead were littering the main road, but he reckoned he could dart around and between them without too much trouble.

He took to his feet, almost relishing the challenge ahead. It reminded him of playing British Bull Dogs as a lad in school. It was a brutal game, where one poor fucker stood in the middle of the playground while everyone else charged them. The one he managed to tackle to the ground had to join him in tackling the others, and so on until the numbers of the 'caught' were heavily outweighing the 'runners.' Lark had always been good at the game, despite his gangly frame. He was good at darting between the players, shaking off their attempts to throw him to the ground.

The dead were a lot less fired up than his mates back at school. It was like playing British Bull Dogs with people who were stoned. They hardly noticed him as he weaved in and out, becoming more cocky as he ran. He tripped a few up, more out of badness than necessity, but his playfulness almost ended in tears. A young girl, probably quite hot in her day, managed to grab his belt. She shook it, as if wanting to steal it from him, or remove it from his jeans. The latter option turned him on, rather inappropriately, but a well placed kick to the stomach shook her off.

Before long, Lark was home free at the petrol station. He bounded through the open door, slamming it shut behind him. He jammed a nearby door stopper into the wedge of the door, stalling the less than enthusiastic dead momentarily, before rolling a large display of tools across the doorway to make it more secure. He reckoned it would hold while he did his 'shopping' at the very least.

Inside it was pretty dark. Lark found a battery operated torch on the floor, thrilled to find it still usable. He was able to shed some light on the situation. The sight of a body, lying across the dairy counter, startled him, at first. As he moved in to inspect it more closely, he realised it had been there for a while. Its hair was thick with maggots and larvae. Lark turned to gag, the stench of the spoilt dairy mixing in with the body's own decay to offer a potent cocktail.

"Fuck," he whispered to himself, feeling the stench clog his throat. He needed a smoke to clear it. Fumbling in his pocket for cigarettes, Lark noticed he'd lost both them and his lighter during the scuffle with Cute Dead Girl. He looked further up the shop, moving to jump the nearby counter, grabbing a box of ropey cheap fags and a lighter from the heavily pillaged display behind the till. He sat the torch on the counter, with his rifle beside it.

He faced out into the forecourt. A single car stood by the nearby pumps. Lark could see the body of its owner inside. He wore a white shirt, with blood puked all over it. Even from this distance, Lark noticed how pristine the shirt was, despite the bloodstain. The man wore glasses, his receding hair combed to the side. He looked surprisingly regal for one of them. The poor bastard had probably died there, quietly. Maybe of starvation or thirst. Maybe from a bite, or some other form of infection.

He lit up, sitting himself on a nearby till assistant's chair, enjoying his smoke. A nearby can of Coke caught his eye, so he stuck the burning cigarette between his lips, reached into the broken cooler, and retrieved it.

He cracked it open, hearing the familiar sound of air escaping from the ring pull. Removing the cigarette from his lips, Lark drank deeply.

He sat the can on the counter and took a look around. The petrol station had been raided many times, little being left on the shelves. Lark lifted the torch, shining it across the shop floor, glass twinkling like stars along each aisle. There was stock everywhere, heavily soiled in dust, puke and random splashes of blood. A single shopping basket lay on the floor, its contents spilling out from each side as if it had been dropped in a panic. It was like some fucked up form of modern art, an exhibition on 'consumerism' or 'post-modernism' or any of those other words which Lark didn't really know the meaning of. But it was colourful. Attractive, even, if you could get past the whole 'death' thing...

Lark wandered through into the back storeroom, finding more joy among the stock waiting to go on the shelves. It seemed past visitors had been in a hurry, neglecting to bother much with the storeroom, meaning Lark was able to secure a can of diesel for the Land Rover. He checked to make sure it was the real McCoy and not some empty can. It felt heavy enough to be real and smelt bad enough.

Lark finished his smoke, watching the dead gradually closing in. They knew he was there, now heavier in number as they made their gormless pilgrimage to the petrol station entrance. Flicking his cigarette across the counter, Lark downed the remainder of the Coke, grabbed the can of diesel, rifle and torch, and quietly made for the back door across from the storeroom. He slipped out without them seeing him, switching the torch off and quietly moving across the forecourt with little interruption. Almost as an afterthought, Lark retrieved his rifle when a safe distance from the forecourt, aiming then quickly offloading several shells into a nearby pump. It went up in flames, almost immediately, the whole forecourt following suit in an almighty whoosh that gave Lark considerable pleasure. Some of the dead caught fire, waving their arms about as if dancing. They moved as if on fast forward, as if the fire was energising them as it consumed them, the yin and the yang of its powerful effect on them.

He sprinted back towards the Land Rover, somewhat surprised by the lack of challenge from the growing numbers of dead on the road. Even those around the Land Rover gave him no trouble, seemingly mesmerised by the flames, moving towards them like flies towards a light bulb. Lark was able to fill up the Land Rover with relative ease, none of the dead in any way challenging him. Bemused, he slipped back into the vehicle.

"Jesus," Geri said, "You certainly left your mark."

Lark laughed, searching his mind for a witty reply but finding none. He needn't have worried, of course. The moment passed quickly, Geri focusing more on the dead's strange behaviour.

"What's up with that?" Geri asked, noticing the dead moving towards the petrol station as enthusiastically as they could manage. None of them were bothering with the Land Rover, anymore.

"Dunno," Lark said. "Must be something to do with the fire." He watched as they continued their slow death march towards the flames. "They seem to love it!" he added, laughing.

Sure enough, a crowd gathered around the petrol station as if it were a bonfire. It was like some pagan ritual. Their actions seemed primal, respectful, even, as they stood in awe of the flames. It was as if they were learning new, exciting things. Sharing an experience that bonded them together in charismatic awe. Some stood with their heads bowed, as if worshipping. Others, incredibly, walked *into* the fire – arms outstretched as if they couldn't wait to feel its destructive heat on their fingers. Like the others before them, these mavericks lit up quickly and noisily, darting amongst the flames, as if born again, before expiring in the very energy that had mesmerized them.

"Jesus," Lark said, unable to articulate himself any better.

"Let's get out of here," Geri said, reaching for the keys in the ignition.

"No," Lark said, placing one hand on hers. "Let's just watch it for a while longer. Just a little while." The heat radiated from the fire, seeping in through the grated windows of the Land Rover. Lark basked in the warmth, noticing a sense of pride within himself which he hadn't felt in years. "I did that," he said, smiling.

...

McFall wandered through the patio doors, keen to escape the summer heat that was making the house almost unbearable. He was starting to feel like a cat in a greenhouse, burning up with sweat from both claustrophobia and humidity. He just wanted to open the back door and look out onto the garden, for one minute. Just to let some fresh air blow in from outside to cool his damp, sweaty, ski-masked face.

He unlocked the glass doors that lead to the back garden, pulling them wide open. He stepped outside like a prisoner being released, the warm, fresh air immediately kissing the exposed skin of his arms, moving through the little hairs, cooling, calming. He could feel it intensely. He hadn't graced the great outdoors since meeting the girl, and he had missed it. He sure as hell didn't miss those... things... but he did miss getting out.

He could hear their moans from the back garden. A glimpse across the fence revealed a middle-aged woman staring through the spaces in the wooden panels as if he were sunbathing naked. He smiled, thinking for a moment that she looked like his wife. She was dressed like her, wearing the same housecoat that he had bought Mrs McFall two Christmases ago.

He moved back indoors, locking them up tightly, checking the lock several times before leaving the patio and returning to the living room. It was still bloody hot, and they had very little water left. He hoped to God the others would be back soon, and that they would come bearing gifts of food and water and, most importantly, more tea bags. He was getting sick of recycling the same one. There was fuck all left in it.

The living room was still hot, its humidity causing him to feel sleepy almost immediately. He lay down on the sofa, lifting the book he'd been reading and straining to keep his eyes open as he tried to read it further.

He fell asleep within minutes, the warm and stuffy heat taking its toll on him.

Before long, he was dreaming. In the dream, he was outside again. Still wearing his balaclava. The dead woman next door was his wife, and she was no longer dead. Their wedding song was playing from an old record player in the garden, and she was asking him to dance. She smiled, reaching for his hand. She was in a much better mood than he'd ever remembered her to be in.

"I see you're still wearing that stupid mask," she said, suddenly back to her old self.

"Still wearing it?" McFall said, confused. "I only wore it from the –"

"Oh, you've always worn a mask," she said, sighing. "I've never known you without one."

The song continued to play, Mr and Mrs McFall swaying gently in its melody. McFall was thinking on what she'd said to him, wondering what she meant.

"I'm sorry I couldn't keep you safe," he said, moving a hand through her thick, dark hair. It seemed like she'd had the rollers in. He could smell the distinctive smell of burnt hair off her.

But she didn't say anything in reply. She just gripped him a little tighter, pulled him a little closer.

...

They closed in on the house, noticing the same crowd of dead there usually was. The few bodies from previous challenges lay on the street, untouched. It was weird to see them there. *Actually* dead. No danger of getting up, of coming back again. But there were others, now, simply taking their place. Geri wondered if their numbers were even larger than normal. Perhaps they were drawn to the constant commotion and sporadic gunfire like flies to light. Just like the others had been drawn to the fire. They knew it was bad for them, that shiny, sharp light. Yet they still wanted to see it, feel it, taste it.

"So, how the hell are we going to do this?" Lark asked, clinging to his rifle like a crucifix.

"Well, just shoot a couple of them and run," Geri said, pointing to the gun. "You weren't so shy earlier."

"Easier said than done," he said. "I was shooting at a larger target back there, but there's at least ten of those fucks out there, and we saw how aggressive they can get."

"At least you've got a fucking gun," she said.

"There's another one in the glove compartment," Lark said. "I clocked it earlier."

"I'll bet you did," Geri smirked. She opened the glove compartment, feeling inside. Sure enough, she struck gold, finding a spare handgun. Nervously, she pulled it out, holding it as if it might explode in her hand any minute.

"You're holding it like a girl," Lark said, laughing.

194

"Shut up!" she cried. "It's not as simple looking as the one in the house."

"Here, let me show you," Lark said, taking the gun from her. "There's no safety on these Glocks, so you've got to be careful."He dropped the magazine from the Glock, noticing it had a full seventeen rounds inside. He removed one, throwing it back inside the glove compartment.

"What are you doing?" Geri asked.

"This is a Glock 17," he said. "Holds seventeen rounds, typically. However, if you limit it to sixteen, you're less likely to find it jamming on you."

"That would *not* be cool," Geri said, blowing out air.

"Far from cool," Lark said, chuckling. He slipped the mag back in, pulled the topslide across then handed it, carefully, to Geri. "Okay, it's good to go. You've only sixteen shots in her, so no John Wayne action out there."

Geri took the gun from him, nodding a meek 'thanks'.

"Be careful, now. Oh, and remember what I said. There's no safety on that bad girl."

"Fair enough," she said. She breathed in, then out again. "You ready?" she asked, turning to look at him.

"Fuck, no," Lark laughed. "Let's just stay here. Forever."

Geri allowed herself a smile. Despite herself, she was warming to Lark. Sure, he was still a prick, but she noticed something different about him back there. Especially when he was staring at the fire. It reflected in his eyes, seeming to release something from him. Something strong and proud. Something she had found attractive. And then there was the way he smiled when he looked at her back then. There was no shittiness about that smile. No mischief or malice.

But a warm stab of guilt drew across her chest, suddenly. She thought back to how they'd left George and Norman out there at the warehouse. She thought of how they would be alone, now, in the dark. Infection spreading through the bigger one's blood like dye through water.

Neither of them had really any cause to be smiling, she thought.

"Okay," she said, breathing in deeply. "I'll open the door on three."

"Three," Lark said, opening his passenger door prematurely.

"Wait, you stupid –" Geri muttered, still remaining where she was. She watched him shoot the first of the dead point blank in the head with his rifle. He wasn't even holding it right, even she knew that, but it seemed to do the job; the sorry looking dead fuck falling to the ground, its blood soaking the windscreen. Another one stirred – this one a woman – but Lark was just as quick to aim at her head and send her the same way. He ran on to the house, banging the door furiously.

"What-do-I-do-what-do-I-do..." Geri recited, uselessly, to herself, finally reaching for the door handle and pushing it open with her teeth gritted. Outside, she could almost taste them in her throat. Their decrepit flesh was not only rough on the eye; they weren't smelling so hot, either. Their acrid stench weighed heavy in the air, and she felt herself gagging.

Most of the dead seemed to be fascinated with Lark's merry mayhem, so she was able to move fairly quickly around them, going unnoticed. What looked like the body of a young boy reached for her, though, just as she made the front garden path. She screamed blue hell at it, shoving her gun in its very mouth and blasting, repeatedly. Bits of its head exploded all over her with the first shot, the second and third finding their way through its devastated skull to shatter the kneecap of a second creature, sending it to the ground, also. Geri kicked the first corpse as it fell, like a mangy dog, backing further up the path.

"Open the fucking door!" Lark was still shouting, banging his hands so hard that they were bleeding.

Geri pressed her back against the front window of the house, both hands shaking. She was pointing her gun in the direction of the remaining dead. They began to close in on them, just like the others downtown, earlier. They were working together. Working as a pack. She could hear their growling, almost harmonising with one another as they closed rank, as if they were communicating. She could smell them, taste them, almost feel their touch on her skin as they ebbed closer.

"Fuck this," Lark spat, turning the rifle in their direction, leaning back against the door. His silenced muzzle flashed once, twice, cutting another two of them down in a haze of scarlet. Geri opened up, too, her gun's sound ricocheting through the street. The blood-soaked chest of an old woman shattered under fire, her wiry legs seeming to lose balance. A young kid, wearing a football jersey and piss-stained pyjamas, lost the side of his ear in a crimson spray. He reached his hand to where it had been, moaning as if the prelude to full-on yapping.

"Jesus fuck!" screamed Lark, a mixture of fear and excitement in his voice. The nerves were affecting his aim. He fired repeatedly at the depleting numbers, his bullets straying high, wide and on target. Eventually, the rifle clicked on empty. He continued to bang on the trigger, nothing happening past a stark, empty round of clicks. "Ah, for –" he began.

Just then the door opened, a ski-masked face appearing.

"Get in, get in!" yelled McFall. He reached out and grabbed Geri by the back of her collar, just as he had done that first day, dragging her in.

Lark rushed past him, slamming the door shut once

everyone was inside.

"Where were you?!" he barked, as the other two joined him in the living room.

"Sleeping," McFall answered, rubbing his eyes through the ski-mask, "until all of this woke me up."

SEVENTEEN

The quarantined flats disturbed her the most. Their doors and windows were boarded up, but it didn't stop the sounds from inside escaping. The hoarse, gravelly growling. The awkward shuffles. The occasional plate or glass falling and smashing. Sharp bangs at the door every now and then. The dead were with her. Inside the apartment block, riled by her every move. Karen knew they couldn't escape, but they still freaked her out. Much more than the ones she could see.

They hadn't ventured as far down as this before. Pat had thought it best to start from the top and work their way down with their campaign of pillaging. The stairwell had allowed them to bypass each floor without moving through it, even when travelling to the entrance of the apartment block. But now she stood in front of flat 23, gripping her handgun tightly.

This had clearly been the scene of a particularly brutal quarantine. The pale, grey pallor of the concrete walls and corridor were stained with splashes of rich, mahogany red. The welding on the metal sheet covering the door looked hurried and unfinished. Karen ran her finger over the join, noticing how bumpy and uneven it was, as if the welder had been rushing the job. A few bolts were missing. Some yellow tape hung off the wall half-heartedly, instead of running the full 'X' across the scene, like most of the other quarantined flats.

Karen noticed the door of flat 27, further up the corridor, hanging open. It was swaying slightly, as if dancing. Her heart was beating in time with the rhythmic slap against the door frame. Karen walked towards it, nervously. She raised her handgun as she moved. A single fly buzzed out of the doorway, making her jump. She raised her gun at it, without thinking, before checking herself.

She looked inside the flat, reluctant to actually set foot in it. A breeze blew out at her, as if one of the windows inside had been left open. A rich cocktail of smells drifted out the doorway. They were smells she was starting to become accustomed to. The thick, heavy scent of sweat. The sickly sweet taste of death, tickling the back of her throat. Rotting food and putrid dairy products. A failed sewage system. All mixed together like some hellish perfume.

Cautiously, heart still tripping, Karen moved inside. The hallway was stained with similar blood splatters as she'd seen in the corridor, slightly more vivid against the floral wallpaper. Pictures and ornaments lay in pieces on the carpet. An overturned vase, still intact, comforted its long dead flowers. Crushed china dogs ground against the carpet like delicate road kill. A smashed TV set lay crash landed on the carpet. There had obviously been a struggle here.

Karen moved through the hallway, glancing towards the bathroom. The door remained closed, a quaint picture of a cottage nailed to the wall beside it. The picture was the very antithesis to the home it had decorated. A quaint, countryside image that no longer said anything about the flat or its contents. It probably said even less about its occupants.

She inched the living room door open a little wider, peering in from a safe distance. The carpets were thick with blood, smeared across the inanely dull pattern like jam. It was as if bodies had been dragged from the scene after a rather violent struggle. Karen began to wonder about the sheer scale of what the flats had suffered before being evacuated. She knew things had got bad. God knows, she was in the heart of most of it, like everyone else still surviving. But she had left home early on, going to the church before things had *really* gone to hell. Now she began to wonder just what those who had stayed at home, or been forced to stay, had put up with before entire housing estates were closed down and quarantined the same way flats were.

A sudden movement behind her made her jump. Turning, gun raised, Karen noticed Pat standing in the hallway.

"Whoa," he said. "Only me."

"Sorry," she replied, lowering the gun. She was still angry at him from before. Angry as well as scared. She had never thought that he could hurt her like that. So violently...

"You didn't wait for me," he said, sounding almost hurt.

"I know," she said, worried of what might happen if she upset him again, "I-I didn't know where you were. I thought you might be sleeping or something."

"Oh," he said. "Fair enough, then." She watched him run his eye over the chaotic looking living room. The smashed television, its glass gathered, for the most part, in large shards just by the fireplace. Curtains wrested from their railings. Creased blinds. An overturned bucket, dried puke hardened in the carpet beside it, next to the smeared blood stains. "What a mess," he said, pursing his lips.

"You can say that again," Karen said meekly. She couldn't even look him in the eye, never mind talk to him comfortably.

"Find anything useful?" he asked.

"Smell the place," she replied, turning her nose up. "Hardly worth even looking for anything eatable." But she wasn't looking for anything to eat. She was looking for somewhere to hide, somewhere that was away from him. She couldn't tell him that, though.

"Fair enough," he said for the second time. It was such a 'Pat' comment. So guarded and lazy, giving nothing away or expressing any real emotion. That was probably why he used it so much.

Another sound disturbed them, this one coming from back down the corridor. It was a high pitched sound, somewhere between a cry and a moan. At first Karen thought it was just the dead, perhaps becoming as scared and frustrated and restless as she was. But when it sounded out again, Karen noticed something unique about it...

EIGHTEEN

"And you just... left them there?" said McFall, after Geri had told him the story. They were sitting in the living room. McFall had made some tea, using a tea bag he had liberated from the bin. Desperate times called for desperate measures.

"Well, it's not like they're locked in the patio, is it?" she countered, "With no food for three days?"

McFall thought about that for a while, then shrugged. He couldn't believe she was still hung up on all of that.

"They'll have everything. An almost endless supply," Lark offered. "Not that they'll need it, of course. That big fucker will be dead within a day."

"You don't know that," Geri said, sharply. It seemed she was obviously feeling guilty for leaving them. McFall was starting to wonder if they should have left her in that damn patio for good. She was too emotional, too unpredictable. And those weren't the ingredients for a quiet life. God knows what she'd do if push came to shove.

"Well, it's pretty likely that you'll pick up a fucking airborne virus from a bite," Lark said, sarcastically. "And, by the way, it wasn't *only* me who decided to leave them, was it?"

"Well, it wasn't me who decided to shoot at them!" Geri yelled back at Lark.

"Jesus, calm down, for fuck's sake," McFall said to both of them, shaking his head. "It's done, now. And probably for the best. That bigger one was a complete prick. I'm glad he's been bitten, to be honest with you."

"How can you wish that on *anyone*?!" Geri screamed at him. "You've seen those things out there! Can you imagine actually becoming one?" McFall thought about that for a second. He couldn't imagine it, really. He hadn't really thought past getting infected, or maybe being eaten alive by them at the very worst. To actually *become* one of them had never entered his mind.

"That other cop will deal with him," said Lark. "George, or whatever his name is. He'd never let his mate end up like that. No one would."

"What about George, then?" Geri asked, antagonistically. "It's pretty fucking likely that he'll end up the same way, with no one to deal with *him*!"

"It's not our problem!" snapped Lark. "Jesus, if you felt so bad, why didn't you stay with them."

Geri put her head in her hands, deflated. It sounded like she was crying. McFall almost felt sorry for her. He never liked to see a woman cry. He'd made his wife cry over the years they were together – mainly for stupid things, like getting into a fight or losing his job. It always made him stop and think when he'd driven her to tears, though. It was like the final straw, the blaring foghorn on a ship rolling in on a rainy night. He always worried she might leave him when she was crying.

"Look," McFall said, sighing, "the whole world's fucked over, love. You can't let this thing get you down. You gotta look out for number one, now. That's the bottom line." He was trying to comfort her, but it seemed to have the complete opposite effect. She immediately jumped up and ran upstairs, slamming the door shut behind her.

"Fucking women..." Lark muttered to himself. "Jesus H Christ..."

"What if they come back?" McFall said to him, speaking even more candidly now that the girl was gone.

"What if *who* comes back?" Lark replied, impatiently.

"The fucking cops!" McFall exclaimed. "They know where we live."

Lark just looked at him, seemingly dumbfounded.

"I think they'll have enough on their minds without –"

"Wanting to fuck over the guys who shafted them, left them to die a horrible death? Come on, mate, you've already said yourself that they're pretty much screwed. They won't have much to lose, then, by trying to get their own back..."

Lark looked scared as the sense of what McFall was saying hit home.

"Okay," he said, finally. "Guess we've got to hit the road, then."

"Do we take her with us?" McFall said, quietly, pointing in the direction of the stairs.

"What?" Lark said, sounding surprised. But McFall knew he'd heard exactly what he'd said.

"I'm only saying, like. She's been nothing but trouble. Might be worth just slipping out, like, and saying nothing."

Lark glared at him, that all too familiar expression of disbelief spreading across his face.

"You're such a dick," he said, finally. "Of course we take her. We're not fucking monsters." And with that, Lark disappeared up the stairs leaving McFall alone again.

He stared over at the TV set in the corner. He suddenly remembered his wife's favourite show. It was a holiday programme, full of sunny beaches and deep blue skies.

She would watch it and then turn around to him and ask him why they never went on holiday any more. Of course, McFall could only say things like *I'm too busy with the taxi driving*, or, *Sure, we have everything we need here*. The real reason, of course, was that McFall was a man who feared change. He liked the status-quo. He liked his routine and he liked having a life that was predictable and safe.

He suddenly felt bad that he hadn't taken the missus on her holiday. He thought of all the cash in the bank he'd clocked up – all worth absolutely nothing, now. He could have used some of that to take her away. It would have made her happy. Now it was too late.

His eyes lingered on the television, a machine unlikely to ever work again. Dust had gathered in a thin veneer over the flat screen. It almost looked like sand.

NINETEEN

"Where's it coming from?" Karen asked.

Pat wasn't sure, of course. The old hearing was never the same since his rifle had misfired back in '87. His orders were to take out a fairly well-known loyalist politician. He had the bastard in his sights, but a dodgy shipment from Libya meant not all the rifles were in tip-top condition, shall we say.

"It's definitely somewhere on this floor," he said, lying, unable to hear the damn noise, at all.

"That's what I thought," she whispered, as if worried whatever was making the noise would run away if discovered. They moved back down the corridor to the flat she had passed earlier that day. Flat 23. As they drew closer to it, Karen's ears seemed to prick up, again. "It's coming from that flat," she said.

"Which flat?" Pat asked, still clueless.

"Can't you hear it?" she said, suddenly perturbed. It was as if she wouldn't believe the sound was real unless he could also hear it.

"Not really," he said, laughing uncomfortably. "My hearing's a bit gone, you see."

But she wasn't interested in Pat's hearing. Her own ear was pressed against the door of flat 23. She pulled her hair back with one hand, still gripping her handgun with the other. She looked like she was tuning a radio station, eyes narrowed in deep concentration.

"What is it?" he asked, "What do you hear?"

"Shhh..." she said.

He noticed the light catching her face, now her hair was pulled back. A huge bruise spread across her cheek, where he'd hit her with the rifle. A sharp pang of guilt ran across his chest, almost causing him to cough. But then she jumped, and Pat jumped with her. Whatever it was she was hearing had sounded again. Only, this time Pat thought he could hear it, as well.

"Oh my God!" she said, turning to look at Pat.

"I definitely heard that," he said. And he had. It was a banging noise, as if someone or something were behind that door. At first he thought it was one of the dead, locked into their death bed, like all the other quarantined. But when he listened more intently, turning his good ear towards the door and tuning in just as Karen had done, he could hear something different. It wasn't just the banging, there were other sounds, too. Not the hoarse, croaking coughs of the dead nor their heavy, sombre footsteps. These sounds were different. They were more animated. More human.

...

Jackson awoke with a start, finding himself on the ground of the control room. His eyes looked around, noting that Gallagher, the private and everyone else was where they had been earlier, all eyes on the monitors. The pilots of the helicopter had returned; both men now sat with the others.

Jackson struggled to pull his tired, wounded body against a nearby cabinet, leaning back and wincing against the sharp pain of the bullet wound. He noticed the shell on the floor. It had gone right through him. It was a clean wound. Yet, despite this small blessing, he was powerless to do anything except keep his eyes fixed on the screen like all the others.

He watched as Gallagher quickly moved to a nearby filing cabinet, reaching to open it before flicking through various bits of paper and card. "We have records, here, of all the new occupants of the target areas," he mumbled to the others. "Even when the project was drawing to a close, it was still thought best to keep the records up-to-date... just in case..."

His eyes suddenly fell upon Jackson. "Ah, you're back with us, sir," he said. "And not in the undead sense, it seems."

"Fuck you," Jackson said, his voice weak and raspy.

Gallagher laughed."Please, Major," he said, returning to flick through the files, as if Jackson were only of limited interest to him. "There's no need to be so rude."

"Sir, you might want to see this," the private said, interrupting them. Both Gallagher and Jackson looked towards the screen. The private had moved the view to outside the flat, again, where Jackson had first noticed the signs of quarantine in the first place. The monitor now showed two survivors, a man and a woman, standing outside the flat as if about to enter. Even though the image was not entirely clear, it was most likely to be Patrick Flynn standing there at the door.

"Patrick, Patrick," Gallagher said. "Looks like you and I are going to have that chat, after all..."

TWENTY

The storeroom was cool and damp. Boxes stood tall and broad, stacked in large cubes throughout the main storage area. A small office ran off the main room, several dusty computers, untouched for weeks, resting on the desks of admin staff who were most likely dead (or undead?) now. Filing cabinets, packed to the gills with archived invoices and stationary, remained locked up tight, as if valuable. They had no value in the new world, though. They would remain locked tight, for the duration of time, never to be opened again.

George leaned back on an opened box, drinking from his liberated bottle of mineral water. The scented candles he'd laid out offered a little light, as well as fighting against the nauseating smell of rotten produce. He pulled himself to his feet, moving to the corrugated shutters that led to the great outdoors. He had locked them tight, earlier. He checked them to make sure they still held. Satisfied, he returned to the crudely constructed bed of his friend.

Norman lay on a brand new camping bed with the tags still attached. His huge frame filled the rickety-looking thing, its legs almost buckling under the weight. He was wrapped in a padded sleeping bag, also new, making him look even bigger - like a caterpillar straining to shed its skin. His face was pale, and his eyes were bloodshot. But he was laughing.

"Do you remember that time whenever you were first made Sarge, Geordie...." he said, "and all the guys in the canteen painted those little Hitler moustaches on themselves..."

George smiled at the memory.

"Sure, mate. I remember." It had been – what – three, four years ago? Yet, it seemed like only yesterday. For George, it might as well have been yesterday that he got the stripes and the much welcomed pay rise to go with it. He still felt he was learning the ropes, still felt he was fresh to the job. Of course, the irony now was that the stripes on his arm meant nothing. The last person to place any value on those three white lines was lying beside him, hanging precariously between life and...

George reached out , as Norman suddenly bent double on the bed, laughing giving way to coughing. Speckles of blood were scattered across the nearby cardboard boxes, like Ragu sauce. George wiped his lips, gently, with a wet baby wipe. The older cop settled back, again, blowing out some air.

"Fuck me," he said, suddenly serious.

His breathing remained heavy and deep. Each cough was almost tangible, as if you could catch it in your hand, like clay. He was drawing close to the end, to the Great Whatever that lay beyond life, and beyond the shadow of life that the virus offered. But Big Norman was laughing, when he could. He wanted to enjoy every last moment of life. He wanted to suck in every last breath that was due to him, fuelling a few more moments, a few more seconds. And it was breaking George's heart to watch him struggle like that.

"And that other time, when we were sent out to that old bloke's house," he said, cracking his tired skin to smile again. "You remember, don't you? The one who had been dead for about four weeks before the neighbours caught a whiff of him..." Norman coughed

211

again, his eyes strained and face full of pain as he bent over. Sweat broke across his forehead, like raindrops on a leaf. George sat down on the cold, concrete floor by his side, reaching forward with a fresh wet wipe, this time to cool his partner's forehead down. "And he was just lying there, wasn't he mate?" Norman continued. "He was just lying there, pants around his ankles... with a clothes peg on his cock."

George allowed himself a chuckle at that one. He remembered the old man well. He'd lived on his own for years. No family, very few friends. His flat had been an absolute fucking mess, suggesting the four-quid-an-hour home help hadn't been putting much backbone into her work. He recalled asking the guys in the morgue why the old boy had the clothes peg like that. They'd thought it was to stop his urine leaking. Seemed the old boy was fighting incontinence, as well as the cancer. In the end, though, it was a heart attack that took him. George remembered Norman shaking his head at that one. Then laughing.

"The things you see in this job. Eh, Norman?"

"You said it, mate..." Norman coughed again, harder this time. "You said it." He turned to look at George, suddenly serious for a moment. He reached out his hand, George grabbing it and holding it tight. It was cold as ice, and clammy. The flu was rinsing every bit of heat and moisture from his body. "We had some good times, mate..." he said. "I'll be honest, though... I thought you were a prick when I first met you. All rule books and regulations. You loved them, mate! You weren't an old-style, get-stuck-in RUC man, like me..."

"Well, I learned the hard way, Norm..."

"You did, mate. But you always kept your cool, though. You never lost it, like me... not until –"

"Don't, Norman. Don't go there..."

"I have to, mate. We haven't talked about it... and –" He coughed harder, this time, and more sharply. It was as if he were puking up knives. As if his tubes and airways were made of barbed wire, now, stabbing him with every breath he took. "And, I think we need to..." he continued in a low, crackling voice.

His face was paling fast. Like there was a hole at the bottom of his feet, all the colour draining out and down some invisible drain. Norman wiped his mouth, a slither of bloody bile spreading across his arm like a dead snail. He looked at it, disgusted by himself. George reached forward with a towel to quickly clean him.

He thought back to that fateful day, the day of the quarantine. George had tried to blot it out, shake it from his memory the way dogs shook water from their hair. But it wasn't so easy. There was too much dampening his conscience. And that little girl's ghost wouldn't let it lie. The scene in the old woman's flat. He could almost smell its mustiness in the air, now. Her husband, lying dead on the couch only minutes before, getting up and walking. The crowds banging against the door. The old man walking towards Norman. The old woman hanging off his arm, screaming. The crowds breaking the door down, coming at him. The gun, raised again in his hands...

"They were coming to us for help, weren't they, mate? Running away from something else. From those fucking –" He began coughing again, having excited himself. He fought for breath, grabbing his chest as if expecting it not to work. "We fucked up," he said, a primal keen escaping his throat. "We really fucked up... They weren't coming *at* us. They were coming *for* us!"

George stood up, turning away from the candid words of his fading friend. He recalled that night like it was yesterday. Or an hour ago. Or two minutes ago. Or right now. The crowds closing in on them. A much healthier Norman swinging his baton without discrimination. He never had been a man to take any shit, George thought.

Then he thought of himself. Standing there, hands clammy. Visor damp with the quickening of his breath. And that woman. The one who'd been shouting at him, the one with the phone. He remembered her judging him, shaking her head. He remembered wanting to give her something to *really* judge. He'd fired at her with anger. He remembered that, too. It was the first time he'd fired a gun with real anger in his heart. He also remembered enjoying it. And not just the act of petty vengeance; he remembered enjoying the aesthetics, too. The shot piercing her neck, tearing through her skin like a knife through bread. How she fell into the crowd, gripping her torn, useless throat, eyes gaping from under her hair like tiny, bright bulbs.

And then they had been upon him, grabbing him, begging him. He was surrounded, people flooding into the room and gathering behind him like a big brother in a schoolyard fight. They wanted him to protect them, guard them, help them. They wanted him to *police* them.

George turned to this friend. He watched Norman pull a small clear plastic bag from his breast pocket. It was full of white dust.

Norman smiled, guiltily.

"Picked it off that wee –" he paused to cough more dagger-sharp phlegm up, "scrotum back at the house..." George had seen Norman take similar bags from people before. He would have pinned them up against the wall, taken the dope from them, then beat blue hell out of them. George had usually turned his head, wandering down a nearby alleyway, at that point. Norman would return as if nothing had happened, sliding into their patrol car and muttering something about grabbing a McDonalds or coffee. It was just one of those things.

"What?" Norman said, spluttering slightly, then wiping his mouth with a shaking hand. "Are you going to judge me even now?"

George had never said anything to Norman about the drugs, but the older cop would have known rightly what his younger colleague thought of it all. It was a damnable offence for a police officer to be involved with illegal drugs. George knew he should have disciplined Norman in the appropriate manner. But, in reality, he had always felt intimidated by Norman. Especially in the early days. It was Norman's age and length of service. His experience. The fact that the big man had survived the very worst years of policing in Northern Ireland. His cynicism about the way things were done now, compared to the way things were done then. He made George feel inferior, even as his superior. He never felt able to question Norman, chastise him, discipline him. Of course, Norman gave something in return for George's silence, his submissive respect. The older cop's loyalty was second to none. He would back George up to a fault. Anyone in the force talking shit behind the young Sergeant's back was in danger of a bloody nose, courtesy of the big man. For George, much of the success he enjoyed (endured?) was due to having Norman watch his back. It was a quiet trade-off between the two men, an unwritten rule. Never questioned nor even verbalised.

Until now.

"I never judged you, Norman," said George. "But I was disappointed in you." There. It had been said. And George almost felt weak for waiting until now. He wondered to himself what exactly was the point in saying something like that to a dying man. A weak man, wrapped in his own piss and puke and sweat like some kind of drunk on the street. He knew he wouldn't have said that to a healthy Norman, to a Norman who was strong enough to stand on his feet and look him in the eye. So, what would it achieve to say it now?

But Norman seemed not to care about those kinds of details. Norman had other things on his mind, other, more important things which needed to be said, needed to be addressed.

"Look at me, George..." he said, his voice growing weaker, his breathing ebbing closer to his chest.

George turned and looked at his partner of five years. He was fading fast. As far from the man he'd first laid eyes upon as heaven was to hell. The formidable man. The intimidating man. None of those things could be said about Norman now, lying on his makeshift bed, crudely wrapped in his stained sleeping bag. The white dust was lying open in front of him, its pure, bleached colour mirroring the pallor of his face.

"You got to go back to that flat... finish business with that little girl. I can't rest until I know she isn't walking around like one of those dead fuckers..."

"Norman, it's too –"

"You got to promise me, George!" he begged, tears glistening in his big, heavy eyes.

George had never seen Norman cry before today, never known he *could* cry.

"Okay," George promised. "I'll do it."

Norman nodded, seeming able to relax more, now that he'd said his piece and got George's word. He seemed to be ushering in death's final embrace, opening the doors of life to allow the Great Leveller a private audience. He reached down to the white dust sitting in the clear plastic bag on his lap. His mouth was hanging open, thick, viscous blood building at the corners of his lips like red jelly. He dipped his fingers in the white dust, messily, like a kid caught in a pie shop. He looked feral. Desperate. In pain. George had seen this before in a dying man. A recklessness. An acute awareness of himself. A final splash of indulgence, just for the hell of it.

He sucked the dust up one nostril like a drowning man fighting for breath. And then, at the end of his arduous fight for pleasure, his hand shook briefly, before falling to his side. His head rolled over one shoulder, eyes still wide and hungry. George wondered if he'd even felt the last hit.

Quietly, George moved over to his friend's bedside. He took the white powder from his hands, using another wet wipe to remove the excess from his nose and mouth. He wiped the sleeping bag where more of the powder had stained like talc. He wiped his collar, his shirt. He wiped his badge. He crumpled the small bag and wipe together and shoved them into another plastic bag, throwing it in the corner as if to discard later.

Then he sat down on the concrete floor again and ran a hand through Norman's hair. It was matted and sweaty, like pond reeds.

"I'm so sorry, mate..." he said, simply. "I'm so very sorry."

...

McFall lifted the dried up teabag they had used and reused as if it were a dead mouse, dropping it into his teacup and standing back as if it might explode. He poured the last of the water into the cup, heated using the camping cooker. Finally, he added two spoonfuls of sugar.

"Where's mine?" Lark asked him.

McFall looked defensive.

"It's the last of the water," he said. "You were meant to bring more back, but you didn't."

"Oh, so it's my fault we've fuck all here, is it?" scowled the tattooed man. "Even though I went OUT THERE," he continued, raising his voice for dramatic effect, "twice, no less, while you sat here on your lazy, fat arse –"

"I've been cleaning up!" McFall countered. "It's not like I've been doing nothing! And, anyway, it's not like I've never done a supply run in all the time we've –"

"ONCE!" Lark shouted over him. "One single run! And all you brought back was a fucking girl! Who may have been infected!"

"Like you're complaining, mate!" McFall laughed.

"What's that supposed to mean?" Lark asked, a baffled look drawing across his face.

"Come on!" McFall said, still sniggering. "I've seen the way you look at her!"

"Fuck off!" Lark said, looking uncomfortable. He grabbed a magazine, flicking through it suddenly. Feigning interest in some article on golf. McFall really wouldn't have pitched him as a golf lover, though. He sat down with his tea, continuing to laugh at his friend's expense, especially when he noticed Lark's face growing red.

"Look, we're all going to have to leave here tomorrow morning," Lark said, clearly in an attempt to change the subject. "How will you feel about that? Going out there, again, eh?"

"No problem," McFall said, as if the thought didn't bother him. "It's not like I can't go out; it's just I haven't had the opportunity."

"Bollocks!" Lark laughed. "You're a chicken shit! It fucking terrifies you, the thought of going out!"

"No it doesn't!" McFall stressed. "I just don't see the point when –"

"When someone else is stupid enough to go out there for you?" Lark interrupted.

McFall seemed stumped by that one, unable to come up with a retort.

"See?" Lark said, leaning back, all proud of himself. "You're chicken shit."

McFall went to say something, but he was interrupted. He reached for his balaclava-clad face. His head leaned forward, as if within a spasm, as if he had lost control for a second. And then he heard himself sneeze, the blast leaving his mouth and staining the woollen gauze of the balaclava.

For a moment, neither man spoke. Both just stared at each other, frozen to their seats.

"It's maybe j-just the dust," Lark said, finally, his voice hoarse and nervous.

McFall said nothing, simply rolling up his balaclava and wiping his mouth and nose.

"Seriously, mate," Lark said, slightly softer this time, "it's probably just –"

But he was interrupted when McFall sneezed again.

Lark pushed back his chair to dodge the blast.

McFall turned towards Lark, his mouth upturned in a panicked gurn.

"Do you think it's just dust, mate?" he asked, eyes damp and leaking through the balaclava. "Really, I mean?" But Lark had no reply. He just sat there, as if still glued to his seat. The magazine still opened beside him at that golf article. Quietly, he reached forward to hand McFall a tissue. McFall accepted it, wiping the corners of his eyes. "It's just the sneezing," he said, his voice cracking. "I'm not crying or nothing..."

Lark got up slowly. He kept his eyes on McFall as he backed towards the door to the hallway. He didn't leave, though, standing for long moments, staring at McFall, as if disbelieving what was happening.

"Sorry, mate." He said simply, eyes still wide as if he'd just seen something shocking and unbelievable. "I'm so sorry, mate."

"It's okay," McFall said, looking down at the table. He lifted the magazine and box of tissues, not knowing exactly why he needed the magazine. He had no more interest in golf than Lark had.

"I'll get you a beer from the van," Lark said, eyes still wide.

"That would be nice, mate." McFall said. "I'll just —" he began, but a third sneeze surprised him, causing him to jump and Lark to raise his arms, as if the blast was like poisonous gas. He shook his head, sniffing loudly then coughing to clear his throat. "I'll just be in the patio," he said, finally.

TWENTY-ONE

"Can you open it?" Karen asked, impatiently.

"It's welded shut," Pat replied, running a finger over the rough line of the join. It was obvious to them both that whoever had done the job had been under pressure. Nervous, even.

"But you can still open it," she said, quickly, "We really need to open it." Pat looked at her like a father might look at his nagging daughter. She knew he needed time to think, time to work out the best way to get the job done. Nothing, to a man like Pat, was achieved through impatience. He wasn't one for taking shortcuts.

He ran his hands over the metal panels bolted across the doorframe of the flat. Karen could see that it had been a rushed job, the bolts only half secured.

He reached into his tool bag, retrieving a wrench. Karen held the torch so that he could see what he was doing in the poor light. Using the wrench, Pat eased out the third bolt from the panel across the door of flat 23. As predicted, the panel swung away, clinging only to the final bolt on the lower part of the frame. It revealed enough of the door for the two survivors to break into the flat.

Once inside, Pat reached his own hand out to help Karen past the metal panel. They moved slowly through the hallway, checking the kitchen first. Pat's torchlight revealed nothing unusual, save the metal panels bolted across the windows. A damp stain ran through the wallpaper, just where the cupboards met the wall. The usual stench of decaying food wafted from the fridge, Karen's nose almost accustomed to it, now. A gas cooker stood next to the fridge, its rings tarred with burnt residue. An empty bottle of water lay on the worktop, as if dead.

Pat slowly opened the door, shining his torch back into the hallway. From her vantage point, Karen thought she could see movement, and it made her jump.

"What is it?" Pat whispered.

"I thought I saw something move," Karen replied.

Pat stepped into the hall, gun pointing alongside the light. His poise reminded Karen of a marine from the footage she had seen on the news. He moved assertively and fearlessly into the hall, ready to pump lead into whatever nasty that presented itself.

Karen followed him, snapping her own torch into action and trying to emulate Pat's poise with her own handgun. Together they searched the living room, finding nothing of interest. From the quality of furniture in the house, Karen thought that the residents were fairly poor. She noticed a photo sitting on the coffee table by the old television set, lifting it and shining her torch on it.

"It's a picture of a woman and a little girl," she said, carrying it to Pat. "They look kinda foreign or –" She suddenly tripped over something on the floor, jumping with the shock of it. The photo clipped from her hands, the glass of its frame splintering as it hit the coffee table. She shined the torch down, finding some glass on the floor. A tin of paint sat at her feet beside the broken glass. It seemed someone had been planning to spruce the place up before everything changed and redecoration became the least of their concerns.

"Jesus, keep it down!" Pat said, irritated.

"Why?" she said, "I thought they couldn't hear anything." She was referring to the dead, of course. Of their blocked sinuses. Of Pat's theory on how that would mean they couldn't hear very much.

"You still need to be careful," Pat mumbled grumpily. He seemed guarded to her, more awkward than ever. It was as if he were embarrassed by what had happened before. By what he'd done to her. Karen began to feel a little sorry for him. She began to entertain the possibility that maybe it had been her fault, maybe her constant neediness had made Pat do what he did. Maybe she'd pushed him too far, leaving him with no choice but to lash out at her, lash out, even, at the helicopter that could, for all intents and purposes, have been their salvation.

She thought back to the church where she'd first taken refuge. Of how she'd shied away when other people tried to protect her. Of how they fought bitterly while she hid, scared and useless. Cowering like a big baby. They had died trying to protect her, died without saying a single thing against her. But Karen wondered if things would have been different were she not around. If they would have managed to survive, managed to keep the dead out and the virus at bay. She began to wonder if she were the one who brought misery to a place. Contaminating everything and everyone she touched, like the flu itself.

A sudden noise shocked Karen out of her maudlin thoughts.

"Did you hear that?" she whispered to Pat.

He nodded silently. He pointed out the living room door and down the hallway, bringing a finger across his lips to silence her. They moved out of the living room, noticing the bathroom staring back at them from the other end of the hall. They moved towards it, both survivors taking care not to cause any noise with their approaching footsteps. The door was closed tight. A sudden knock against it startled both survivors. It was the sound they'd heard from the living room.

"Okay," Pat whispered. "I think there's one of them trapped in there."

"We should check," Karen said, "because whatever I heard from outside sounded more human. You heard it yourself, too."

Pat nodded, another knock confirming his diagnosis of the situation. It was a hollow knock, weak and lethargic. Not frantic, like what Karen would expect from a trapped human. Pat pointed at the door handle with his handgun, standing a safe distance from the door. He motioned to Karen to stand back.

He fired twice, blowing the handle into pieces which fell onto the carpeted hall floor.

The door suddenly swung open, revealing the heavily bloodied and bile-stained body of a woman, who stood glaring at them. She moved suddenly toward Pat, but he fired another two shots, splitting her head in the same way he split the door handle. The woman fell to the ground, her body jerking, momentarily, before falling still.

"Was it the woman in the photo?" Karen asked, realising her heart was racing with the action.

"Probably," Pat said.

"I really didn't think the sounds I heard were from... one of them," she said, unable to take her eyes from the body.

"Okay," Pat said, turning away from the fallen body. "Sure, we'll take a quick look –"

But he paused, standing stalactite still in the corridor, eyes fixed on something further down. He fell completely silent, and Karen followed his gaze to see why. She noticed a figure in the darkness at the other end of the hallway. She lifted her torch, instinctively, finding the shape of a little girl, probably six or seven years old, looking back at her. Her tiny, chocolate brown eyes were wide and hungry looking. Her mouth and nose were swollen and caked in dry blood.

Pat looked at her, not seeming to know what to do.

The child suddenly started to cry, the way normal, human children did. Karen realised it had been this very sound she'd heard from the flat.

"My God..." Pat said, rubbing his mouth. "She's alive. *Really* alive"

TWENTY-TWO

She woke up with a start.

She'd been dreaming about George and Norman. In the dream, Norman looked frail, about twice his age. He was running awkwardly through the streets of Belfast, as if trying to flee the dead. But it wasn't the dead he was fleeing. It was the living. George, Lark, McFall and herself hunting him. Growling like animals as they gave chase. Foam drooling from their mouths, as if possessed.

Geri noticed light pouring in from the curtains. It couldn't be that late. She pulled the duvet back, realising that she was still wearing her jeans and t-shirt. She couldn't remember getting into bed. God, she must have been so tired. Slipping on her trainers, she moved quietly out of her room and crept down the stairs. She heard a sound coming from the kitchen. She paused, noticing her heart leaping for a second. Gingerly, she moved into the kitchen to investigate.

She noticed a man in the patio, but not someone she recognised. He was squat, stocky, with thick, curly hair. He sat calmly at the patio table, drinking beer. He didn't look like an intruder. In fact, he looked comfortable. Almost familiar. She wondered, for a second, if he were someone whom the others had met while she was sleeping.

She noticed the revolver sitting at the kitchen table. She reached for it slowly, checking, quickly, that it was loaded. Against her better judgement, she moved to open the patio door.

The man looked up, noticing her.

"No, don't open it," he said. His voice was familiar.

Geri froze. On the table was a balaclava. Beside the balaclava was a box of tissues and a magazine. A used tissue lay on the floor beside the table. It was stained with blood. The man sneezed. He followed up the sneeze with a laugh. Tears filled his eyes, and she wasn't sure if they were from sneezing or crying.

"It's not hayfever," he said, smiling. His smile was warm and attractive, and that surprised her. She had never thought he'd look like this under the woollen mask. She'd thought he'd be ugly, even stupid looking. She'd treated him as if he were ugly and stupid.

"I'm sorry," she said, pressing her hand against the glass.

"Don't be," he said, still smiling. He lifted a can of beer from the table. "Lark brought me it," he said, grinning comically.

Geri smiled back. "What'll you do?" she asked, not sure what else to say. She'd never had much of a rapport with McFall. None of them had, apart from Lark, maybe. There was no point in trying to pretend otherwise.

"Have another a drink or two," he said, "Lark brought me a few." He took another swig, burping at the end of it. "Then, when they're done, I was hoping to go out with a bang." He pointed to the revolver in her hand. "All those films you see," he said, looking at the gun as if it was something rare and precious, "tell you that you have to shoot them in the head." He looked up at her, and she could see that his eyes were red and puffed. "I don't want to be one of those things," he said, choking slightly.

Geri felt a lump gathering in her throat. She didn't want to lose it, not in front of him. It would seem insincere to shed crocodile tears. It would also be selfish. He didn't need that, now. She didn't know what he needed, but it wasn't that.

"You better go," he said, almost as if sensing her discomfort. "Probably best you leave the house. I think Lark's gone, already. Just leave me that revolver"

She pressed her hand against the window, again, as a goodbye. It left a clammy print on the glass which blurred her view of his face.

Geri sat the revolver on the kitchen table then moved through the kitchen into the hallway. Moving back upstairs, she retrieved the Glock handgun Lark had found for her earlier, pausing to pack a few things into a bag. Lifting both bag and gun, she went back downstairs, reaching the front door. She looked out the small window. The Land Rover was still parked where they had left it, just outside the house. Lark had obviously not taken it when he'd left. She thought she could remember leaving the keys in the vehicle. Several of the dead hung around, as if bored. She felt as if they ruined the moment she had just shared, seemingly oblivious to the ill-fated McFall. For some reason, Geri thought they should be doing something different. Bowing their heads in respect. Anything, really, to offer their condolences. Gloating, even. But to just ignore him like they were, carrying on as they always did, seemed indulgently callous.

She opened the door, making sure to close it behind her. She didn't want those fuckers ruining McFall's last hours. Hovering like hawks over a dying man. One of the dead stirred, moving for her with an aggression she hadn't sensed in them, before. She aimed her Glock and fired, piercing its head with the bullet. A part of its brain split from its head, and it looked surprised, momentarily, before falling to the ground like a sack of potatoes. Another looked up, but seemed reluctant to challenge her. It was as if it were aware of the danger, acting with self-interest. She maintained her aim while moving towards the vehicle. The thing didn't move, still glaring at her suspiciously as she moved. Another one surprised her from somewhere else, but she managed to kick it away while reaching for the passenger door of the Land Rover, firing at it as it stumbled away, blowing out half its chest.

She slammed the door, once safely inside.

A figure to her right scared her, and she raised the gun almost instinctually.

Lark was sitting in the driving seat, staring into space.

"Jesus!"she said, lowering the gun. "You gave me a fright. I thought you had left already."

"Did you see him?" he asked, tears streaming down his face. It had made his eyeliner run. It looked like he was crying tears of ink. As if his tattoos were leaking, somehow, through his eyes.

"Yes," she said quietly. "I saw him."

He looked at her, smiling sadly.

"I didn't call you," he said. "I kinda forgot. Sorry about that."

"It's okay," she said.

"He's a dick," Lark said, suddenly.

"I know," Geri said, agreeing. "So are you."

"I know," he said, choking a short guffaw of laughter back like an overexcited child. Then he buried his head in his hands and cried. He cried hard, the tears shaking through him as if boiling over. Geri placed a hand on his shoulder, gently, as if to steady him. As if to stop him from literally falling apart like a broken doll.

For a few moments, they just sat there in the Land Rover. Him crying, her holding him. The dead peering in through the windscreen, like shoppers looking at a shop window. The sun was dipping in the sky, as if about to retire for the night, but wanting to offer a few words of condolence before doing so. Finally, he was still, raising his head from his hands as if he had nothing more to give. She took her hand from his shoulder without saying anything.

"I feel bad about the cops," she said. "I dreamt about them when I was sleeping."

"Yeah?" Lark replied, wiping a tear from his eye.

"Yeah," she said. "I don't want us to lose what makes us human. We'll be one step closer to those things outside if we do."

"Maybe," he said. He didn't seem to care. "Do you want to go back to the store, then?"

"Do you?" she asked him.

"I just want to be away from here," he said. "I don't care where we go."

She looked at him in a different way. The fading light cast a flattering shadow across his tired, solemn face. She realised that he was handsome in a rough kind of way. And his tattoos... she hadn't really looked at them properly, until now. One of them stood out to her. It was an antiquated looking samurai, Japanese style, on his forearm. It had one eye looking up as it held its sword aloft. It looked sad, somehow, while still embroiled in the fight. It was like its eyes told one story while its sword told another.

"Do they hurt?" she asked, reaching forward and running her finger over the samurai. He jumped, as if her fingers were tattooing him, then, relaxed, again. She noticed the hairs on his arm standing on edge.

"That one did," he said.

TWENTY-THREE

George sat on the cold, hard, concrete floor of the storeroom, leaning his back against a couple of boxes of bleach. In one hand was a half-empty bottle of warm vodka. The other hand held his handgun. Opposite him lay the body of his colleague and – perhaps – friend, Norman Coulter.

George could hear the movements of the dead outside. They were gathering at the storeroom entrance like vultures around a carcass. He reckoned they would be hard pressed to get in. However, the noise of their attempts was enough to disturb him, preventing him from sleeping through the night. Of course, he was unlikely to sleep soundly beside...

He would never in a million years have thought that he would have to keep this type of vigil over Norman. The kind where a gun was required. If anything, he'd have expected things to be the other way around – the big man loyally standing over *his* body, waiting for it to stir before, solemnly, putting a bullet through *his* head. But here they were, and that just wasn't the way things had rolled.

He wondered how long it would be until he, too, contracted the virus. Falling ill, no one but himself to put a bullet through his brain. It was so hopeless that he reckoned he'd probably have done it right after putting

Norman down, but he'd made a promise to a dying man... and that meant something more than ever, now. It seemed that in a world like this, patrolled by Death itself, even more respect was demanded for those who had passed.

He recalled a time, when he'd just joined the force, being the first to arrive upon a random shooting. Rarely, for Belfast, it wasn't a sectarian attack. Just a pub brawl gone nasty, ending in one party going home for his shotgun before returning to the scene. The perpetrator even had a licence for the gun, which at the time had struck George as odd.

George had been working the graveyard shift, receiving the call just after 1:00am. He got there pretty quickly, even before the ambulance. One man was lying on the road, the other simply standing mutely with the shotgun in his hands. Punters surrounded them as if it were some kind of street theatre being acted out. The wounded man was almost blue by the time George got to him, but he tried to keep him talking, applying pressure to his wound as he chatted aimlessly about nothing. The man knew he was dead, though. It was almost as if he could feel the life drain from his body, knowing exactly how much he had left and how long it would take to fully empty. He said only one thing to George.

Tell my wife she was right.

George remembered feeling burdened with the words. He didn't know what they meant, but he knew that he had to pass the message on. Exactly as it had been told to him. After all, he thought, if it had been my wife, I'd want her to know the exact words.

He waited until the funeral, a sombre affair made all the more grim by the typical Northern Irish weather. He spotted a young woman at the front of the small crowd. He remembered thinking how pretty she looked in her black dress and feeling guilty for even thinking it. This was a woman mourning, he reminded himself, not some skank at a night club.

George approached the woman, asking if she were the widow. She cried, reciting the word 'widow' as if it was a sudden realisation of what the day had been about. As if George talking to her made it all the more real, an event that meant something beyond the graveside. George introduced himself and passed on the message. *Tell my wife she was right,* he said slowly and clearly. He even remembered smiling, once it had been said. He had practised the smile in the mirror before coming out. But she never thanked George for the message, nor did she express ingratitude. She simply nodded before being led away under an umbrella.

Later that week, George heard from Norman of another tragedy. *Remember that bloke you were called to who had been shot?* He said. *The one from the bar brawl?* George would never forget it. *Well,* said Norman, *the wife's only gone and done herself in and all. Seems she couldn't live without him.* Later George discovered the truth. She'd accused him of cheating on her with her best friend. He'd vehemently denied it, storming out for a night on the booze. It was the last she'd seen of him.

A sudden sound snapped George out of his daze. He looked to the bed in front of him. The big man's eyes had opened, and his body was shaking, as if recharging. He coughed up some phlegm from his lungs. It slid out of his mouth like drops of red paint. He stared at George for a while, as if surprised to see him. George waited for a moment, taking another heavy swig of vodka.

The big man was on his feet, stumbling around as if he, too, were drunk. He looked at George as if about to say something, but then forgot what it was.

George rose to his feet, grip tightening on his handgun. For some reason he felt suddenly angry with Dead Norman. It was as if he were disappointed that he was no different to the rest of the dead fucks outside. No smarter, no more able to articulate himself. A part of him thought Norman should have had more class than them, more dignity. But he stumbled about just as aimlessly, grunting and sniffling exactly the same way a hundred or thousand others got on.

Finally, George couldn't take anymore. He walked over to Norman, aiming the gun squarely at his head. His aim needed to be steadied, what with the vodka's influence. He fired once, twice, cutting two clean holes through the big man's head, staining the tall, cardboard tower behind him. Norman fell faster than he'd gotten up, his arms flailing as he collided with the boxes. And there he lay, sprawled over the dusty storeroom floor and blood stained cardboard, like some kind of giant, bloated spider. But he was finally at peace, finally able to rest.

George stood silent for a second, drinking the moment in. His eyes lingered on the big cop's body, as if the shock of his death were finally sinking in. A heavy clot of grief stiffened his chest. He felt tears well up in his eyes, his throat suddenly swelling. Without even realising what was happening, he suddenly found the gun in his hand rising, travelling through his lips, into his own mouth. The barrel was still hot, and it scorched his lips. But he seemed to be numb to that, numb to everything. The gun rested in his mouth for a moment, George's finger trembling on the trigger. He knew he'd made a promise, but it seemed to mean nothing to him anymore. What was the point, anyway?

(tell my wife she was right)

Who would know, who would care? Norman certainly didn't look like he cared about anything much anymore.

He could taste the warm, acrid metal of the gun on his tongue. Almost sweet against the harsh, dry taste of vodka. He mostly longed for it all to be over, but another part of him, minute though it was, fought to stay alive. Finally, the gun hand fell to his side, again, before leaving his grasp, entirely, clambering against the hard concrete. And George fell down beside it, knees cracking, heart breaking. He lifted his head, looking to the beams across the storeroom ceiling. But his eyes were dry, now. And he had no release.

TWENTY-FOUR

"She must be starving, the poor wee pet," Karen said, mopping the little girl's face with yet another baby wipe. Several spent wipes littered the carpet beside her; Pat noted the amount of dried blood on each with his trademark furrowed brow. He was suspicious of this child. Sure, he didn't mean her harm, but it was pretty clear to him that she had either suffered the flu or was still suffering from it right now. How she'd managed to survive, he didn't know, but he questioned just how safe it was to be around her.

Pat called Karen out of the room. She came at once, as if scared not to. Pat felt a moment of guilt before reminding himself of *the greater good*. The necessity in keeping a tight rein on a girl like Karen, a girl given to spontaneous excitement that could very well kill her. He suddenly realised that he would hit her again, if he needed to. Only to protect her, of course.

(spare the rod spoil the child)

He closed the door, looking in on the little girl and smiling. She smiled back, her eyes radiating innocence like some kind of heat.

"Has she said anything yet?" he asked Karen, once they were alone.

"No," Karen replied, breathless and obviously very excited by the new development. "I don't think she can speak, though. Or if she can, she probably doesn't know any English."

"You have to be careful, you know," Pat warned.

"What do you mean?" she asked, baffled.

"She's had the flu," he said, keeping his voice low, as if worried the little girl might hear him through the door. "We don't know how safe it is to be around her."

"She's just a child!" Karen said, agitated in a guarded way.

"Yes, but a child who was so close to death that they decided to quarantine her!" Pat stressed, again. He began to wonder if there was any common sense in Karen's pretty little head. Of course, Pat knew the little girl's arrival into their lives gave Karen the purpose she so badly longed for. So her spectacles were going to be very much rose-tinted about this whole thing. And that worried Pat, because, regardless of how good her intentions were, it would do no one any good if either she or he contracted the flu. Even the little girl would lose out.

But Karen continued to pout, despite this. It was as if she knew just how much sense he was making but refused to acknowledge it. This wasn't a world for her, Pat suddenly thought. There wasn't a selfish bone in her body. A girl like Karen was born to nurture, to look after the needs of others. If she'd been born into a different side of the community, Pat reckoned she'd have ended up as a nun.

"So what do we do?" Karen asked, her manner short and to the point. Any kind of rapport they once had was now lost.

"We keep in her in that room and that room alone," Pat said, adopting a similar manner. "And when you go in, you wear one of these," he showed her a packet of surgical masks in one hand, "and when you go out, you wash your hands with some of this," Pat said, pointing to a plastic container of anti-bacterial wash in his other hand.

Karen nodded, retrieving a mask without protest. She slipped it on before walking back into the room. Pat did similarly, following her. The child was waiting for them, smiling at him as he entered the room. It was hard not to allow your heart to be melted by this child. She was utterly adorable. Once cleaned up, Pat could hardly take his eyes off her, such was her beauty and innocence. Her mahogany brown hair and dark, chocolate eyes lit the fuse of her porcelain skin. If he still believed in God, he would have seen her as something of a miracle, a sign that not all was lost.

And that was the thing, of course. Karen hadn't thought this far ahead, obviously, and Pat was keen to discourage her from doing so. But this little girl was more than just a miraculous survivor of a killer virus. She held hope for the future in other ways, too. Within her blood could very well be the answer to the whole sorry mess. The reason she had survived. The reason her body had rejected the viral attack on its defences. Something different within her make-up that offered hope for all that remained of humanity. This little foreign girl could hold the cure, the very key to humanity's survival. In her blood, there could very well be the foundation for an anti-virus.

The little girl was walking around the room, now, picking things up and putting them down again. In her hand, she held a bottle. She sipped at its tip it like a comfort dummy every few seconds, hardly draining much of the juice inside.

She wandered over to the window, standing on her tip toes to look down at the ever-increasing tide of bodies below.

"*Mirtis*," she said, pointing.

Pat looked at Karen. It was the first they'd hear her say since finding her.

"*Mirtis*," she said again, a sad look drawing across her dark eyes.

TWENTY-FIVE

They left the house on the Lisburn road almost immediately, Lark keen to get away before they heard the inevitable gunshot from within. It was dark, though, and it seemed foolish to do anything brave in the dark. So the unlikely duo found a safe-ish spot in which to park, halfway down the M1 motorway, tucked under a recently constructed underpass. They settled down for the night, feigning sleep in an attempt to coax in the red-stained dawn.

Geri didn't think she had slept at all. Her eyes felt too alert for sleeping, even when they were closed. But she must have nodded off at least briefly, finding herself dreaming as the gentle light of morning roused her stiff body.

It had been a different dream than before. This one featured only her and Lark, sailing the Land Rover as if it were a boat, through a sea of flaming bodies. She thought back to the petrol station from before. How it had flared up, loudly. Noxious, black fumes bellowing into the blue-sky palette like black ink. And the dead, moving towards it as if hypnotised. Her dream was just a replay of that, she reckoned. Nothing more, nothing less.

"You awake?" she said to Lark. But she knew he was. His reflection in the window gave him away, his eyes hanging open, as if held there by clothes pegs. His pupils hardly visible, the whites heavily bloodshot. He looked so bad that Geri considered, for a moment, that he might have taken ill during the night. Contracted the flu, just like everyone else she had known.

He turned around, looking at her and smiling faintly, before rubbing his face with his hands.

"Fuck," he said for no reason at all, then yawned loudly. "Did you sleep?"

"I think so," she said. "Not much, though."

"Me neither," he said.

Geri looked out the window, surprised to find none of the dead hovering around the vehicle.

"*They* must have slept, though," she said, smiling.

Lark laughed, "The sleep of the dead."

They sat silently for a few moments, staring out at the empty space around them. It was comforting to see none of the dead there, for once. You could almost pretend that they no longer existed. That they had rotted away in the night. Or evaporated, somehow, like ghosts. Sucked up by the rising sun like the shadows of life they were.

"Geri," Lark said, and she realised it was the first time he had addressed her by her name. "What happened the other night –"

"Don't," she said, turning her face away from him. "I don't want *that* to define me. I don't want the pity, the stigma or any other bullshit that comes with being a 'victim'... so don't..."

"Okay," he said, simply. "I won't..."

"It never happened," she said sternly, turning to point a finger at him.

"Right," he said, hanging his head.

For another moment, nothing passed between them. They both stared at the empty motorway in front of them, as if they were alone. As if they were separate, in some way, from each other. Like two trees standing side by side.

But then Geri leaned forward, gently kissing Lark on the cheek.

"Thank you," she whispered. "For what you did..."

His eyes glistened as he continued to stare ahead, unflinchingly. It was as if her kiss had turned him to stone or ice. Geri suddenly felt very aware of herself, aware of how the dynamic between them was shifting and how uncomfortable that made her.

"Will we hit the road?" she said, purposely killing the moment, busying herself with keys and seatbelts.

Lark turned his head, smiling cheekily, the way he always did. It was as if the moment were forgotten to him, also.

"Sure," he said. "Let's see if your porky pie mate's still in the land of the living."

Geri shook her head, laughing. The joke was in poor taste, but she welcomed it as a return to their normal rapport. She turned the ignition, firing up the Land Rover and moving it quietly out onto the main M1 motorway. The roads were empty. The real reason for this, of course, was nothing to do with ghosts or shadows or the sun. The stark reality was that few of the dead saw much point in wandering too far from the sparsely populated life that the city boasted. There was nothing on a motorway that would normally be of interest to them, and they clearly hadn't found their way to Lark and Geri as yet. Geri wondered, briefly, how far and wide their sense of smell – or vision – could reach. They already suspected they were pretty much deaf. Had their other senses been heightened, therefore, overcompensating for a bereavement of sound?

Before long, they pulled up just shy of the storehouse where they had left the two cops. It was obvious that the cops had attracted some unwanted attention, a band of the dead accumulating by the shutter doors, as if awaiting some great event. As if queuing for the opening of a shopping centre or some concert. Geri almost felt sorry for them. Their heads were hanging limply from their necks. As if they were fast asleep on their feet. They looked tired, bored. Geri began to wonder what it would be like to be one of them, to be trapped in a body that seemed somehow familiar, yet ultimately alien to you. To be a pale imitation of that which you crave. Warm flesh, human blood. Was their tireless campaign motivated by mere jealousy?

But Lark didn't seem to see anything in their hapless poise, apart from inconvenience.

"Great," he said, shaking his head. "Just what we fucking need."

Geri laughed her plaintive thoughts away.

"What?" he said, as if she were laughing at him.

"Oh, nothing," she said. He was clearly a man to bring you right back down to earth, were you ever to need it. "How's your aim?" she asked him.

"Eh?" he replied, looking bewildered. She wondered if he was still waking up.

"Your *aim*," she reiterated, handing him the rifle from the back. "I found this in the glove compartment," she said, feeling around and then retrieving a telescopic scope. "It probably attaches onto the rifle, some way."

As she watched, Lark fixed the scope into place. He pulled the cocking handle of the rifle back halfway to lock it into place. He slapped in a fresh magazine and pulled the handle loose, allowing it to shift forward again, chambering a round. Geri wondered how Lark seemed to know so much about firearms, recalling the mini-lesson he had given to her, earlier, regarding the handgun. Although he didn't seem as proficient with a rifle, he still appeared to know how to fit it together.

"Two months in the Army," he said, as if reading her mind. "They threw me out for dealing dope."

Geri laughed.

"Were you ever *not* a dick?" she asked facetiously.

"Okay, wind down that window," he said, once the rifle was ready.

Geri did as she asked, Lark having climbed into the back seat to lean across, allowing the lengthy rifle barrel, with fitted silencer, to slide out of the window. She watched as he struggled to find a suitable position, to get the rifle where he needed it to be in order to freely move.

"Comfy?" she asked, sarcastically.

"Not really," he said. "Look, I'm going to have to get out. I don't have enough free rein in here. Not when taking out that many." He scrambled back into the front seat, rifle slung by his side. He reached for the door handle.

"Be careful," Geri said, touching his arm.

He looked at her, shocked, as if she had spat on him.

"Listen, I'm a crack shot with this bad girl," he said, protesting.

"Like hell you are," Geri scoffed. "Maybe the pistols, but you're shit with a rifle!"

"The fuck I am!" he said, laughing with her. "Just you watch, sweetheart. I'll have those filthy dogs downed in seconds."

He climbed out of the Land Rover, running around to the other side in order to lean across the bonnet, facing his targets. His first shot surprised Geri. Regardless of the silencer, she still felt herself jump with the rifle's slight shake reverberating through the vehicle. It was a good shot, though, tearing a clean hole through the head of a middle-aged woman on the periphery of the main pack. Her body fell without protest. None of the others seemed concerned.

Lark began to carefully work his way through the rest of the pack, aiming for the heads each time. His shots were mostly on target, picking the dead off one by one like grazing cattle. Some strayed wide, though; Geri heard Lark swear as he no doubt felt the pressure of his boast to her. The last few began to stumble towards the Land Rover, seeming to sense the danger was coming from there.

"Shit," she heard him say as he couldn't seem to get the next few shells to hit anywhere close to their targets. He was panicking, and it was making *her* nervous, as well as him. His next shell hit one of them in the chest. As Geri watched, it stumbled backwards, tripping, before scrambling back onto its feet, drunkenly. She watched as Lark struggled with his rifle, the dead thing ebbing ever closer to the Land Rover.

"Shoot it!" she shouted, unhelpfully, out the windscreen as she locked her door.

"I'm trying to," she heard him say back," but the fucking gun's jammed!" She watched the wounded dead fuck move towards him, its eyes as blank and lethargic as ever. As it drew closer, she realised it was wearing a police uniform, and for a horrible moment she thought it might be George (it was too small to be Norman). But it was bald and older. That much she could tell beneath the calloused face and ground-in gore.

Lark continued to struggle with his rifle, aiming then shaking it when the shell didn't fire. Eventually he turned it around, approaching the dead cop with the rifle acting as a club. He struck it across the head, using the rifle's butt. It fell to the ground, landing on its back, arms stretched up as if to protect itself from further blows. Geri watched Lark club it like a wounded dear, the sounds of each blow growing softer. She noticed the rifle butt get thicker in rich, scarlet grime, each time he lifted it. But Lark kept going, pouring a lot more effort into the action than seemed to be required.

"Stop it! She cried through the window. "It's dead, for Christ's sake!"

She could see another one coming for him, but he still seemed lost in the moment, as if caught in some kind of death trance. He continued to beat on the dead cop's head with a fervour she had never seen before. It was as if all his anger, all his frustration was being taken out in this one brutal, repetitive action. And he seemed to be enjoying it, too. Maybe that's what worried her the most.

She yelled at him again, more furiously, still too frightened to open the Land Rover door. Yet her shrill, banshee-like shriek seemed to be enough to snap him out of the trance; Lark turned to face the nearing dead fuck at the last moment. He stepped back, pulled the rifle into place and aimed towards its head. Miraculously, the clubbing seemed to have cleared the gun's jam, two shells finally leaving the barrel to hit home, blowing chunks of hair and brain out of the dead fuck's head with final, angry precision. Still aiming, he turned on the remaining pack, downing them with similar success.

As Geri looked upon the ten or so bodies scattered across the tarmac grounds, she breathed out a sigh of relief. Finally, she opened the door and stepped out of the Land Rover, noticing how her entire body was shaking from head to toe. The sun was still beaming in the sky, and she could feel its heat on her face. It would give her more freckles, and she had far too many already. Plus, it was meant to age you, she thought. As she looked upon the nearest dead faces, lying before her, she could make out sun damage on their faces, too. The rays hadn't been kind at all, scorching their already parched, prune-dry skin, creating little bubbles. Geri looked up at the sun, narrowing her eyes against its fierceness. She wondered briefly if it were somehow on their side, equally as angry as humanity was at the ugly, messy dead littering God's Great Earth.

She looked to Lark, noticing he hadn't moved or spoken since she had got out of the car. He was still standing over the cop's body. She walked towards him, and he turned to face her.

"I think I knew that one," he said, quietly. "He picked me up downtown, once. He was a real prick."

Geri laughed, pushing a hand against him, playfully. Soon Lark was laughing, too, all previous signs of malice having faded away.

...

George woke to see the sun shining in from an opened shutter. He could make out some blurred shapes and grabbed his handgun, thinking the dead had somehow managed to breach the storeroom. But as his vision cleared, he realised it wasn't the dead who had disturbed him. He first noticed the bright red hair of Geri, reflecting the sun. She was standing in front of him, also holding a handgun, as if prepared for the worst. He next spotted Lark, the tattooed freak standing on the edge of the entrance, nearby, smoking a cigarette.

"You came back," he said before adding, sarcastically, "how nice."

"I felt bad," she said. "Listen, what I did was very wrong, George. I know that now." She seemed sincere. He could almost read the guilt in the freckles scattered across her face. Like Braille. "But I got scared, God help me. Surely you can understand that?"

But George gave her nothing.

"And what about him?" he said piously, pointing at Lark. Lark looked up briefly, but said nothing. He took another drag of his cigarette, looking out into the sunshine. George noticed Norman's rifle slung across the tattooed man's shoulder. A number of bodies lay across the ground, outside.

"He lost his friend," Geri said. "Maybe he's had an epiphany."

George laughed.

"You mean that idiot with the balaclava?" he said, viciously.

Geri shushed him, clearly disappointed by his insensitivity. But he didn't care. Any last trace of 'caring' he had managed to keep within him was all but washed out, now. His only reason for not sticking the barrel of the Glock in his mouth and pulling the trigger was the promise he had made. A promise he wasn't even sure was worth keeping.

(tell my wife she was right)

He noticed Geri looking over to the body on the ground, covered with an old blanket.

"Is he...?"

"Dead?" George said, "Yes."

He checked his gun as he spoke.

"And dead again?" he added, "Yes."

George walked towards the shutter, looking at Lark and raising the gun.

Lark saw him coming, chucking his cigarette and putting his hands up, in appeal.

"Fuck's sake, mate!" he said, falling and scrambling along the floor.

George fired, clipping a quietly confident dead fuck on the side of the head behind Lark.

Lark looked back, shocked at the approaching threat. He pulled his rifle from its sling and finished the thing off. Another creature appeared to its left and Lark fired twice to stall it, as well. He struggled to pull the shutter down, George moving in to give him some help. Between the two of them, they managed to get it down, just before another couple of dead fucks made it to the entrance.

Lark looked at George, nodding in what George took to be gratitude.

George nodded back.

"You need to watch your back," he said, quietly. "Always."

Lark looked uncomfortable, slinging his rifle again and moving back into the store.

"Don't be such a dick," Geri said, approaching George as Lark moved away. "It doesn't suit you."

"Oh, and it suits *him*?!" George said, pointing at the retreating Lark.

"That's not what I meant," Geri replied, curtly. "And you know it."

"Well what *did* you mean, then?" George said.

"I meant you're a man of integrity. A man who doesn't need to get on like that," she said, looking him straight in his eyes. She reached a hand to check a tear erupting from his face, more out of frustration than anything else.

"Well, the world's changed," George said, pulling away from her. "And I'm changing with it."

Geri looked sincerely disappointed. George didn't think she had the right to be disappointed with him. After all, she'd left him here to die, shooting off with that... thug. With all they'd shared together, that was unforgiveable in his book. But his book was getting murkier by the day. His book reflected the world it was being written within, a vivid, horrific reflection of its backdrop. A book of death, of darkness, of sadness. A book sure to end both soon and horribly.

TWENTY-SIX

As the sun continued to rise, gently pouring light onto the outstretched streets of a reluctant Belfast, the few survivors left continued to wrestle with growing numbers of dead. Some, like Sergeant George Kelly, had all but given up their struggle. As the dead got progressively more vicious, the virus within them vibrating through every vein, artery and organ, the tired and malnourished living became jaded. Many couldn't cope. A single gunshot at 7.05am seemed to illustrate this, ringing out in Belfast's centre as yet another survivor gave up the fight.

Yet for every man and woman putting a bullet through their own head or poisoning their last shot of whisky, there were others still struggling on. Still thriving on the longing to be free again. Castlecourt, one of Belfast's largest shopping centres, was overrun with the dead. They poured through crudely constructed barriers to breach the final respite of the living. A small pocket of survivors huddled together in a storeroom, few supplies left to see them through to the next day. In Templepatrick's airport, a group of the living, including some survivors from the nearby army base, fought fearlessly to hold back an increasing tide of dead fucks. They had held the airport for days, weeks. They were preparing planes for departure but needed just a little more time... just one last push...

For many, it seemed hopeless and pointless to keep going, but survival instinct alone kept the few mavericks thinking, planning, conspiring. It's what had kept men and women going for years, through wars, famine, love and loss the world over.

It was all that was left now.

But for many it was enough.

Throughout the world, the virus ran amok. But humanity fought back, bitterly, kicking against the threat of extinction like a dying man fighting for breath. Every last moment became precious or pointless. The coin could land on either side, the glass either half-empty or half-full. But someone, somewhere had refused to give up. Someone, somewhere fought to keep themselves and others alive. Someone, somewhere clung to hope like a drowning man to driftwood. And it was enough to see through another day.

...

They pulled up by the tower block at Finaghy, George driving while Lark and Geri sat beside him in the front of the Land Rover. A large housing estate sprawled out before them like a grand canyon. An echo waiting to happen. In the end, this estate, like many others, had been completely evacuated, its remaining inhabitants packed into a bus and shipped off to one of the many rescue camps they'd heard were springing up across the countryside. The estate was now empty, save the dead and a number of parked cars.

Lark marvelled at how the cars were parked so neatly, as if their owners intended to return for them someday. He wondered if they had thought the things that were important to them, the property they had accumulated, the houses and flats they had filled with... stuff... could all be taken with them to the grave. Stacked high, like some Egyptian Pharaoh's tomb. To be enjoyed in another life.

"Here it is," George said, pointing at the block of flats opposite.

Lark looked out the dirty windows of the Land Rover, eyes narrowing at the sight of countless dead crowding the entrance.

"It's going to be hard getting through that lot," he said.

"Are you sure the place is secure?" Geri added, "Because we could always try somewhere –"

"No," George said firmly (a little too firmly for Lark's liking). "This is going to be the best place to hole up."

Lark didn't trust the cop, never would. He knew Geri thought it was because he hated *every* cop, and she was right, but for Lark it was more than *just* that. His radar was definitely shouting ding-a-fuck-a-ling at this shit. Seemed to Lark like the cop had a vested self-interest in this place for some reason. He just wondered why.

So he decided to ask.

"Why this one?"

George looked at him the same way the other fucker had looked at him during that night they were all drinking.

"It was quarantined fairly early on" he said, "Just before they decided to evacuate people. It's going to be locked up tight. It's also likely to have cupboards full of canned goods and bottles of water. People were panic-buying around that time."

"How do you know it was quarantined?" Lark pressed.

"Because I helped do it," George said, without emotion.

The quarantines had scared the shit out of Lark. Even the word 'quarantine' freaked him out. He was reminded of those dark days, all too recent, once again. Vicious and desperate attempts to prevent the spread of the virus. Men and women, sometimes whole families, literally being sealed into their homes and left to die. Reports of mass executions followed, the government's measures moving from extreme to despicable as their diminishing grasp of control slipped further and further. Finally, rogue police and soldiers patrolled the streets, enforcing their own brand of martial law, executing anyone who displayed symptoms or just looked funny at them. It was people like Lark, people who could move below the radar, who fared best during this time. Cynical enough to see through the bullshit promises of preventative medicines on bureaucratic posters, signposting to Emergency Medical Facilities in the rural areas. He had seen some people give in, desperately seeking out these camps with promises to return with food, anti-viral medicine and supplies. But Lark never saw them again. And he sure as hell wasn't going to follow them. He was a glass-half-full kind of bloke, and it had stood him in good stead so far.

"I don't like this," Lark said, sniffing.

"I don't care," George said.

"Oh, for God's sake," Geri snapped angrily. "Grow the fuck up. Both of you. You need to put this shit behind you. Seriously! It's the only way we're going to stand a chance out there!"

But Lark couldn't agree with her sentiments. He'd seen way too much to believe that forgiveness was the cure-all in this situation. Sure, he would go along with whatever kept his arse safest. But it was only because it suited him. It also seemed to be what Geri wanted. And that was important to him, regardless of whether he admitted it to himself or not...

"Okay," he said, dryly, "I'll be good." He smiled sarcastically at George before looking out to the harem of dead that gathered around the tower block. Some of them were breaking off from the main herd and moving towards the Land Rover.

"Any ideas on how to make a dent on this lot?" George said to the other two.

"Sure," Lark said, lighting up another cigarette to the displeasure of his fellow survivors. "I know a way that'll work a treat."

...

Pat peeked out the window, careful not to disturb the blinds too much. His eyes were fixed on the police Land Rover, like salt on a wound. It stood out from all the other vehicles. Large, adorned in armour plating and wheel guards. Obnoxious and threatening, even now.

He hated it. He wanted it gone.

The sight was met with a different reception by Karen. This was great news to her.

"Do you see it?" she asked. He turned to look at her, finding her fully dressed and wearing make-up. Her clothes were stained, as if she had spilt paint on them. Her hands were messy.

"Yeah, I see it..." he sighed. "Where were you, by the way?"

"Nowhere," she replied, innocently. "Just in the room, painting the wall. I've got to make it nice for _ –"

"Well, just stay away from the windows," Pat said impatiently. He didn't care what she did, as long as she didn't draw any attention to them.

"But why?" she said, looking at him as if confused. "It's a police Land Rover out there. Don't you see what this means?"

"It means trouble," Pat said looking at her as if she didn't understand something simple. "It always means trouble."

He remembered the first time the police had come for him. He'd been holed up in a safe house in Dublin. It had been after one of his most brutal operations, a bomb placed by the side of the road as two police Land Rovers had passed.

They had been outside, just like now. His wife had gone out the door, screaming and shouting at them, calling them all the bastards of the day. Several heavily armed units had circled the area. They grabbed her, pulled her down to the ground, gagged her and removed her like some kind of inconvenience. Later, her account of the ordeal would anger Pat. It would stoke his dampened flames, rekindling an old anger. And he would kill again because of it.

But that night, Pat was upstairs, weighing up his options. His son, now a young man, had sat at the top of the stairs, looking down at the front door in the hallway below. He was loading a revolver, hands shaking, face perspiring, as he worked. He talked of how they would never get past him, how Pat should stay where he was.

He was thirteen years old, and he was loading a revolver.

Pat simply laid his hand on the lad's shoulder, bending down beside him.

"It's over, son," he said, smiling.

His son just looked up into his eyes. Pat knew he would have been happy to give his life for him, and he'd never felt as proud of anyone as he felt of young Sean that day.

He'd gone quietly, then, but he wasn't so sure he was going to go quietly now. He'd seen what those bastards had been up to in the final days. The quarantines. Rounding people up like dogs. Dragging them off to 'rescue camps', where cures and vaccines and food all waited for them. All lies, of course. Death was all that waited for anyone. He'd never trusted cops or government types before, and he sure as hell wasn't going to trust them now.

Karen moved towards the door, an excited look across her innocent, young face. But Pat reached it before she did, placing his arm across to block her from leaving.

"Don't do this," he said firmly.

"What do you mean?" she said, smiling as if stupid, as if unable to comprehend the very words he was saying to her. "They're outside. We've got to let them know we're here."

"They don't give a damn about you," he snapped back, feeling the anger rising up within him. "We sit tight and let them pass."

"What are you talking about?!" Karen said, grabbing his arm and trying to get past.

"I'm talking about what was happening when you had your head buried in the sand!" Pat said, visibly and uncharacteristically riled. "The quarantines. The death camps. The executions. Don't you remember *any* of that?" There was every chance she did, but was, somehow, blotting it all out. Now, of course, she only saw the police Land Rover through rose-tinted spectacles. Perhaps, Pat thought, she *needed* to see it that way. If not for her own benefit, then for the benefit of the child.

"Let me past!" she yelled, beating her fists against his chest. But Pat grabbed her roughly, slapping her face the way men used to do in the movies when women became hysterical. She screamed at him, tears erupting from her eyes like tiny fountains. He immediately felt bad, but he couldn't let his guard down. He needed her to be scared of him, needed her to do what he told her. This was important; it wasn't just her life at stake, or the little girl's, but his as well.

(the greater good)

She reached again for the door, but he hit her again. She fell by the kitchen table, smacking her head against its rough edge. The little girl was crying now, her tears almost harmonising with the tears of Karen, now on the ground, rubbing her head. There seemed to be noise everywhere. Blood was seeping through Karen's fingers where she'd hit her head. Pat moved to check the wound, but Karen was suddenly on her feet.

"Th-they've come for us," she said, her breathing stunted, "They've come because they know how important the child is. She's the answer, Pat. She's got the cure in her blood. You know it, and I know it!"

"I wish that was true!" he said, almost shouting. "But it isn't... God help me, it isn't even *near* true! You have no idea what they'll do to that little girl if they get their hands –"

"They'll help her!" Karen countered. "They'll help her, and they'll help everyone else! Don't you see?! How can you be so blind?!"

The little girl went for the door, stressed out by the high tension. Karen went after her, but Pat moved to stop her. She grabbed the handgun on the table, pointing it at him as he drew closer. His instinct was to reach for the gun, take it from her hands, but she fired before he could do that, the bullet shattering his neck at point blank range.

Pat fell to the ground, grabbing his mangled throat. His body was jerking in spasms, blood spurting from his neck in jets. He felt himself blacking out, his heart beginning to slow as his life continued to drain. He was shocked by what she'd done. Shocked by the bullet wound in his neck, the blood escaping from it. Shocked by the once pretty, naive child holding a smoking gun in her hands...

(thirteen years old, and he was loading a revolver)

...but deep down, buried by all the other emotions racing through his dying heart, he was also proud. Proud of the fact that she had the gall to stand up to him. Proud of the fact that he thought she could now look after herself.

He noticed Karen by his side, placing her hands around his neck. She was crying, screaming. Trying to stop the blood escaping from his wound. But it was too late.

"Stop bleeding!" she yelled, between huge keening sobs. "Stop BLEEDING!"

"It's o-o-okay..." he stuttered, still in shock. "Just... j-just don't trust –" But his voice failed him, his eyes blacking out and his head rolling to one side as life quickly evaporated from his body. Like steam from a teacup.

...

"Did you hear that?" asked Lark, his head peeking out from the Land Rover's roof hatch.

"What?" called George from the back of the vehicle, dragging two canisters of fuel.

"I heard something. A gunshot, I think," Lark muttered.

"Plenty of those around," George said, heaving each can up to the other survivor.

"Okay," said Lark, forgetting all about the gunshot. "So I'm just going to tip these over the sorry bastards. I'll try to cover as many of them as possible."

"I just hope it works," George said, casting Lark an uneasy look.

Lark just smiled. "It'll work a fucking treat, mate," he said, still sucking on his cigarette precariously. He uncapped the fuel canisters, slapping the thick, heavy liquid over as many of the bodies as he could. They were about four deep, meaning he got plenty of mileage out of the first canister. A single hand reached out for his ankle. Lark pulled his leg away, steadying himself before trampling the overzealous dead hand with his steel-toe capped DM boot. The stupid bastard hardly reacted, simply falling back into the crowd, hand mangled and face drenched in pungent petroleum.

"Okay, first one's away," Lark called into George, holding his cigarette with one hand, banging his other on the roof. "Take us closer to the tower block."

The Land Rover kicked into action, moving gently through the crowd, closer to the tower block. Bodies crumpled against it, turning to stare in at the driver as if appalled they were pushing up a queue. George parked next to the crowd of dead hovering by the entrance.

"Okay, same again?" George called up through the hatch.

"Same again," Lark shouted in, still sucking on the butt of the cigarette. He unscrewed the cap from the last canister, emptying the contents over the second group of dead, liberally. They hardly reacted at all, some giving out a slow annoyed murmur, others silently suffering the humility of it all. Once done, Lark patted the roof again. Within seconds, George appeared at the hatch, again, looking at the dampened and strongly smelling heads of the surrounding dead.

"Hey!" Lark said, his face suddenly upturned with concern.

"What?" George asked, nervously. "What's wrong?"

"I know that guy..." Lark said, pointing to one of the dead. "Done a little time with him in the tank, back in the late nineties."

"The *what*?!" George said, brow furrowed in confusion.

"The tank," Lark reiterated. "Rehab," he said when George still looked bemused. "I did a spell in there after all the E-tab shit was big. I'd gotten pretty into it, so I

259

went in the tank for a bit to dry out. Shook like a fucking junkie for weeks. But, I met that guy in there. He was alright. We had a laugh."

The cop shook his head.

"You had a laugh...?!" he repeated, shaking his head. "Your world," he said, "is so very different to mine."

Lark just looked at him, smiling as he toked on his dying cigarette.

"Okay," George said, looking back at the crowd of fuel doused dead. "What now?"

Lark lifted the cigarette butt from his lips, breathing out a volley of smoke across the cop's face.

"We light them up," he said, leering as he flicked the cigarette into the crowd.

A nearby dead fuck caught fire immediately, the poor bastard reaching its hands to its hair as if to thank Lark. The stupid fuck went into manic mode, dancing around like a bitch in heat, infecting one, then two, then ten others with the same viral fire that it had contracted. And so the fire spread. The first group of dead, doused by the first canister, hurried back towards the commotion, and they too caught fire. Soon, pretty much all of them were succumbing to the flames, rushing to and fro, as if excited.

Lark dipped back into the vehicle, looking out the windows for an alternate view.

"Ha! Do you see them?" he called to the others, like a school child sharing a joke. "Stupid fuckers!"

"Brilliant," George said, almost as if in disbelief. "Simple but brilliant."

As they watched on, the herd thinned considerably, some of the dead completely overwhelmed by the flames, falling to the ground. Others turned and, rather bizarrely, tried to escape the flames consuming them by falling to the ground and rolling. It was as if the damn things were learning, evolving, seeking to preserve their

260

pathetic un-lives. The three survivors watched in silence, perhaps disturbed by how much they could relate to the plight of these evolving unfortunates.

"We need to move quickly," Geri said, distracting them all from the crass view before them. "Before they burn out."

"Okay," said George, reaching for his rifle. "Everyone ready?"

...

He parked the Land Rover away from the tower block, lest it, too, catch fire like the dead. All three survivors hurried out, grabbing whatever supplies they could manage and moving quickly towards the entrance. George urged everyone to check their weapons and be ready to use them as they drew closer to the carnage.

The crackle of flames and pungent whiff of petrol was thick in the air, smoke billowing across the front car park like thick vanilla. It was like a scene from some '80s pop video or a cheap and nasty horror film. George was reminded of innocent days gone by, suddenly, and he held the memory close as he approached the tower block.

"Get inside," he shouted over the commotion, "Quickly get inside!"

As they approached, the front doors of the tower block suddenly opened, revealing a young woman and little girl. George's mouth hung open as he saw them, unable to believe that someone would be so stupid as to exit the building given what was happening.

"Get back inside" he yelled at the two survivors. "What are you doing?!" As he drew closer, the face of the little girl became clearer to him. "Jesus Christ!" he said out loud. "That's –" His legs suddenly felt weak, heavy as the realisation sank in. This was the little girl he had quarantined, the one from flat 23. He was sure it was her. God knew, he couldn't forget her face. The olive skin, those chocolate eyes. He'd dreamt about her every night since. His mind wouldn't... couldn't lie to him. "G-get back inside!" George screamed at them again, his voice hoarse and cracking this time.

But it was too late; the dead, some still burning up like faulty fireworks, moved towards the doors. Some of them had already clambered through. The young woman looked confused, emotional. She hurried the little girl towards the approaching survivors, stopped, then turned back as George continued to yell at her.

Lark was first to reach them, throwing his bag of supplies at a nearby dead fuck who had almost managed to grab the little girl. He bustled the two back indoors, turning and firing at some of the surrounding dead as he inched his way through. Geri caught the door just as it was closing, managing to squeeze through, also. She held it open for George, who finally reached the entrance just as more of the dead were closing in. George could hear more gunfire from within, Lark seemingly still busy. But a burning hand grabbed for him, making contact with his backpack and pulling him outside. As George fought to loosen the straps on the pack, the lucky bastard managed to connect its jaw with his one of his fingers, sinking teeth through flesh and drawing blood. George turned to it, blowing a hole through its skull in anger, at point blank range. He was baptised in its blood, pausing to spit pieces of its brain from his mouth. He pushed through the entrance, falling on the floor in front of the other survivors.

More of the dead managed to break through the double doors, spilling into the corridor of the ground floor. Some of them were still on fire, infecting others and the building around them as they stumbled against the wooden doors and bodies alike.

George felt himself being helped from the ground by Lark, of all people, the two men following the women and young girl as they headed for the stairwell.

"Go!" Lark called, half at him and half with him to the others. "Get up those fucking stairs!"

They stumbled through the fire door, George's heart beating heavily as he moved. He could feel the dampness of sweat all over his skin, just like his last visit to the building. A claustrophobic stumble through these corridors was simply history repeating itself. A sick and twisted version of déjà-vu, the dead having multiplied and consumed with demonic fire for the replay.

Halfway up the first round of stairs, George stopped in his tracks, turning back down.

"What are you doing?" Lark called after him.

"The door!" he yelled, "We need to lock the fire door!" But it was too late. Several of the dead were emerging through it as he reached the first flight. "Fuck!" he said, turning back towards the stairs. "Fuck, fuck, fuck! They're in! Keep moving!"

While the others hurried on up the stairs, George stopped in his tracks. He looked at his finger, noticing how it was already inflamed and smarting. A blue vein protruded along the ridge of his hand, as if a wire was buried under his skin. It reminded him of one of those old horror movies. It looked fake, comical. Sighing, George turned to face the incoming dead.

"Hey," shouted Lark, slowing down on the stairs. "What are you doing?"

George frowned, lifting his hand. "I was bit," he said, simply.

Lark just looked at him, shaking his head and tutting.

"Fuck, I'm really sorry, man..." he said, genuine concern etched in his face.

"Sure you are," George said, smiling ironically. But he had misjudged the young tattooed man. Lark turned to go, before looking back as if he'd forgotten something. He stepped down a few stairs, extending his long, wiry, tattooed arm to George to offer a handshake. His eyes told George it was a sincere gesture.

"You're alright, so you are," Lark said without sarcasm.

George accepted, shaking the other man's hand firmly.

"Well, you're still a prick." He replied, smiling.

Lark smiled back, still shaking George's hand.

"Just look after *her*," George said, knowing Lark knew exactly who he was talking about.

"I will," Lark said. He turned, quickly.

"And the little girl –" George started.

Lark turned back, shaking his head in confusion.

"I think –"

"You think what?" Lark pressed, impatiently.

"Never mind," George said. It couldn't be the same one; it simply couldn't.

As Lark moved up the stairwell, George turned just in time to see several of the dead emerge from the corner of the first flight. They looked excited, taking the stairs like children visiting a castle for the first time. George almost felt sorry for them, their stupid, tortured faces swarming towards him. It seemed that hunger constantly plagued them. But were they ever sated? Or was it like an itch that you couldn't scratch?

The first one reached him. It was a middle-aged man wearing a dark suit. He looked sombre, tired, like he had just come back from a funeral. *His own funeral, maybe...* George thought. He kicked the man against a couple of others, sending several of them humorously back down the stairwell. The others swarmed towards him like bloated wasps. George guessed he wouldn't be keeping his promise to Norman, after all.

"Alright lads," he said, raising his Glock. "Let's be having you."

...

Karen didn't know the couple following her, but she was pretty sure they weren't police. The one wearing the white vest top had his arms and chest tattooed, and his face was full of metal. He had a shorn head and huge black rings circling his eyes, as if drawn on. The police didn't look like *him*, that much was for sure.

They continued up the stairwell, Karen flinching each time she heard a shot from further back. Her own mind was cloudy, confused and over-stimulated. She could feel her heart beating fast, almost tasted it in her mouth. Images of Pat, of the dead, of the little girl were mish-mashed across her blurry eyes as she scrambled up the stairs.

There was another shot, then another, punctuating every couple of steps she made up the stairs.

"What's happening?"she asked the other girl. The woman had red hair, and her face almost matched it. Sweat broke across her brow, one bead for every freckle.

"That's what I wanna know," she answered, looking to the other survivor.

"Just keep going," said the tattooed man to both of them.

"I can't, I'm knackered!" the woman said, panting. "And where the hell's George?"

The tattooed man grabbed her roughly by the arm.

"I said keep moving!" he yelled, supporting her as she stumbled.

They reached flight ten, Karen heading out of the stairwell and down its corridor for the flat she had shared with Pat. The others followed her. She set the little girl down, fumbling for the keys in her pocket. The door had seemed to lock automatically when she had last closed it. She paused for a moment before opening it, suddenly remembering that Pat would be in there, his body crudely wrapped and hidden in his bedroom. But they had no choice... there was nowhere left to run to.

"In here!" she shouted at the others. She pushed the little girl in, following her into the flat's hallway. The other two followed shortly after, the tattooed man closing the door tightly behind him.

"Jesus fucking Christ," he said, doubling over on his knees to catch his breath. A scream startled all three of the survivors. "Ah fuck," he said, "what now?!"

The little girl had run into the kitchen but was now retreating. Following her, Karen could make out the form of her old friend, Pat. His head hung from his neck like some crude, horror version of that Swing Ball game she used to play as a child. His mouth was still moving, teeth jittering and eyes searching as he moved.

"Oh God, no..." Karen said, frozen to the spot. The blanket was hanging off him now, like some kind of cloak. Pat moved in her direction, somehow attracted to her in particular. She felt unable to move, as if she had unfinished business with him, as if there were something which she could say that would make up for all she had done to him. "I'm s-sorry!" she cried, tears breaking from her eyes to stain already reddened cheeks.

But Pat didn't seem to accept her apology. His rough, calloused hands formed a strangle hold around her neck. She fought against him but stumbled over a nearby chair, both her and Pat hitting the ground. His head fell at her face. His mouth feverishly danced beside her, searching for her flesh, his teeth finally digging into the side of her face like a dentist drill. Karen screamed, reaching for Pat's head, fragilely attached to his head by that single strand of veins and arteries. She tore his head from his body with a single tug, stumbling to her feet quickly, as if the floor were covered in spiders. Pat's body flailed around the floor like a demented freak before finally stopping. She ripped his lockjaw head from her cheek, feeling it tear even more flesh from her face as it came away. Crying uncontrollably, she threw his head to the ground as if it were red hot.

From the corner of her eye, she could see the two survivors leading the child back into the hallway. The door hung open, and she rushed to follow them, a huge flap of skin hanging from her face where Pat had worked on her. She ran back to the stairwell. It was rammed full with the dead. Some of them were still burning, the stench of charred flesh thick in the confined, small space. Parts of the building had caught fire, and it seemed to be spreading as the dead continued to crowd the stairwell. They swarmed around her. She tripped, falling, several of the dead dipping to reach for her on the stairs. Others simply stepped all over her to continue moving upwards, attracted by the promise of more warm bodies ahead. But soon the impatient amongst them, those who wanted flesh right now, were upon her, like hyenas around fallen prey.

Among the crowd, she saw the cop from earlier, struggling against them with his baton. They were trying to drag him to the ground, but he fought to remain standing. He caught her looking at him, just as the teeth of the first one tore through the flesh of her thigh. He reached his hand towards hers, and she grabbed it tightly...

...

Lark was carrying the little girl, dragging Geri with his free hand. Sweat was getting in his eyes, and he could hardly see more than two steps in front of him. He slipped on the stairs, almost falling. His DMs were even struggling against the smoothness of the cold floored stairwell.

The little girl looked at him, her huge brown eyes full of fear. She cuddled against his shoulder with her head. It made Lark uncomfortable; he never had been a big fan of kids. *What the hell am I doing?* He thought to himself.

"I can't go much further," Geri cried, almost a dead weight on the other end of his arm.

"Not far now," he shouted back for the fifteenth time.

"Ahhh!" she shouted suddenly, and he felt her let go of his hand.

Turning, he saw her sprawled on the ground, having slipped. He cursed, wondering why girls insisted on wearing shoes without grips. It just didn't seem practical to him. The dead were almost upon her. Setting the child down, Lark reached quickly for the Glock 17 shoved into the belt of his jeans. He pressed his finger against the trigger, firing repeatedly at the faces that weren't human. Several exploded, their dry skin and bone scattering across the nearby walls as they stumbled back against their brethren to cause the domino effect Lark was depending upon. He reached to help Geri back onto her feet.

"Now stay up, this time!" he yelled in her face, aggressively.

She nodded, moving upwards with a renewed sense of vigour.

A couple more flights, and they realised they were on the top floor of the tower block. They left the stairwell, entering the corridor. Geri fumbled with the locks of a few nearby flats, failing to get in. Lark tried another lock, once again unable to shift it.

"Fuck!" she yelled, "Where do we go, now?!"

He didn't know. He looked around, his eyes travelling

360 degrees. Nothing. They were at the top of the building; the only way out seemed down. He looked at the nearby lift, wondering if it still worked. Unlikely, he thought. Definitely not worth taking the chance. He breathed out heavily, heart bouncing in his chest as if about to explode. The incoming dead were hot on their tail. He could hear their approach, sniffling and snorting like a herd of swine. Their flames were spreading; Lark heard the distinct sound of windows from the stairwell blowing out against the heat.

They were fucked. This was the end of the road.

He looked to the little girl, wondering if he should kill her or Geri first, in his final act of mercy. But she seemed disinterested in the dead, instead glaring at him and pointing at a maintenance door at the end of the corridor.

Lark followed her gaze, straining his eyes.

"That's it!" he said, as if having invented something new and wonderful. He handed Geri the gun. "Keep them busy!" he said.

Leaving her to size up to the approaching dead, Lark struggled with the maintenance hatch. He managed to open it, finding and then pulling down the ladder as fast as he could manage. A couple of shots rang out behind him, reminding him of how close the ever-increasing numbers of dead were. Lark lifted the little girl, roughly pushing her up towards the first few steps of the ladder.

"Climb!" he shouted at her, as if she was deaf. She seemed to understand, quickly disappearing up the ladder. "Come on!" he yelled to Geri. She had run out of bullets and was proceeding to throw the gun at the nearest of the dead. Turning towards his voice, he watched her run towards him, spotting the ladder almost immediately. "Go! Go!" he shouted in her ear.

Waiting for Geri to disappear, Lark booted the head of several of the dead closing in. They fell against their peers, not collapsing, due to the thickness of the crowd. He leapt quickly onto the ladder, following Geri's feet. Another one of the dead fucks managed a lucky grab at his ankle, but his DM boot – some of the most sensible footwear he'd ever known – did a fine job of pummelling the unfortunate back where it belonged. He continued to climb the short distance up towards the rooftop. Once atop, Geri and Lark flipped the rooftop lid over the ladder and sealed it as tightly as their human hands allowed them.

They fell back onto the roof, breathless. Lark looked at Geri, sweat drying on his skin with the cool air of the altitude. She looked back, and for some reason unknown to either of them, they both started to laugh.

...

They could still hear them, just below. Their grumbling coughs. Their aimless meandering from one end of the corridor to the other, confused and frustrated to have lost their prey. It was as if someone had called the game to a close. *Hide and seek is over, kids. Everyone back to class.*

The sound of the spitting flames had paled, but Geri was still worried that the whole building might eventually go up, the dead rebounding off each other like human firelighters. It was a small relief to feel the pitter-patter of rain. Geri quietly thanked whatever god was listening for that small mercy, hoping it would be enough to stall the flames. She sat on the rooftop, sheltering against a nearby brick enclosure as Belfast's run of warm weather broke in the inevitable down pouring of rain. For Geri, the rain not only fought against the onslaught of fire, it was also a sign that change was in the air. With so much bad having happened, she was hoping the change would be for the good.

She held the little girl in her arms, rubbing her exposed skin to warm her up as the rain strengthened. The child made no cry or complaint. She seemed still, content even, allowing the rain to bounce off her face as if it were bathwater. Geri knew nothing about the child. She didn't even know if the other young woman, the one she had communicated with very briefly before her untimely death, had been her mother. But she felt something radiate from the child, a positive energy. Even now, Geri felt warmed by her embrace.

But there was something special about this child on another level. A human level. As if, in surviving this whole mess, the child would be destined to view the world differently. The little girl lived in the moment, and there was nothing more magical than that. A warm embrace from a stranger or the cooling splash of summer rain upon her face was probably enough to lift her. And in lifting herself, she also lifted Geri.

She looked out onto the dampening rooftop, noticing a warm mist rising from the rainwater already. It reminded her of the moment, her omen, in the bath, just before George had arrived. He had later told her that they'd known there was life in the house due to the steam escaping the bathroom window. It was a change in her fortunes, then, and she was willing to bet that the mist lifting from the gathered pools, now, was equally promising.

Opposite them, Lark stood, legs spread-eagled, pissing over the side of the rooftop. Geri smiled, realising there was absolutely nothing magical about *him*. He was as grimy as the sludge gathering around her, formed by years of rain and sleet and pollution. But he was suddenly precious to her. *Salt of the earth*, she thought, smiling to herself.

"Haha! Come and get it, you dead fucks!" he mocked.

"That's foul," Geri said, still smiling.

"Not half," he laughed, continuing to let out what seemed to have been building for far too long. "You know what's *also* foul?" Lark said, turning to look at her as he shook himself dry. "All of that..." he said, casting an arm across the horizon in indication. "All of the world's loves, hates, joys and sadness eaten up by some fucking flu virus. And here we are, top of the fucking world, without a prayer of ever defeating them. Standing in the wind and fucking rain, while they're running around in the flats below. Warmer, dryer and probably a lot fucking happier." He looked across the skyline, and Geri could see a poignancy draw across his face. She wondered if he were thinking of McFall. "It just ain't right," he said, shaking his head before tucking his cock back into his pants.

But Geri hugged the child tight and smiled, no longer seeing their situation the same way as Lark. Perhaps he was right, in a way. Perhaps they would die up here, unable to fight their way past the dead lining the corridors. Or, maybe they'd think of some way out of this mess. A simple but effective solution. A keen sharpening of their human senses and intelligence to come up with an answer to a seemingly unsolvable problem. It was what humans always did in desperate situations. It was what would make them the more superior race, in the ongoing struggle between the dead and the living.

But it didn't matter, either way. In her mind, sitting here in the rain, she had already made it. She was a survivor.

But the same couldn't be said for all of them. Her heart sank as she thought of George. She didn't even know his surname. In fact, she knew absolutely nothing about him. They had shared little more than a fleeting glance across a table. A random and awkward conversation or two, played out on a bleak landscape. And then he had been lost to her, before the significance of him in her mind, in her heart, could be realised.

"Wait a minute..." Lark said, drawing her out of her moment. He was looking at the surface of the rooftop. The rain bounced ferociously off his shorn head, yet he didn't seem to notice it, such was his concentration. He walked purposefully across the length and breadth of the rooftop, staring at the ground.

"What is it?" Geri said, standing up and shielding the child from both the rain and whatever threat Lark was anticipating.

"On the ground," Lark said. "There's something written on the ground..."

Geri looked down, finding a huge stripe of paint at her feet. It seemed to spread across the entire rooftop, and she was unable to read what was written from where she stood. She thought suddenly of the other, now-dead, girl's paint-splattered clothes. Lark had climbed up on the small enclosure, looking down on the rooftop with better perspective.

"What does it say?" she asked him, shouting against the growing intensity of the rain.

"Wow," he said. "This is fucking mad..."

"What is it?!" Geri persisted, growing impatient.

"It says 'WE HAVE THE CURE'..." he said, looking at her, confused. "It's huge..."

Geri looked down at the little girl. She didn't know how, but she knew, she simply *knew* the little girl was special. That the message on the roof had something to do with *her*. She pulled the child even closer to her, frightened in case she would somehow disappear, dissolving into the rain, as if made of ice.

"It's the child," she said to Lark, confidently. "It means the child."

...

Jackson's eyes flicked open, immediately stinging against the harshly lit room. He had been dreaming, and the dreams hadn't been good. In his dream, Gallagher and the other men were sitting at a long table, dining. It was a medieval style affair, and they were all dressed in their Sunday best. A silver platter arrived, brought in regally by the dead colonel, now seemingly a butler. The colonel lifted the lid with his skeletal hands, revealing Jackson's own head on the platter beneath. In his mouth was an apple, as if he were merely a wild boar, slain and cooked for the pleasure of the gathered men. Gallagher seemed delighted, his intake of breath and polite applause encouraging the other men to join in and praise the main course. But Jackson was still alive, now able to see them from his new resting place. He tried to spit the apple from his mouth, but it seemed fixed there, as if glued to his teeth. He screamed with his eyes, noting how each of the men looked back at him, still clapping and praising him, as if he should be proud to be on the table, proud to be on a silver platter.

He fought his way back from unconsciousness, his waking eyes straining to accustom themselves with the artificial light. He was in one of the interrogation rooms, strapped into a chair, naked. The last thing he remembered was being shot, and then waking on the floor of the control room. He couldn't remember how he'd got here. He felt terrible, nauseous. The room was almost freezing, the bite of cold air shivering through his tired, old body, clammy sweat breaking on his brow. He looked down at the wound on his shoulder, realising it was patched up. His eyes then fell upon the cold, undead stare of the colonel, strapped into a chair directly opposite him. Or what was left of the colonel. He was little more than a stump of flesh, a torso with a head, but little else. His limbs and organs were spread out in sealed, bloody plastic bags along a nearby table, where Gallagher was working. He turned as Jackson tried to shake himself free.

"Ah," he said. "Just on cue." He was still wearing the blood-stained plastic suit that seemed to now act as his surgical gown. He held a syringe in his gloved hand. "You are to be commended, sir," the doctor continued. "That shadow you spotted on the video monitor... well, it was a little girl. " He walked over to another table, setting down the syringe and removing his gloves, carefully, before lifting a particular file. "Ah, here we are. Flat 23. Brigita Fico is the last name on record for residency of this flat. A Slovakian. As you're aware, we launched a pilot project with Home Office for keeping track of particularly irksome illegal immigrants. Just after the peace process broke, and our standard surveillance project was no longer needed. Miss Fico was one of our first targets. Of course, the funding was pulled before the project really got off the ground," Gallagher paused and looked into the air, regretfully, "but we never delete any of our files, as you know, sir. Information is power, in this game.

"Last we heard, young Brigita gave birth to a little girl called Brina, six years ago... just before the project came to an untimely halt." Gallagher continued to study the file. "Brina seems to be your shadow," he said, finally looking up at Jackson. "Quarantined, having taken ill, but now, seemingly, alive and well..."

Jackson struggled against the straps.

"She's just a child, Gallagher..." he heard himself say, the words heavy in his swollen throat, like boiled sweets. He coughed, suddenly, thick phlegm breaking across his lips. "For God's sake, man..." He was thinking about his own granddaughter. The alcohol in his system was all but spent, inviting back the things he had been trying to blot out. Things like how he hadn't talked to his own little princess since the shit had hit the fan. Or how he didn't know where she was, how she was.

But Gallagher looked at him as if genuinely hurt. It was the most emotion that Jackson had ever seen cross his face.

"The girl is *vital* to my continuing work, sir," he said. "Work that hopes to guarantee the very survival of the human race," he stressed, "so you can be sure that we will do whatever needs to be done to keep her safe."

"You're a fucking monster!" Jackson spat, looking at the results of Gallagher's *experimentation* with the colonel on the table. He had no reason to believe that he would be any less enthusiastic with the little girl. "You leave her alone, or I swear, I'll –"

"You'll do very little, sir," Gallagher interrupted. "Apart from assist me in my work." He sat the file down, walking to the corpse of the colonel, fondling his brittle hair affectionately. "He was a good officer," Gallagher said. "Perhaps even more useful after death than he was before it. I've learned a lot from the work I've done with him... " Jackson thought he'd finally lost it. Gallagher was never the full shilling; he'd always known that. No one could be so consistently callous, so utterly without emotion, without having some sort of defect. It wasn't human. But as the doctor continued to caress the torn body of the still functioning colonel, as if the ragged rump of flesh and bone were his pet pooch, Jackson realised that whatever humanity had been retained by the doctor was all but gone. "Do you know that they will devour even their own bodies?" Gallagher mused, studying Jackson as if he were the audience in some sort of seminar. "Watch this," he said, waving a finger in the air. He walked back to the table, humming to himself as he went. He picked one of the bloody bags, retrieving an unidentifiable body part from it by carefully unwrapping the plastic. He then returned to the colonel, now writhing hungrily in his chair. As Jackson watched on, wanting to take his eyes off the scene, but strangely unable, Gallagher proceeded to feed the colonel what seemed to be the dead man's own flesh. The colonel ripped shreds from the bone, like a starving animal. "So, I know what you're thinking," mused Gallagher, still feeding the colonel almost maternally, as if he were a sick child. "You're wondering why they don't hunt each other, in the wild..." Gallagher's hands were jerking dangerously close to the colonel's mouth as he continued talking. The dead man's hunger was ravenous, devouring every scrap of flesh vicariously. "Well," Gallagher continued, "my theory is that they have some sort of collective mentality. A respect for the herd, if you like. They don't hunt each other because they enjoy a certain sense of belonging, if you like." Gallagher raised an eyebrow at Jackson, as if to underline his next point. "Much like us," he said. "Only sheer desperation will force them to act as the good colonel is acting, therefore..."

"Alas," Gallagher said, leaving the fleshy bone hanging from the colonel's teeth, "he's no longer of any benefit to my studies. I need another specimen, Major, and that's where you come in."

"W-what are you talking about?" Jackson gasped, struggling uselessly against the straps.

"I've injected you with the virus," Gallagher said. "I need another dead subject, shall we say, to test little Brina's alleged immunity. So, in reality, it is not I who should be pressed regarding how gentle to be with the little girl. No, sir. It will be you."

"You bastard," Jackson said, tears dampening his eyes. His whole body became consumed by anger and fear.

"I didn't need to inject you, of course," continued Gallagher, unfazed by Jackson's outburst. "You would

277

have risen, just like all the others, if I had left you to die *naturally*, shall we say. However, I want a specimen that is *purely* infected, if you get my meaning. A specimen that is completely and utterly consumed by the virus, so to speak."

"H-how could you do this?" Jackson spat bitterly at Gallagher. He could feel the flu racing through his system. He coughed suddenly, choking on his words as if they were sharp in his mouth. He felt himself gagging, about to vomit. A gob of blood seeped from his mouth like oil. He didn't want to be one of those things. He didn't want the guilt of destroying another child's life, after what had happened with Flynn's boy all those years ago. This was not what was supposed to happen; this was not how a man was supposed to die. He looked at Gallagher, searching for any hint of benevolence, any faint glimmer of humanity within his cold, sterile gaze. But the doctor simply looked back at him, as if answering a simple question with a logical answer.

"The greater good, sir," the doctor replied politely, in answer to the question. "I do it all for the greater good."

EPILOGUE

Edward Samuel McFall sat at the patio table, spent tissues gathering at his feet like fallen petals. Several cans of beer, crumpled up like old napkins, lay beside them. His balaclava lay on the table next to the golfing magazine. It was still doused in heavy-scented herbs. It was still useless.

He was drunk. *Drunk as a skunk*, as his old mates at the taxi rank used to say. He was also cold, shivers racing through his body like electric shocks. An all consuming wheeze shook his chest, like a box full of rice, and he almost gagged on the bloody phlegm that came with it, drooling through his lips and teeth like juice from a drinks machine.

He began to laugh, the delirious humour giving way to a coughing fit. He spat another glob of blood into a tissue and dropped it to the floor. And then, when he was done laughing and spitting, McFall began to cry.

He knew he was dying, and it made him sad.

The revolver sat squarely on the table, defiantly within reach. It was fully loaded, all six chambers carrying a shell each. McFall was ready to use it. He didn't fear it. In fact, it comforted him. But he wanted to keep its saving grace for the very last moment. He wanted to rinse every last trace of life from his tired, unravelled body before picking that gun up.

You see, McFall didn't want to be one of *them*.

He looked out the back patio door, into the garden. The rain peppered the windows like sweat, but he could still see clearly out onto the overgrown lawn. It was still empty, still clean of them, apart from one. And she didn't count, because he didn't fear her. She was the one who looked like his wife, and she was glaring in at him through the glass, as if baying for his attention. She must have found a way through the next-door neighbour's fence. How she'd managed that, McFall didn't know. *But love conquers everything*, he said to himself, laughing. She didn't see the funny side of it, of course. She remained still, motionless, as if bored or huffing. It was just the way his wife would have stood, if she hadn't already fallen asleep, whenever he came home, late yet again, from taxi-driving.

She always wanted to go out, *to go dancing*, as she put it. Especially at the weekend. But that was his busiest time with the taxi-driving. It was the time you made the most money. Still, he'd promise to be home in time, phone her and tell her to get all dressed up, only to get that 'one last job' and find himself rolling through the door past 1:00am, finding her angry and upset, wearing her best togs. Or even worse, curled up, fast asleep on the couch. Because that meant the bollocking he was due would wait until morning. Maybe even get drawn out for days.

The dead fuck outside was still wearing the housecoat that he'd bought for his wife two Christmases ago. Through the dirty glass, she looked even more like his wife. He knew that it wasn't her out there, standing in the rain as if at some sort of protest, but for his last few minutes of life, he was willing to pretend it was.

What harm would it do? he thought.

McFall looked her in the eye, still in his seat at the patio table.

"Not wearing a fucking mask now," he said, a cackle of laughter breaking from his bone-dry lips. "This is me, now. The real fucking me. And it's about time you met the real Eddie McFall." There were a few things he needed to say to her, a few home truths that she needed to hear. Things that he needed to get off his chest before he gave up the proverbial ghost. The guys at the taxi rank had always said he'd been too soft on her, and he was beginning to see their point. He let her away with murder.

"Listen love," he croaked, every word like a dagger to his throat, "If you had got off your fat, lazy arse and got yourself a job, instead of moaning at me," he paused to cough more blood into yet another tissue, "well then, maybe... maybe I could have worked less hours."

The dead thing looked back at him, still huffy. Still pouting. Still fucking ugly.

"And that's another thing," he said. "Always fucking complaining about no sex. No sex?! Fucking look at you, love," he laughed as if the boys at the rank were behind him, cheering him on. "You're no Pammy Anderson, are –?"

His last word was lost as he felt a sharp stab to his chest, as if his heart had taken a turn for the worse. He had always meant to get his cholesterol checked out – too many hours spent sitting on his hole in a taxi cab, shovelling Chinese down his gob. His body shivered, an ice-cold wheeze raging through him like a cold river. He felt like he was dying; he knew he was dying.

McFall reached for the revolver, finding that his hands were no longer doing what his mind told them to do. Instead, they lay on the table. Useless, sleeping on the fucking job. His breathing intensified, his lungs almost collapsing with the lack of support from his weakening heart. He felt himself slipping away, even though he didn't want to slip away. He still had things that needed to be said. And he sure as hell didn't want to end up as one of those...

His head hit the table like a dropped melon. The skin across his forehead cracked, but no blood flowed from the wound. His eyes closed, a last act of dignity in a world where anything even resembling dignity was rare as hen's teeth.

But two hours passed.

And then his eyes flicked back open again.

Acknowledgments

I'd like to thank everyone who has supported my writing over the last couple of years.

I'm particularly grateful for the ongoing support and encouragement of Ryan Fitzsimmons, Gardner Goldsmith, David Moody, Mal Coney, John McMahon, Hannah and Andy Nutter, Tariq Sarwar, James Melzer, Dr Pus, Patty Smith and everyone at Snowbooks.

Finally, I'd like to thank Rebecca and Dita for their love, patience and belief in what I do.

About the Author

Belfast born, Wayne Simmons has been loitering with intent around the horror genre for some years. Having scribbled reviews and interviews for a variety of zines, Wayne was delighted to release his debut horror novel, *Drop Dead Gorgeous* in November 2008 (republished by Snowbooks in February 2011). The book was received well by both fans of the genre and reviewers alike.

Flu is Wayne's second horror novel.

In what little spare time he has left, Wayne enjoys running, getting tattooed and listening to all manner of unseemly screeches on his BOOM-BOOM Box.

Visit Wayne online at waynesimmons.org

Also by Wayne Simmons

Drop Dead Gorgeous

available from Snowbooks
February 2011

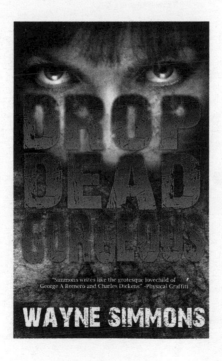